Lost Souls

By Ronald J Butler

Lost Souls

By Ronald J Butler

First published 2024- Ronald J Butler

This edition published 2024 by Ronald J Butler
Moreton Bay, Qld
Australia.
Copyright © Ronald J Butler 2024

The National Library of Australia Cataloguing-in-Publication

Author: Ronald J Butler

Title: Lost Souls

ISBN: 978-0-6486022-0-0

Genre. Historical, Society, Fiction.

Disclaimer: This story is based on historical events in our society, melded with a childhood lost in care during 1960's- 1970s in Queensland. Reference to persons living or dead is coincidental.

Cover designer and artwork by Gloria Lebrocq Butler
The front cover artwork shows a wardrobe that depicts the desolation of young children confined within.
Font Times New Roman 12pt. Heading Font Retro Vintage by Nimarna Visual.
Printed and bound in Australia by Ingram Spark.

A catalogue record for this work is available from the National Library of Australia

Dedication

Gloria, my wife for your love and support in getting this book out of the closet.

To my son Taren, A sanitised tale of times past. Which may or not be helpful.

The families of Hopelands and Chinchilla for your generosity. There are many that are worthy of mention that would fill another book.

Acknowledgements

A special thanks to Professor Emeritus and author Gary Crew, for your guidance and inspiration, and the supportive interaction of Bribie Island Library writers and authors group.

Prologue

Little did I imagine that in six short months, my world would crumble, and my life spiral into despair. When you have no choice, giving up is not an option.

Fun times

Like most other kids my age, I lived in the moment without a care in the world. I chose to spend my spare time outdoors, daydreaming under the shade of our mulberry tree. Today was no different except for an invasion of bloody-minded, green ants rudely disturbing me. The little buggers had overrun my favourite spot and had decided to explore a new world up my shorts. This galivanted me into instant action, desperately brushing most of them off and bolting for the house to change my underwear. Mission accomplished, I wandered about to see if Mum wanted some help. She hardly ever took a break; I might be able to distract her from never-ending chores. Of household appliances, we had none to ease the daily life of my mum.

Our home was a low-set white stucco three-bedroom structure, not what one might call a palace. The house was part of the grand design of the salubrious satellite suburb of Inala in the early 1950s. A housing commission estate that fell short of the hype. I shared this place with Mum and Dad, two aunties, and three older brothers: Illy, 13; Ike, 11; and Elan, 9, myself and my sisters, whom I called the fairies as they often disappeared. The oldest sister, Maggie, got married - a thing girls seemed inclined to do. The middle sister, Murein, was run over by a train at Woolloongabba railway station and lost one of her legs. She survived and went on to be a talented seamstress. The youngest sister, Lizbeth, was her faithful companion and was constantly by her side.

The Penguins recently kidnapped these two sisters [my pet name for the nuns in black and white habits] and were returned every other weekend. There were three other older brothers, and one lived away after military service. He was soon to be married to his beautiful sweetheart with long black hair. I don't remember the other two, as they were often on walkabout, wherever that was. So, if we all lived here together, this place would burst at the seams, with seven boys including myself, three girls, mum, dad plus two aunties. We could have had our own cricket team with reserves and me as the mascot. Ours was a crowded household at the best of times.

'Hello Mum, Aunties, anyone around? Are you hiding? Has everyone run away? Where are you?' My home was seldom quiet, and I shared it with people who liked fun and gossip. Just where were my brothers anyway? They were the creators of endless mysteries. The word *mystery* became a favourite of the three at-home brothers. When they were asked about anything, it was always a mystery, which to me was rather curious, as they all seemed to have such bad memories.

'Hey! Where're you all hiding?'

A silent house was scary, so I yelled louder. What was that chill in the air, a boogie man? Crap, the penguins could be sneaking about to capture me; not bloody likely if I can help it. Survival was the motto of this family: be quick, or you're it. My brother's scary stories began haunting me even in the daylight. I was not staying inside a moment longer and bolted out to the footpath to sit peacefully on the gutter in the sunshine and ponder the problem.

Now Mum was either at one of the neighbours or up the street at Aunty Lil's. She wouldn't go without me if she went to ask for a food parcel from the Salvos. When times were tough, which seemed to occur more often lately, the Salvos food shop was a place of last resort. The two aunties were at work, and Dad might have been either at the Woolloongabba shipyard or his TAB job, which was the one he enjoyed the most. It wasn't a school day, so where were my brothers? They often left me behind partly due to my age and my toe-stubbing habit, which annoyed them. I frequently kicked as I walked, making my toes bleed. My brothers were blamed for this lack of care, and Mum would give them an earful. So, they nicknamed me Stumpy, for I often stubbed my toes running after them.

Being the inventive minds they were, they made up a little ditty. "Poor old Stumpy's dead for eating mulberry bread, get a bit of charcoal stick it up his arsehole, poor old Stumpy's dead, and on it went in similar unflattering terms," much to their amusement.

Most likely, they are up to one of their money-making rackets. Come to think of it, they were talking about a fete; that might be where they are. Our dog Cesar is missing, and he would follow them to hell and back if given the chance. He took his guard duties quite seriously, always on alert to mark anyone who threatened us. While the brothers were at school, Cesar would hang out with me; perhaps I was of more interest to him than watching the chooks through the fence all day. The only place the fete could be is at the Inala primary school. It was a bit of a hike for me, wandering up Buddelia Street. At least the roads were cool enough to walk on in bare feet. Shoes were a rare item, and who wanted them anyway? It became a hot foot shuffle on the heated road surface in the summertime when even the tar would melt. My life revolved around the golden rule: look out for bottles. Each one earned a halfpenny when returned to the shop.

Dropped coins were like mana from heaven or someone's holey pockets. A penny and, even better, a threepence would be just short of a miracle. It was a long walk for my short legs, and I was close to chucking it in. Then something stuck to my left foot: a piece of old paper with bubble gum, a sticky sweet substance that was difficult to remove once it was on you. I sat down to pull it off and rubbed my foot briskly on the grass to remove the rest of it. The paper then stuck to my shorts, and I noticed a number ten on it—the highest number to which I could count. It wasn't monopoly money, that was for sure; maybe it was real. Holy cow, I'm rich, you little beauty! With this newfound wealth, I took off up the grass footpath, potholes be damned. The screams and music confirmed I was on the right track. This was the first fete I'd ever visited, and I'm free to run wild. Being thirsty and hungry, I made a beeline for the first food stall.

'Mister, please can I have a hotdog with sauce and a Sunny Boy ice block.' The hairy old troll peered over the high bench, glaring at my cheeky request.

'Yeah, that will cost you 5P. Do you have any money? Where's your parent's kid?' Handing the paper note, I pointed to a large lady looking in my direction. With the hot dog in my hand, I put the Sunny Boy, a frozen soft drink in a sealed triangular carton, inside my shirt for safekeeping. Then I turned to walk off.

'Hey kid, take the change; your mother will get cross if you don't return it.'

'Thank you.' I stuffed the coins in my pocket, started munching on my hotdog, and slowly walked over to where the lady and her children were standing.

'Where is your mother, young man? You shouldn't be wandering around here alone.'

'Over there with my sisters,' I pointed towards the merry-go-round and headed in that direction. *Boy, these adults are stickybeaks; they sure ask a lot of questions.* My new life of easy gains and good times had a downside.

'Penny, a ride! Shouted the ride operator man.'

'Here, one for me!'

I gave him the coin, jumped onto the merry-go-round, and sat down in a large cup and saucer thingy. Two older girls partially occupied one side and didn't seem to mind my joining them. Now I could suck on my Sunny Boy ice block. Round and round we went, making me a little dizzy, and I began to feel sick. Finally, it stopped, and I staggered off, dropping what was left of the Sunny Boy.

This wasn't one of my better ideas, stuffing my face and getting on a fast-spinning ride. I rested on a worn grey wooden bench and checked that the money was still in my pockets. It shouldn't be easy to go just because it was easy to come. My eyes bulged; this was more than big sister earned in a week. All these coins added up to ninety-six pence [today's currency A$ 0.96c]. I had better watch out for robbers and gang members; they'd find me an easy target. For my own safety, I'd better find my brothers soon. Some copper might come and grab me by the ear; they would be suspicious of a short-arsed big spender.

'Last tickets in the cake raffle, drawn in 15 minutes, five prizes, a penny a ticket,' the lady called out. Her stall had been selling cakes for the school P&C raffle to raise funds for the local Girl Guides and Boy Scouts clubs.

'I'll have one, please, lady. 'I handed her a sixpence. She gave me a coloured ticket and change. I waited impatiently for about 15 minutes, and then Mother Nature got the better of me. I started to hop about searching for a toilet. With few choices, I found a hidden wall, the perfect spot for a young lad, and returned to the cake stall.

'Orange ticket—number something. Last draw. Hurry to get your prizes,' the lady called out.

'Me, me, mine is orange,'

'That colour is lemon, young man. Please give me a look at it. Aren't you a lucky little fellow? You've got the right number for this cake here. Mind you, carry it carefully. Where's your mom?

'Yes, thank you, lady. She is over there.' Wow, a sponge cake. Mum will be pleased.'

It was a long walk with such a big box. Stuff looking for the brothers, I'm off home. Out the gate, down the footpath and homeward bound. As I ran across Rosemary Road, a car slammed on its brakes, tyres squealed, and a horn blared. Then someone yelled out.

'Look where you're going, stupid kid.'

What's his problem? How am I supposed to see over this great box? He should be watching where I'm going.

'Rickie.' It was one of my big sisters and her boyfriend out cruising in his FJ Holden. 'What are you doing running around up here? That car almost hit you.'

'Sorry, sis, I gotta get this cake home to Mum.'

'Where are the boys? Why aren't you with them? How did you get that cake?'

'Steady on, Sis; I can't answer that many questions. They're over there somewhere; you wouldn't believe it.'

'Probably not; get in the car, and we'll take you home.'

How cool was this—a ride in a big car and a cake—things that dreams are made of? The ride home was full of questions, and I had few answers. I began to see why most things were mysteries with my older brothers. We pulled up outside the house, and Sis ordered me out.

'Now you face Mum and leave me out of your story.'

'Thanks for the ride home, Sis. Bye Johnny,' I took off into the house.

'Hi Mum, where've you been?'

'What Rickie! I've been looking everywhere for you; I only went next door for 10 minutes, and you disappeared. Your brothers are out looking for you; where have *you* been?'

'Mum, you wouldn't believe what happened. I found some money up the road on the footpath. I won you a cake at the fete raffle, went on a merry go around and lost some of the money; these are left.' Handing her the four two-bob coins was a lot of money for our family.

'Then Sis and Johnny found me and gave me a ride home in his FJ Holden; it was cool! I tell you what, I am stuffed! I hope you like the cake, Mum?' It's had a bit of a hard time on the way home.

'You're a worry, my boy; I don't know whether to hug you or belt you. It's a lovely cake. Where did you really get all this money?'

'I told you; a ten bob note on the footpath up the road. I went looking for the boys and bought myself a drink and this cake for you at the fete.'

'It's a lot of money. Anyway, you know you're not allowed to go anywhere alone; wait till your father gets home. Now go to your bed and stay there and watch your language, young man.'

'Aw, Mum.' Even when I do good things, I still get into trouble. Luckily, I kept the one shilling and five pence as Cracker Night is coming soon. I hope Mum forgives me before Dad comes home. Otherwise, I'm going to be in for it. A few hours later, Mum came into the bedroom to talk to me.

'Rickie, I've decided not to tell your father about your disappearing act and will tell him I won the cake in the school raffle. As for the money, it will be our little secret. It will be difficult to trace who might have lost the money. Just about everyone would put their hand up if I asked.

I know your brothers are scarce with the truth, so you'll not have to worry about them dobbing you in.' [slang for telling on you]

'Thanks, Mum, I'm sorry for worrying you.'

Another of my escapades that ended well for me this time. Kids did disappear without a trace, which worried my mum. Innocence comes with its perils; I couldn't read the newspapers, and television was restricted. We had a rented television in our house, with a coin box on the side to operate it. To do this, someone had to have money, as a shilling was required to run it for eight hours. There were only two channels, and these were in black and white. Limited movies were shown, mostly cowboys and Indians. Other times, it was music game shows and the regular six o'clock news. Screening is from midday to ten pm; after that, you get test patterns. Primarily, our entertainment comes from the radio, which has a variety of music and immensely popular radio shows. Our limited record collection could be played at any time of the day on a second-hand, valve-operated Radio/ gramophone donated to us by a neighbour. This record player was built into a low sideboard and was a stylish piece of furniture, even if I say so myself.

We were fortunate to have a local picture theatre within walking distance from our house, which is how we generally got anywhere. If you knew someone with a motor vehicle and the money for the admission fee, there was a drive-in picture theatre in the next suburb. Johnny had a car, and sometimes he would take us. We got to sit in the comfort of his car and watch two movies on the giant screen. The voice and sound effects came from an outside metal speaker on the car's door. Other entertainment came from school plays, choir groups, and mischief to add variety to our lives. The last activity was a rite of passage, and we boys became quite good at it.

Sporting clubs were the bare-bones set-ups. Consisting of a playing field, a scoreboard, and a corrugated sheet metal shelter. This was for sale of soft drinks and hotdogs and a toilet block. But all these things cost money to participate in, which was relatively scarce in our family. Even to make a phone call, the only choice was a brisk walk to the nearest coin-operated public phone. These were situated on the footpaths, community halls and shopping areas. Public phones were mounted within a red glass and timber square box-like booth, a small shelf, and a helpful phone directory. Once inside the booth, a caller and anyone else who could cram in was protected from the weather. My preschool childhood was a laid-back existence. Kids got to spend daylight hours outside playing, where we made up our own games. I especially liked it when my brothers swam in the local creek; here, we could catch yabbies. Hanging from a high tree branch was a long rope with a rubber tyre attached, and we would swing out on it and dive bomb into the creek.

My brothers had to lift me to reach the tyre, swing me out, and yell when to let go. I would jump in and get dragged back to shore as I could not swim. I was never afraid to do this as I trusted them to rescue me.

Our mode of transport was exciting as I got to sit on the handlebars of my brothers' pushbikes. They flew around corners and down steep hills with me yahooing along the way. We'd go miles for adventure, and mischief usually found us. One day, my brothers were out to something, so they sent one of their mates to pick me up from home. I jumped up on the bike's handlebars, and we went racing along. Within sight of the park, I yelled out to my brothers just as a car pulled out from a side street. The bike swerved, and I went headfirst onto the road and cracked my head. Safety and helmets were optional extras. After that, I don't know what happened; someone called an ambulance, I suppose. My cyclist would've been petrified my brothers would beat him up. This was a sign of things to come; my head getting dinged and whacked. You might think it would knock sense into me.

The following week, we went searching for free fruit. This grew outside the boundary of nearby fruit and vegetable farms. Unfortunately, only a few small watermelons were outside the fence; the best ones were on the farmer's side and looked delicious.

'I can crawl under the fence and get some for us.'

'No, wait, Rickie,' Ike replied.

He grabbed a stick and pushed it past the fence onto a single wire running not far off the ground. Then there was a bang. That day, I learnt why my brothers constantly warned me not to go to those farms alone. Between the dogs and shotguns, I would always keep my distance from the fences.

Cracker Night

The most exciting night of my life occurred in November and was the next best thing to Christmas. The night skies were filled with smoke and unbelievable noise, lit up by multiple colours. Fireworks were bought from any local shop, and no age limit or license was needed. We were following an age-old tradition of blowing stuff up. Guy Fawkes Day was a historic event in 1605 A.D, a bonfire night in the United Kingdom where, according to history, a chap named Guy Fawkes plotted to blow up the House of Lords. We might've been direct descendants of this colourful fellow.

Locally known as Cracker Night in Australia, it was the greatest love of kids and the dread of parents. If you've not experienced it, you've missed one of childhood's highlights. What a racket and fun, a memory that lingers whenever I see a fireworks display. In the 1950s & sixties, we kids saved our pocket money if we were lucky enough to get any. Chores around the house weren't part of the deal; if they weren't done, a swift clip in the ear or a boot in the backside resulted. Ingenuity was how we made pocket money and encouraged young entrepreneurs. I was almost six, a big boy, so I pestered my brothers to give me a paying job. Well, they did, and I got paid in crackers.

Their four primary sources of my brother's income were centred around the following activities.

1. Horse manure fertiliser was sold in hessian sacks, and we delivered on our homemade cart to nearby neighbours' gardens.

2. Seasonal fruit: mangoes, grapes, and watermelons, all farm-fresh and sold at mate's rates.

3. Fresh honeycomb from local beehives: the beekeeper paid us for keeping the weeds down around them and protecting the hives from would-be thieves. Smart man.

4. A newspaper run in the city if you were of the correct age.

It was a mystery to me how my brothers got all these things done when they were supposed to be at school all day. Our stash of fireworks continued to grow and were safely locked away in the outside shed. I was itching to get my hands on some. I knew a particular rooster in the chook pen would've enjoyed them rather than attack me. That mongrel rooster seemed to take a particular liking to peck my feet whenever I went in to collect the eggs. It was a massive surprise when Dad came home early one afternoon with a big box.

'Hey, Dad, what've you got there?'

Dad explained that he suddenly acquired the surprise box of fireworks while working down at the wharf with his mates, the painters, and the dockers. It's a big secret. Can you keep a secret?

'Yes, Dad, I'm the best secret keeper going.'

'Mind you do, young fella.' Hmm, another mystery, it seems all I ever do around here is keep secrets. The box was full of exciting, explosive devices for cracker night. Dad was a bit of an expert on explosives after serving in WW11 in the South Pacific and Papua New Guinea, 1942 – 1945. He was never in the best of health ever again.

The way Dad explained the sudden appearance of the surprise box of fireworks was that he acquired them while working down at the wharf with his mates, the *painters and dockers*. These men were busy working when boxes fell off the back of a truck near them. Despite the men yelling at the driver to stop, it drove on. It certainly was good luck for us, though; the household budget seldom stretched to extras. Poor old dad was often left to clean up this type of mess and would bring surprise boxes home occasionally. The more crackers we had, the better.

What a night we had as brilliant colours lit up the sky, wizzes and bangs everywhere, skyrockets in every direction, absolute bedlam. The dogs in the neighbour took off and didn't come home for days. One of my little skyrockets in a milk bottle fell over as I lit it, and off it went across the road to the neighbour's yard. They were surprised, which I was most pleased about, as they'd be right shits at times. The night might have been a momentous success, till one of my skyrockets hit the half-full cracker box, which blew up, thus ending our entertainment spectacularly. The night sky lit up, as did the side of the house. Dad turned on the hose; my brothers grabbed

10

the water buckets that sat around in case of emergency. This was part of Dad's danger plan, something he often went on about. Lucky for us all, he was prepared for accidents.

Mum grabbed me and fled into the house. 'Rickie, are you ok? You were close to the fireworks when they all suddenly blew up. You could've been badly hurt.'

'Gee Mum, we are missing all the fun.'

The fire brigade arrived and hosed down the blackened side wall of the house. Fortunately, it was stucco cement and not flammable. Though not so fortunate was Mum's pride and joy, her beautiful lawn became brown and crunchy to walk on. Even the coppers showed up as they were fond of our family. They often dropped in for a chat with Mum and Dad about community events and the wellbeing and whereabouts of my brothers. That evening, they were most interested in blown-up letterboxes nearby and exploding pumpkins. These had been left on the front porches of nearby houses. I'm unsure why they thought we would have known about such things.   I enjoyed their visits if they gave me a barley sugar, a twisted lolly stick, known to cure the ills of most young children. That cracker night was talked about around the suburb, giving my brothers bragging rights for ages.

How it all happened was another one of life's mysteries, although everyone had an opinion. Our lives continued, peppered with drama, sometimes involving the emerging street gangs. My primary education was at *Richlands Primary School*. In my imagination, I could spend all day playing with my brothers. Who would have thought it would be taken up by bossy adults telling me what to do all day? I made new friends and enjoyed the storybooks the teachers read to us.

We had a big Christmas party at school, with total attendance. The teachers did some fundraising to buy us ice cream, lollies, and soft drinks. The local farmers donated cakes, watermelons, and sugar cane, which was great to chew on. That was the best part of the whole year. It was a sweet memory of school, in contrast to getting the cane for misdemeanours, that's for sure.

The Paper Run

A noisy, smoky red van pulled up outside our house, its wheels squealing, and then a side door rattled open.

'Get in, boys. There's no time to lay about; there are papers to pick up and sell,' the driver called out.

'No worries,' Illy replied.

We all piled into the van and headed off into the big city. My imagination was in overdrive, as this was a covert operation. I was supposed to stop home with one of my brothers to look after me. Stuff that when there was money to be made. I was certainly too young to sell newspapers on city streets at any time, let alone in the evening. Still, why worry? Details were often a hazy subject anyway. I had been practising for weeks, yelling out 'Paper, Telly, City Final' around the house. Mum wondered if her youngest angel was going nuts. I asked her to teach me to count small change like we were shopkeepers. My reward was dripping on bread when I got it right. I would have got more than dripping if she'd twigged to my little game. Arriving in the city, we picked up the bundles of newspapers and dropped them off at our marshalling point. A city block that bordered Elizabeth and George Streets, then up to Queen Street and North Quay in Brisbane. This was their turf, and they strenuously defended against those who coveted it.

Illy was training to be a boxer and eventually entered the Golden Gloves competition. The other two brothers were often sparring partners, so it didn't pay to annoy them. My brothers got to have all the fun, being amongst these buildings, trams, trolleys, buses, and people wanting newspapers rushing everywhere.

'Don't stand there gawking, Rickie. Grab a couple of those papers, follow me, and don't wander off,' yelled Illy.

'Ok, Illy.'

The first night was a bit of a blur. We got home just before Mum and the aunties returned from their weekly bingo game. I had a quick bath and was in bed before they knew. *Wow, I had a real job, selling my 12 Brisbane Daily Telegraph newspapers one evening a week.* This was exciting, and I would get paid real money.

The following week, business was slow on the streets, so I wandered through public bars. The places were packed, the men were noisy, and one rude bugger yelled out.

'What's that kid doing in here?'

'Leave him alone; he's only trying to make a few bob!' someone quipped.

'Get out of here, kid. You'll have the coppers in shutting us down; give me your papers; how much do I owe you?'

'Thirty-six pence, sir.'

'Here's your money and a tip, now get!' yelled the barman.

'Thank you, sir.' *Wow! Sold the whole lot in one go. I'm getting the hang of this sales racket.* I wondered why the brothers didn't sell all their papers in pubs. Pubs had to shut at 6 pm on the dot. These were severe drinking sessions with standing room only. On the final bell, it was skol time. Then off they would go to catch the bus, train, or tram merrily home, pissed to the eyeballs. A few remained and sipped their last drink behind closed doors. This was probably something Dad did, as he never got home until after eight when he went to the pub.

A few weeks went by before I'd discovered a park wishing well. It was situated slightly off my brother's designated area. My brothers paid me threepence for selling my newspapers. On the other hand, the wishing well often donated around two shillings each Wednesday evening to my pockets. Of course, expenses were involved: a stick from a garden, chewing gum, and sometimes lost newspapers. With this tool, I would spear coins through the wire mesh covering the pond. I left my papers sitting on the side of the pond with a rock on top. Generally, they sold themselves on an honest basis. I was on my way to riches, or so I thought, until one evening, I was rudely interrupted.

'What're you doing with that stick in the pond, young fella?' asked a copper as he grabbed me by the ear.

'Selling papers, sir.'

'Yeah, right. What are you doing here at this time of the evening? Where are your parents?'

'Hey, my papers are blowing away,' he turned to grab them. I took off. Stuff the papers, I got out of there. Thank heavens for the big crowds rushing to get home; I managed to disappear. So that ended my newspaper career. My brothers twigged to who the coppers were looking for.

Over the next few months, my mother became ill and was admitted to the hospital. Her illness, *Huntington's Disease,* was misdiagnosed, and she was transferred to a mental institution. Dad's health went down, and he was placed in the care of the Repatriation Hospital Kenmore. The next time I saw my mother was seven years later, the night she died. I was thirteen and taken to a place called Wolston Park Hospital. The place would depress the most positive of people. They drip-fed her for the last three years of her life in that hole of a place. By the time I got to see her, she had been in a coma for some time. Before this, not one person told me she was still alive or took me to visit her. Four members of my family would pass away with the same disease over the years.

The Dark Road Looms

With our parents out of the picture, my days running wild on the streets was exciting, though not without risk. We would seldom return to the house as it was being watched. The power was turned off, the cupboards bare and recently someone had begun to remove our furniture, clothing, and personal family documents. The loss of these documents would sever my connection to extended family for the future and from the past. We all were getting thinner just drinking borrowed milk and eating dry Milo powder from a tin. Camping on mattresses laid out across the floor was losing its appeal. Someone must have seen us creeping about with lit candles in the evenings, as early one morning we were swooped on. Police officers and other busybodies from Children's Services Department had us surrounded. Their actions started a domino effect either by good intent or overzealous ambitions, we were taken into custody. I had just turned six and the next day, my brothers and I found ourselves before a children's court. *A place that was frightening to me. Were we criminals?*

There were quite a few people milling about the place, adults arguing over something. They all had an opinion that is for sure. The large bloke in his royal costume sat up on the high throne. He was the boss and would on occasion wave a hand in our direction. What they were arguing about was lost on me, with people sitting, standing, and waving pieces of paper about. Best I could make out, some sort of auction was going on with a show of hands. In the end one of my older brothers and his wife won me. Someone else won Illy, Ike, and Elan. No one ever told me what happened, where they went and why at the time.

My life took a drastic turn. Under the Child Protection Act, there were diverse bylaws that separated children from their families. One of which covered the situation where a child was deemed, temporary without a home. Then you became a ward of the state. A situation that would fracture my life forever, to the point that I've always felt alone in the world. Seldom would I form a close attachment to another human being. This was something I began to accept as normal; people kept disappearing out of my life and I never knew why? I got to live with Marl and Eta at Acacia Ridge, where I was quite happy, and discovered I didn't like peas and made them disappear, into nearby pot plants or under the table. I attended the local State Primary School and during the holidays we'd go camping and put up a huge canvas ex-army tent. wherever there was a spare spot on the beach.

At the time, if you did not have a car, you could catch a train from South Brisbane station and travel all the way down to Coolangatta beach. There were lots of activities for us, building sandcastles, swimming in the surf puddles, making new holiday friends. The adults played cards or went swimming, and surfing on their "woodies." a nine-foot timber surfboard. Dancing to rock and roll music was extremely popular and partying on the beach with the adults. We had a great time, often falling exhausted onto our canvas stretcher beds. Even rainy days were fun, I'd help Marl dig a trench around the tent and we'd run around throwing mudpies at one another. He'd dealt with all types of weather and conditions when he was in the army, so nothing seemed to faze him.

Not long after my seventh birthday in 1962 I got another shattering surprise. This one involved the machinations of child services again. I thought I was going to see my three brothers at a college out in some coastal area. When that big black limousine arrived to pick me up, I felt special. The car was driven by a chauffeur and accompanied by the housemaid or so I imagined. Off we went on a long drive, through Brisbane city and Fortitude Valley, passing electric trolley buses and trams. Further on we passed some big houses that overlooked the river, at some high point I got a glimpse of the ocean.

Passing by a cemetery, the road ahead looked dark in the shadows of overhanging Jacaranda trees. I sensed an eerie feeling as the driver turned right at a T intersection. Going between open huge wrought iron gates, with the sound of gravel crunching under the tyres, gave me goosebumps. The car came to a halt at a large roundabout bordered by huge pine trees. Excitedly I jumped out of the car and strained my neck to look up at this spooky, two storey large brick building with wide timber verandah's. *Wow* I thought, *look at the size of this joint.* There were many of these places throughout Queensland. This one was built up high on the slopes of bushland that fell away across to mudflats on the horizon. Here amongst the mangroves was the breeding grounds of millions of mosquitoes that would relish feasting on us all, young and old for decades to come.

Trapped

Out of the shadows a nun appeared, greeting me with a soft voice. This place might not be too bad. They must be friendly to look after my brothers. Taking my hand, the nun led me unsuspectingly into a future beyond my understanding. Out of the bright sunlight, we passed into a cool, dimly lit, silent room adorned with religious statues. I was seated at a small, round, silky oak table with a glass of milk and biscuits. A kid doesn't have to be told twice, so I tucked in while the adults chatted in the next room. One of the huge timber doors behind me suddenly slammed shut, the sound booming throughout the building. I was beginning to feel creeped out. There was little solace in biscuits, so the last one disappeared into my pocket. When I heard a car start up outside my concern stepped up a notch. I stuck my head out through a side doorway, only to see a long corridor with two nuns coming towards me.

Crikey, I was in the den of the penguins.

'Stay where you are young man.'

'I came to see my brothers; do you know where they are?'

'Yes, be a good boy and you will see them soon, there are a few things we need to talk about first.'

'What! Who are you to tell me what to do? I'll tell my brothers on you,' I replied.

'You be quiet, and do as you are told,' a nasty nun snarled.

'Why?'

'Sister, will you take him over to the little boy's section and settle him in,'

'Come along, Rickie, we shall go together to find your brothers.'

The young nun talked softly to me as we walked down the hallways. Out we went through a walkway lined with plants, the sides of which were enclosed with timber lattice. Diamond-shaped dappled light spots shone through, giving it the appearance of a peaceful place. Further along, we stopped at a huge room filled with clothing and assorted coloured boxes.

'Good afternoon, sister' the nun said to another one sitting inside at a sewing machine.

'This is our new young charge, Rickie Battler.'

'Hello Rickie, Welcome to our home, would you like a barley sugar?'

'Yes please.'

Barley sugar worked a miracle in distracting me as we walked along, the nice nun pointed out various places. Chapel, big boys' section, little boys' section, a school over there. This place was massive with buildings for lots of activities including a farm, dairy, bakery. Although interesting, I was on a mission and my driver might get impatient waiting. I wanted to spend time with my brothers before heading home. Wrong, I've been sucked in! Nice nun handed me over to a bean stick nun, who took my barley sugar away.

'Now, young master Battler, let me show you around and explain our rules, Ok.'

'Um, ok.'

'Speak UP, and your only answer should be, YES Sister, do you understand?'

'But!'

Whack, whack! with her giant hand.

'Ow that hurt, why're you hitting me?'

'Be quiet; naughty boys are not tolerated here. Another sound and you'll be in trouble. Listen up and follow me!'

I was shown toilets, dormitory, multi-bathtub room, a changing room with many wooden pegs fixed to the wall. All the pegs had clothes hanging off them. Then onto a pharmacy/infirmary area and big playroom with a TV set at one end.

'Lastly, out there is the playground, where if you behave, you'll be able to go out to soon. What do you think of your new home?' asked Stringbean nun.

'But I'm not staying, I only came to visit my big brothers, so I don't want you wasting my time.'

'Come with me,' I was dragged into the bathroom and belted with a leather strap.

'Stop! My brothers will beat you up!'

A swift kick in the shins with my new shoes should sort her out. That only served to increase her excitement and she continued hitting me. Then I was stripped of my clothing and shoved into a bath full of chilly water. This weird person stuck soap in my mouth and eyes, rubbed something in my hair that hurt like hell. I was screaming and crying, while trying not to drown in the bathtub. There were a few of the other kids around the doorway and verandah, yelling and screaming out to other nuns.

'Sister, if you please, I can take over from here,' another nun had entered the room and closed the door.

'This is the rudest, naughtiest boy I've ever met,' said the nasty nun.

'It's nearly afternoon teatime. Perhaps you'd like to go over to the convent, while I finish here." Stringbean departed without another word.

'Now, young man, calm down; I'll not hurt you. Let me get the soap out of your eyes.

'Stand up, please, so I can pour some clean, warm water over your head to wash all the soap off. Now, hold this damp washer over your eyes. I'll dry you off and get you some clean, dry clothes, but I need you to help me, OK?'

'What did you say?' The soap in my ears made it hard to hear. I dried off, wrapped a towel around myself, and went into the pharmacy room. She rubbed some Dettol on a minor cut, which made me jump. I don't know if it makes germs come off, but it gave me the urge to hurry up. That stuff stings.

'Now I need you to be a good boy so I can look after you. Can you do that for me?'

Still crying, I blurted out, 'But why are people hurting me? Why am I here? I only came to visit my brothers for the afternoon and then go home.'

'Rickie, I'm sorry; this should have all been explained to you before you came here.' So, we'll get you clean clothes, and then we can have a talk.' Into the changing room, we went, 'Here, these look about your size...' The sister gave me clean clothes, with a number E17 on them. All the clothes were second hand. Re-used until they were only fit for cleaning purposes. She showed me a clothes peg with the same number. 'You'll need to remember your number, ok? When you change, your dirty clothes go in that big basket in the corner. Your clean clothes will be on this peg number. Do you understand Rickie?'

'Yes sister'

'Don't worry, you'll get the hang of it, just follow the other boys.'

'Can I see my brothers now?'

'Come with me and we'll talk about a few things.' So off we went back past the pharmacy, and into another small room with four beds.

'This is the infirmary, where you'll sleep for the time being. You'll be perfectly safe here.'

'Yes, but my brothers are waiting!'

'Rickie, sit quietly while I finish telling you what is happening. Now your parents are both unwell and in hospital. They'll be there for quite a while, so you'll be staying with us.'

'Really, but they will all miss me, Sister.'

'No doubt they will, your other family members aren't able to take care of you anymore. They've asked us to look after you and I'll talk to mother superior about visiting your brothers, Ok?'

'Yes sister.'

'You've had a long day, have a lie down on that bed in the corner. I'll bring you something to eat, dinner time isn't for a few hours. No need for you to go to the dining hall tonight, Ok?'

'Yes sister.' Which is about the level my vocabulary shrank to. Seldom in life would I ask anyone for help. Why would they bother with me? Best not to waste my breath and get doors continually slammed in my face. Bothering people was a sin, I would soon find out.

That's how I became number E17, I used up a lifetime of tears that night. Nobody wanted me anymore, according to what I was told. Seldom in life would I ever feel close to anyone. All the doors where I thought I was welcome had now closed. Given no choice I learned to accept that I was on my own. The months rolled by in a drudgery of routine existence of a closeted life where at times us kids would be locked in cupboards for varying offences. Before long I forgot to care about anything or anyone, including me.

The only thing I owned were my thoughts, which self-preservation decreed I kept to myself. For many years of my life, I rarely spoke, unless asked a direct question. A personal survival plan: don't give anyone anything that can be used against you. From this point on the rare conversations, I would have with others were often shallow and uninformative. No one cares so no one needs to know. If I tell them what they want to hear, maybe they'll leave me alone. If not plan B might be strike first, strike fast. Fight or flight became a way of life, except there was nowhere to run to.

Somewhere along the way my ability to smile vanished. If on rare occasions, photos were taken, I would stand behind someone else. Friends have commented on this annoying habit. Smiling was no longer an instinctive reaction and became a staged exercise for me when requested. Laughter was my medicine; thank God I never forget how to laugh at the absurdity of my life.

Laughing at most things may have seemed quirky to some people and infectious to others. This behaviour became my way to survive, and it skewed my perception of the world. Without a mentor or protector, I had to make the best of the hand that life had dealt. Wishing and hoping were a waste of time. I have learnt to exist in a very controlled environment, an ungenerous incarceration due to no fault of my own. This place like many others was a detention centre despite the public façade.

Segregation

During daylight hours, our group of ill or injured boys was segregated on a verandah. When the nuns were occupied elsewhere, other kids would peer through the railings, hoping for gossip. One day, a fat boy appeared on the other side and asked, 'Hey, who are you?'

'Rickie, who are you?'

'Nigel. What happened to you?' Nigel was quite chubby in comparison to his scrawny mates. He must have an inside track to extra food, which might come in handy one day.

'Come back later. Lot of big ears around here.'

Smirking, he gave me the thumbs up. 'See you later, Rickie.'

Nigel and his followers went off down to the back of the playground. No doubt to gossip about the flogged newbie and embellish the story to their hearts' content.

Nigel popped up again when a nun called out, 'Bath time, year one first.'

This routine was conducted by school grades one through four, with sick kids being last. Bathwater was changed every so often. Waste not, want not, was the idea.

'Hey Rickie, how ya going?'

'Hi Nigel, what's up?'

'Why did you get a flogging? You're a bad boy, hey?' Straight to the point, this habit became ingrained in us all. We never learned subtlety. On many occasions throughout my life, people found it annoying. If you don't want the truth, why waste your breath asking me?

'Nothing, I'm a saint, mate. She asked a lot of questions, that one's a real sticky beak, going on about God knows what, so I told her that I was leaving.'

'Then what happened?'

'She just started whacking into me, and I told her to stop, or my older brothers would bash her up.'

'And then what happened?'

I gave her a swift kick in the shins. Smarted her up, that did.'

'Holy cow, that would've made her angry; you shouldn't have done that!'

'Yeah! well, great time to tell me now. She went nuts, started whacking me with her belt, and then I swear she was trying to drown me in one of those big old bathtubs.'

'Is it true that the cops took her away?'

'Probably off to the loony bin if you ask me.' This would improve my street cred around here if the rumour got about. Things had a habit of growing out of all proportion to the facts. These kids just loved a good story.

One of the nuns called out, 'Nigel, get away from those boys and get ready for your bath.'

'Yes, sister, see you later, Rickie,' and off he bolted.

'Bye, Nigel.' We became friends over time, which came in handy. His being a bigger boy discouraged some of the bully boys' attacks on me. Over the years, I realized that he was a few slices short of a loaf, but he had a good heart.

It was about a month before I could see my big brothers. They were just on the other side of the main verandah. In the big boy's section, no more than twenty metres away from me directly. I was taken on a confusing route to the meeting place, which was held on a wide verandah with a bell tower perched on the roof. I was so excited as it was almost two years since I'd last seen them. My brothers stood on one side, while I stood on the other with nuns in close attendance.

'Illy, Ike, Elan, I have missed you so much.'

'Hello, Rickie,' they all said in unison.

'Can I come over there?'

'No, stay where you are!'

'Why?'

'Because big boys' and little boys' sections aren't allowed to mix.' None of that made any sense to me.

'What?'

'The sisters don't like us all to get together, Rickie,' said Illy angrily.

'Stuff that.'

I ran to the other side, and that created chaos. The nuns shouted, and more kids got involved. It was not one of my best ideas. They dispensed their displeasure upon us with canes and straps until control was regained. I, on the other hand, was dragged off to receive penance as only the truly righteous can deliver. The process of divide and conquer in this place of intimidation and confinement would affect all our lives.

The rest of the world carried on, unaware of our plight. We faded into history as a *"forgotten generation."* I was not offered another supervised opportunity to visit my brothers. They would soon work out a covert visitation system, sometimes in tandem with the official sibling gatherings on Sunday afternoons. Outside that boundary fence, the world we had known ceased to exist, and I joined the legions of *Lost Souls*. My life from then on settled into a monotonous routine, marked by the ringing of bells, both large and small.

Our dormitories were big, freezing in winter and hot in summer. They consisted of a low-set timber construction on short stumps with external weatherboard walls. Tongue and groove timber lining were used on the inside. The ceilings and floors were timber lined and topped off with a corrugated tin roof. The side walls had large sash windows, which allowed some breeze and a multitude of mosquitoes to pour in. Double timber & glass French doors at either end. The external one remains bolted most of the time. Our internal furnishings consisted of two rows of steel bed frames with stretched wire bases and a stuffed horsehair mattress on top. These mattresses were packed quite hard, and you'd regret it if you decided to take a flying leap onto one. A timber two-drawer side table separated you from the next kid. Each dormitory had a small cubicle in the corner, where one of the nuns would sleep. To be close by her fifty to eighty little angels for the night. At 6 am, we woke to the joyful sound of bells and slid from our beds to kneel for morning prayers that sometimes drifted to a creation of my own.

"Little bells stop your swinging; it's hell when you're ringing; if you just fell, all would be well, especially on a freezing winter's day." God treated my little prayer with disdain. Then the morning rush was on; then off to ablutions, get dressed, make your own bed and the corners better be tucked in at the right angles. No time to dither just get in line. Don't be late or a whack would make sure you weren't often at the rear.

Glorious Food

Our breakfast consisted of watery porridge, a type of ceravite colloquially known as *bird seed*, toast, or bread with butter, and, if we were lucky, jam or vegemite. It was all washed down with a mug of steamy, weak tea. Then, we returned to our residential area to clean our teeth, wash our hands, and get in line for school.

Morning break provided a small bottle of milk, which was the best part of my day. Then, back to our lessons, a wack with something was inevitable, almost a ritual. The reasons were many; if you fell asleep, daydreamed, didn't understand, looked out the window or failed to achieve expectations. It was the Whack, Whack, which brought you back. Any poor soul who had learning disabilities was considered a slacker. The sisters' regimental routines would've done a sergeant major proud. We all tried not to look at the clock as this was a dead giveaway that your attention was waning.

Waiting for our lunch break was agonising as we were always hungry. We downed with gusto as food was a welcome pastime for whatever was served, sandwiches, some meat stew, and damaged fruit sometimes. Winter was special as we also had soup, which always warmed me up. If you turned your nose up at what was on offer, you went hungry. This place was diet control central, and my physique, after being here for close to six years, was on the skinny side.

At 11 years of age, I weighed sixty-eight pounds, a fact discovered while idling time away at a railway station on one of my rare health excursions. To be fair to these nuns, they would put in long days to feed and care for us. They, on the other hand, received little government financial support and precious little thanks. Some of the nuns were nasty and had anger management problems; most were okay and strong-willed; they had to be to survive us. Still, as childhoods go, it left a lot to be desired.

After lunch, there was usually ½ hour for playtime. On offer were two swings, a monkey bar, several old car tyres, and bare spots to play marbles for several hundred kids. A mind-numbing pastime.

Meals were served with constancy. Fridays were fish days, a food I was forced to eat; it made me ill, and I vomited. I later discovered that I was allergic to seafood. It was a matter of eating it or starving; I chose to starve. Wasting food was a sin. In my first year here, I was the target of abuse for wasting decent food. Floggings taught me one thing that's for sure, get more innovative. Another boy might eat my fish for a bribe. Once a month, maybe we would receive a treat: homemade ice cream. This was an item of trade, which ensured my fish meals disappeared.

The only reason we moved to another table was when new boys arrived. Newbies started the endurance of their new life in the spotlight, seated at the front table. It was then that existing boys would shift. I'm not sure how the nuns worked out this checkerboard game. After about three months, good old Nigel solved the problem for me. He convinced another boy he'd be much happier exchanging places with me. I ended up on Nigel's table, the centre one, in the back row near a window, without attracting too much attention.

Finally, I was at a table where I knew the kids well. We kept each other's secrets and, over time, formed our own covert group. Don't give anyone up, or you copped it from all of us. My plan, which they'd appreciated the humour, was to catapult the fish out the window by hitting the edge of my plate. *Which meant that I now had to eat my own ice cream.* The window was generally left open, except one time, it wasn't. Then, the flying fish made a loud noise, hitting the glass. Nigel threw a piece of buttered bread at the head of a kid on the next table, causing quite a stir. One had to think quickly about this place.

'What's all that racket out there? You boys sit down this minute,' the charge sister called out.

There were less than 10 seconds to act before she got from the servery, past the alcove and out through the locked access door. Quickly, I dragged my chair to the window, straining to push it up to the first catch, and then I threw the fish out.

'Why're you standing on that chair, boy?'

'Cats sister.'

'What cats?'

'The cats outside are fighting, sister; I was just trying to close the window.'

The wild cats were used to their Friday night fish dinner and were a little upset it was late. It was always a good idea to keep to the facts and add a little embellishment to improve my chances of survival.

'Get down from there at once! You boys at table three, what're you fighting about? Sit down this minute and be quiet. Now, who started all this?'

Typically, they all pointed at one another, as no one seemed to know who started throwing bread. There were two ratbags at that table who had been giving me grief on separate occasions. I figured fair's fair, and revenge is best served cold.

'Right, Table two, with Cat Boy as your leader. Collect all the plates and place them on the servery.'

'Yes, Sister,' I replied.

This was an easy job; twelve tables, each with ten kids, created a lot of washing up. Oh, what joy this was to hear, as it was our table's turn to wash up. I could almost hear the words she was going to say.

'Table three, you're on wash-up duty tonight!'

'But sister, our turn is tomorrow night,' one of them complained.

'Good! Practice makes perfect. The rest of you boys, pass your plates to the end of your table, and don't dawdle, cat boy!'

'Yes, Sister, hurry up, guys, we're getting out of here.' *You beauty sister, I'm a jolly good fellow, and so said all of us.* This meant they would all owe me favours for a change.

'All right, the rest of you. Stand quietly, go outside, and line up in silence.'

'Yes, Sister,' they all called out.

'Silence.' This was an implied threat.

Unfortunately for those table three mob, night-time roster duty meant you got to wash and dry all those dishes, cutlery, pots, and pans, then stack them all away. You also had to sweep and mop the floors and carry rubbish bins down to the outside holding area. All this you obviously loved to do out of the goodness of your heart— just marvellous. It also meant you missed TV, and things would only get worse if you were late for bedtime. Dawdling is a sin.

Fun for Some

We merrily trudged off to our common room for two hours. Here, we had free time to play board games, do card tricks, read comics, and watch TV. Nigel and I liked crosswords and simple secret code puzzles. The nuns selected most TV shows. The nightly news was a must-watch educational program. Astro Boy or the Jetsons got our attention, and Monkey Magic or sometimes Pick a Box, which was a new game show. Then come 8.30 pm or close to it, the TV was turned off.

It was time for bed, to clean your teeth, and a nun dispensed toothpaste. Then, off to the toilet, wash hands and say nightly prayers before bed. This kneeling business on hard, bare floors was doing my knees in. Life around here is no bed of roses. Lights went out at 9 pm; woe betides you if you're late back to your bed. Tardiness was one of the 101 things that were a sin. Sleep and silence were the rule; get caught, you're a bloody fool. Some poor bugger was always crying in this place, misery and pain their constant companion. If they became the target of the current crop of bully boys, a biffing for any slight misdemeanour, imagined or otherwise, was forthcoming.

Now I lay me down to sleep; I wish to God to get these creeps. How is it done? Please give me a sign. Nothing big would suit me fine; it's beginning to look like I'm running out of time. Thank you, God; I hope we agreed that giving them hell would be best for me. One of my many creative nighttime prayers, which I hope heaven hears.

Some of the fortunate boys possessed a torch, a handy item that could be used to read comics under the cover of the sheets. Keen ears listened out for the signal. The bangs of closing doors and the tap-tap sound of a nun's shoes on the timber floor. A God-sent early warning to let us little angels know to feign sleep. Mornings brought new misery for any of the boys who'd wet their beds, which was about twenty per cent of the kids. Empathy was in short supply. Often, they copped a slap from the nuns and a swift kick from any other kid who slept near them, which did little to reduce their misery or level of anxiety. Counselling was a non-event. The end of a stick had more immediate and effective outcomes. Educational motivation was a physical thing backed up by psychological harassment. My ability to adapt was beneficial to my existence. This game of life had diversions and perversions of abuse of a physical, psychological and, at times, sexual bias. The last was a subject we were naïve about. Trusting others was a bad idea, and the rules were fuzzy, changeable as the winds. Our possessions were few, friends rare. They could be used against you should an opportunity arise for someone else to benefit.

Participating in activities was how to fit in here, like hiding in plain sight. Knowledge was king; any advantage I'd gain was kept to myself. One thing I never shared with anyone was that I possessed a photographic memory. Most of the time, I played dumb to distract undue attention. Being top of the class had disadvantages; being slightly above average was cool. It was good to have some other high achievers gain the limelight and deal with the prize. This ruse prevented me from being a target. However, it would annoy the nuns and cause them to wonder. Unfortunately, life can throw curve balls, as being a passenger in a car accident later in life would severely dampen this ability. Then I discovered what most of the population already knew: that learning required a lot of effort. I was suspicious of the intentions of everyone at this stage of my life. The adults may have felt they were doing an excellent job. Who was I to tell them any different? Ungrateful kids received particular attention, which would harm one's well-being.

Destiny

I accidentally bumped into a girl today while running to catch up with the rest of the mob. We both seemed to have the same idea: run fast without looking, which resulted in both of us ending up on our backsides on the timber verandah.

'Sorry, are you ok?' As I bent to help her up.

'No, I am not you silly boy! Now I am in more trouble for being late. I don't like this place,' she replied.

'Me either. Maybe we can keep running out the gate?'

'I have already tried that; it doesn't help much.'

'My name is Rickie, What's yours?'

'Gloria.'

'Tell them some boy tripped you over and run away, might help.

'Are you nuts?'

'Bye Gloria, see later, alligator.' Then we both took off.

I don't know what happened to that girl. She disappeared.

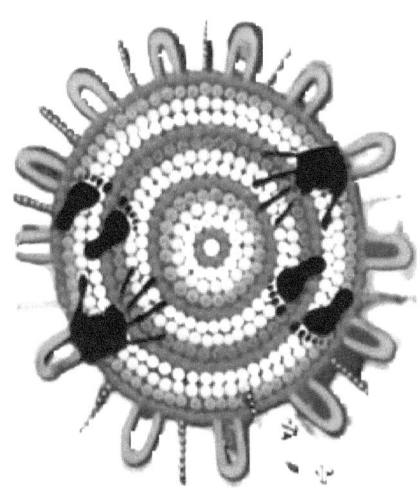

DESTINY CONVERGENCE

Social Interaction

I disagreed with this sibling separation rule, and a plan B was needed. My eldest brother, Illy, had left and got himself a job in the meatworks. No farewells, just gone. A secret code became our *forte*. In an orphanage, it's a matter of trusting God and few others. My brothers' mates would pass the coded message on to their younger siblings during official family visits.

Good old Nigel: God bless his soul, provided me with a secret pathway. He was, by nature, inclined towards adventure and mischief. His hidden route was a crawl space, confusing to others. There were different exit points on the other side depending on your purpose and the nun on duty. It was important to look up through the verandah board gaps for any unexpected watcher who may bring the game undone. We became each other's lookout to discourage other boys and on alert for overtly attentive nuns. Each of us varied our route so as not to leave drag marks in one spot. On our prearranged days, I would grab Nigel's hidden cardboard sled, a shabby, flatted cardboard box that often smelt of cat urine. This added to its allure as the smell kept others from confiscating it. A homemade tool of necessity to keep the red dirt off our clothes, which would be a dead giveaway.

When I came out from behind the hedge on the other side, I could roll out unseen. Here, I would wait for my brothers, whose habit it was to walk around that general area. Each would go past separately as a ruse designed not to attract attention.

Sometimes, for the hell of it, I'd give the in-house high jump event a go by attempting to climb over the high wooden boundary fence. This was the ultimate challenge for me, the final frontier known as the forbidden boundary, guarded by our minders. This earned me a flogging with the cane, an instrument favoured by teachers in every school all over Australia. It got so bad that kids were proud of how many cuts they got each week; it can be dumb being tough, but we were short on games. On one such occasion, my brother

Ike saw this nun flogging me, as I wouldn't let go of the fence. He came to my rescue and grabbed her from behind to dissuade her cruel intentions. With one arm around her and the other on the cane, they both fell to the ground, and Ike yelled out.

'Stop Rickie!'

'What?' I let go of the fence and ran over to help, snatching the cane from the nun.

I managed a serve or two on my tormentor before another nun took it off me. Like most things in life, actions have consequences, and our tormentors take them seriously. Unfortunately, this time, for both of us, it came with an extra sting. For me, it is more of the same pain, both physical and emotional. Ike was shipped out to Wilston Youth Detention Centre, a demonic place in comparison. His charge, according to their version of the event, was he'd made a violent, unprovoked attack on a nun. I wasn't to see him again till I was about nineteen. Only one of my brothers remained, and by the time I was old enough to move up to the big boy's section, he would be gone, too. Elan would shift to a De La Salle boarding college under some scholarship arrangement. No one ever told me that my brothers were leaving or where they went. I was on my own, again. This was an act of mental torture. Now everyone I had cared about was gone.

Some kids had all the luck. Their families came to visit them most Sundays. I would on occasion, watch them through a gap in the courtyard fence, which was depressing. Out there they'd laugh and play with their own real family. *How normal it all seemed; did I ever do that?* The front courtyard gardens were another forbidden zone to the rest of us. In the beginning, my father came to see us but was discouraged from continuing. Another underhanded tactic the authorities used on visiting relatives. The concept was that visitors would only make us feel more miserable when they left. It was nowhere near as damaging as the feeling of abandonment. Being lonely can be changed, being left all alone creates a dead spot deep inside you that never goes away.

The golden rule that children should be seen and not heard; had a purpose. It was a behavioural practice suitable for restrictive control by Child Services of the time. How could they muddle through their day if they were constantly redirecting impertinent questions from parents or the public? To thwart the endless minions, a process was conceived that required innumerable levels of disassociated redirection forms. To be completed and taken to a different department to be stamped and returned for review. These workers dreamed of moving up a level that required they met their quota of T's crossed and I's dotted. It was their sworn duty to implement this process with determination, dedication, and, where necessary, procrastination. Their looking into things became legendary and eventually became the job itself. Achieving useful outcomes was for smartarses who were reassigned to the records dungeon. At the other end of the scale were us annoying kids; we were told to put a sock in it.

Around 1963, Dad came to visit my brothers and me. It must have been quite a road trip for him to travel from Kenmore Repatriation Hospital by bus, train, and bus again to the majestic mudflats amongst primeval mangrove swamps. This came as quite a surprise, having previously been told he had died.

After 1964, I must have fallen into the too-hard basket. Rarely did I have a visitor, being the only one of us boys left here. My brother Elan came a few times from his new college at Scarborough. This wasn't far away as the crow flies, though certainly a long, tedious journey by public transport. The ungenerous Christianity of the brothers in charge curtailed his free time; a scholarship apparently did not extend to external family activities. They required him to use his spare time doing chores, and there was no such thing as a free lunch. I must remember not to accept such a gift should a similar opportunity arise.

We are going to have a special Christmas lunch, according to the rumour mill. If true, we all highly anticipate it. Be thankful for small mercies. Some older girls who worked in the kitchens told me they'd gone out with the nuns to local food vendors. Cafes, bakeries, and restaurants kept their leftovers to help support the orphans and the homeless, a noble cause till some spineless wanker stuffed it up. Other girls would sort through fruit bins to save the unspoiled parts and make stewed fruit and pies. These were a real treat we'd occasionally have. Other times, maybe custard, sago, tapioca, or jelly. I always thought they were delicious, regardless of the origin of some of the ingredients. To all the girls, thank you.

The nuns, through their fundraisers and the help of generous, goodhearted people, struggled to provide us with little above the basics. Growing children are naturally ravenous creatures; our quantity-controlled diet barely touched the sides as we scoffed food down. These special dinners, as they were colloquially called, would almost start a riot. The rush for anything special created a herd mentality; the fear of missing out galvanised us starving munchkins.

One day, something extraordinary occurred: we went into the city to see the hit movie, *Mary Poppins*. Any kid misbehaving had Buckley's chance, as the seats were limited. A special bus trip took us to the Wintergarden Theatre, situated on Queen Street, Brisbane. This was a salubrious, richly furnished establishment with a marble ground floor and a central walkway of deep red carpet that led patrons to the stalls section. We were cordially greeted by a bevy of stylishly dressed usherettes, who escorted us to our seats. I, like most of the other kids, were overawed by this attention and, for a brief time in our lives, felt like someone cared. We received a frozen chocolate-coated ice cream in a cone, a soft drink, and a small bag of lollies. Our faces grinned with the enormity of these treats, and when the big screen lit up, we sat dumbfounded. For a few short hours, I was swept away into a magical world. While watching the big screen, we escaped our dreary lives and revelled in Mary Poppin's magical world. Here we could dream how wonderful children's lives might be, if someone loved and cared about them.

Good Times are Rare

On two occasions, I remained here while most of the kids enjoyed freedom for a few week's holiday. The place felt like a ghost town, with silent buildings and a lot fewer adults. As the saying goes, a change is as good as a holiday. I fared better over the following years and was billeted out to a variety of foster parents, not knowing what to expect. A background on them would've been helpful as their locations were many and varied. A family from Wavell Heights took me with their kids for a Christmas holiday at the beach. The father had built a plywood caravan, and it was a lot of fun to camp in. One day, I told them I'd heard on the radio that Elvis Presley had died, aged forty-two. I must have been tuning into the future. They had a laugh, thinking I was a peculiar kid. Years later, I was right. I often had premonitions of impending danger to others or myself. I'd learnt to keep those thoughts to myself as one time I slipped up, and some kids became quite hostile towards me.

There were other families where I had a fun holiday and was spoilt rotten, as they were quite wealthy. They owned hotels, car garages, or shopping precincts like TC Beirnes in the Fortitude Valley. One of them owned a newspaper. Somehow, I didn't fit into this elite cadre. My ideas on fun stressed them out. How different my life could be if I were adopted. Mostly, these foster parents were kind, generous in spirit, and treated me well. Out in the suburbs, there was one odd couple who would creep me out. I felt uneasy being by myself with the bloke. I was happy to leave and return to the orphanage.

During the Christmas holidays of 1965, I was sent out to stay with a rural family who owned a grain farm at a place called Formation, a fly spot on the map near Jondaryan, Queensland. It was here that I first realised I preferred country life. Along with a couple of other boys, we enjoyed spending time on the tractors and helping with the farm work. When receiving presents from these families, I felt ashamed, as I had nothing to give them in return. I would leave those presents behind when I left. We didn't have personal possessions in the orphanage, and if we did, they would disappear. Occasionally, I would receive cards from these families or a relative. Birthdays were a thing to keep quiet about as others celebrated it by giving you a punch or a kick or two to mark the occasion.

Some of the cards held money but were opened, and inside, a dollar amount was written. Once, I thought to inquire about this while standing in line. The kid in front of me got a clip in the ear and a belting for asking a similar question. This saved me the trouble; I would no doubt get the same answer. The nuns held onto the money, and we can spend a part of this each week. If you'd been naughty that week, you missed out on buying lollies at the *'little shop cupboard'* on the verandah. Small things bring great joy when you have nothing.

This was a lesson in the reality of economics as the nuns kept a concise record in their little book. One possible reason for this was to remove an incentive for any of us to run away.

In this, they were correct, as any escape required opportunity, timing, and cash. I kept the holiday money hidden in my secret space. Then, I had the funds to explore the unknown for a few hours of freedom, which is not the same as running away. Once, I got on the wrong train; instead of going to Sandgate, I was heading into the city. So, stuff it, I went to a suburban picture theatre at a place called Toombul and sat in a row with some noisy kids. It felt like a normal thing to do, sitting there eating popcorn like everyone else. On my return trip, the attention of a nosy conductor checking train tickets motivated me to jump out at the next station. This made for a long walk back, so I stuck my thumb out to hitch a ride.

Eventually, someone stopped, a huge hairy biker…'Where are ya going, kid?'

'Hello, umm, up along that long road over there, it goes up past the cemetery.'

'Get on,' no helmets needed. It was a noisy bike, but this was cool! *One day, I'm going to get one of these.*

'Stop just here,' I said as I jumped off the bike outside a house across the road from the cemetery.

'Hey kid, you going to be, ok?'

'Yep, No worries, thanks.'

'You need a better story if you're going to run around the place.'

'Huh, Ok.'

The biker took off and turned at the next intersection. As it was late in the afternoon, I ran the rest of the way and could've sworn that I'd heard a motorbike rumble behind me. Back to my hidey-hole, I changed my clothes to orphanage ones. I had them hidden in a bag in an old dead tree. Then my luck ran out as I bumped into a nun in my haste to blend in with the mob.

'Hello sister, have you had a nice day?' It was bath time, and no doubt I was in deep shit.

'Where've you been?'

'I fell asleep under the building, sister' I replied. As I had put dirt on my clothes, face, arms, and knees, it was worth a try.

'Must of been some sleep you've missed lunch as well.'

'Yes, sister, I was exhausted; I might be coming down with some bug.'

'You're coming down with something all right and weren't under this building. I had some of the boys look under here; explain yourself.' She was determined this one, a bloodhound with the scent up her nose.

'I was under the first classroom area, over there.'

'What in the dear lord's name were you doing there? That's outside your boundary, young man.'

'I was looking for lost marbles, sister.'

'That is a likely story; move yourself and get into the bathroom.'

I don't know about the truth setting me free; it'll most likely attract more crap in this place. Being the lesser of two evils, my story was rewarded with a belting, bath, and no dinner. The more I jumped around, and yelled, seemed to reinforce their belief that it was a lesson well earned. Even though the belting stung, the pain diminished. In time, more fun might be gained from mischief. One can only pray. Most of the kids who did run away were soon rounded up by the coppers. The result was a return trip here to face the music and flogging for good measure. Some were then moved onto places of more pain and suffering with foreboding names that struck fear into our hearts: Wilston, Riverview, Westbrook, or special schools like BoysTown. Some kids just seemed to disappear off the face of the earth and were never heard of again. This was the historical nature of the nefarious underbelly of institutional supervision as they dutifully conducted their care of minors.

Did we get up to mischief? Every chance we got. Did we get caught? Not enough for us to stop trying. Kids are what they are; adventures are a rite of passage, even when some of them scare the hell out of you.

In time, justice was served in full measure to our in-house bully boys; our own secret brotherhood gleefully delivered this. Our guerrilla tactics proved most successful in dealing with these ratbags. They never knew who got them, which was just as well. Loose lips would bring us a mountain of grief. The nuns were often too busy to keep their eyes on us all the time. God was on our side, it would appear; let's face it, we needed all the help we could get. Our survival as functional human beings depended on it. We had our scrounging expeditions to find extra food and whatever else we could get our hands on. The rubbish tip, repair workshop and an old disused woodwork shed supplied us with an assortment of raw materials, which enabled us to create some homemade weapons and the occasional toy.

Our favourite was Shang *eyes,* a useful weapon. It was a crude form of slingshot, something we could easily hide. These were pivotal to attenuating our prey, the slovenly bully boys, whose confidence was being eroded by unknown sporadic attacks. Their attempts to extort information gained them little more than running around in circles. No one besides us knew anything, but that didn't stop others from telling stories to curry favour. Besides, dobbing in someone would only make any kid a pariah, a sure path to a painful existence. Violence was an unseen undertone that permeated all our daily lives.

The golden rule is that silence will bring you peace; anything else, watch out. The three monkeys' rule is that you should say nothing, see nothing, hear nothing, and sure as hell, it was useful not to know anything either.

Even when the kid beside you had a pillow put over his head, and others punched the crap out of him. If you were questioned, you were fast asleep at the time, along with all the other little angels. The foolish fellow had obviously fallen out of bed while having a bad dream and injured himself. To counteract this, a few of us formed the Justice League, which consisted of Raga, Petra, Chris, Bobbie, me and, on occasion, Nigel. He was now in the new special school set up for kids with learning difficulties, and he wasn't always part of our activities. We'd tell him disinformation at times, which he would naturally let slip to the nosey ones; this worked to deflect interest in us. On the other hand, he could be trusted to keep a big secret as he loved being part of something no one else knew. We learnt at a young age that division of knowledge effectively minimises damage to us all.

It was nearing the end of our final term in the little boy's section, a change that offered new beginnings. Maybe a better life, but it was unwelcome to our group. In the next term, after Easter break, we'd move up to the big boy's section. This would bring new challenges as we were little fish in a bigger pond. Fear of the unknown was a major reason why some kids ran away rather than face the gauntlet. I would, too, if only I had somewhere to run to. It is best not to dwell on these things, as they can defeat you before you even start. Chill out, daydream, whatever it takes and watch you don't walk into a fist in the meantime. Sometimes you bluff your way through, dazzle them with brilliance or baffle them with bullshit, whatever works. The main thing was to survive in my original condition, preferably. Sticks and stones can break my bones, and I will never feel quite right again.

Rural Life Beckons

I spent this Christmas holidays on the farm at Formartin with one other boy. He went by the nickname *Jai*. He was an Aboriginal boy, one of the most relaxed people I've met. We had a great time out there, although we didn't stay with the original foster parents. The mother was having a baby, so we were billeted in another house on the property where the husband's two older brothers lived. These guys were ex-soldiers and lived frugally, eating the same things every day, which didn't particularly bother us except for one thing. The older of the two used to leave his dog, a Doberman Pinscher, in the house yard to keep us out, or so we thought. It may've been because their tobacco started to dwindle mysteriously. We drove that dog crazy, as one of us would stir it up at the front fence while the other ran through the back door. Jai was much faster than me. The dog nearly got me a few times as I felt its breath on my arse.

One day, the dog was relocated out under a tank stand and chained up, probably because it was cooler. We heard it barking, growling, and going crazy, and then it went quiet. So, we went to see what was happening, and the dog lay on its side whimpering. I took a chance that it was not a ploy of the dog to attack us and gave it a pat. It died within minutes. The culprit, a black snake, lay nearby, chomped up but still moving; Jai sorted that out with a shovel. When the brothers returned and found their dog dead [and the snake], they sadly buried the dog under the tank stand. These blokes didn't take us out on the farm equipment much, unlike Vince and his wife would do most days. Sometimes, we got bored just sitting around, and borrowing a few smokes alleviated the problem. I had not smoked before, so it was a new experience for me. Buggered if I knew why anyone wanted to cough their guts out while choking on smoke. Still, it's a rite of passage to experience.

On Sunday, we all went into town to mass and a social chinwag with some of their relatives. The drive home included a stop at the

Jondaryan garage to get a few necessities, one being Weiss mango bar ice creams. A last delightful distraction, as tomorrow we would return to the children's home. Jai and I became mates over that holiday and remained so for years to come. In the home, Jai was a part-time friend with the biggest smile, and you could not help but like him. I say part-time, as he usually spent most of his time playing marbles and won nine times out of ten. My game was the reverse; usually, I lost more than I won. When we returned, he was back to his favourite game.

'Hey Jai, winning?'

'Hey bro, play a game?'

'Nah, got no marbles.'

'I'll lend you some of mine and show your sorry arse how not to lose so much.'

'What, how?'

'We'll go and play over there past the swings, come on.'

'So, what's the big secret? Blackfella magic.'

'Nah, you white fellas are plain dumb. You can't see what is right in front of your face. See this. It's my secret basher, a coloured steel ball that will knock quite a few marbles outside the ring, no matter what you hit.'

'So that's how you win so often.'

'Hey, I got talent, bro. I almost fall asleep playing you lot. The best games are usually at lunchtime when everyone's in a hurry. Take your shot after me; make sure no one else picks up the basher, ok?' Over time, I slowly built up a good stash of marbles, being careful not to win too often.

'Jai, here's your basher back. Thanks for the loan, as it's given me some status amongst some of these losers. Anyway, tomorrow is the big day for moving up to the big boy's section.'

'You know anyone over there? Otherwise, it's going to be another shit fight, just to be left in peace,'

'A few, some younger mates of my brother Elan and five boys from here, what about you?'

'No doubt they'll shift me along; everything around this place is a pain in the arse. I wish I'd some of my cousins here; we'd own the joint.'

'Well, in the meantime, before you become king, you're stuck with me; that's better than nothing.

'Yeah, I suppose so. Thanks, Rickie. 'No worries; we white fellas might need your wisdom. What do you reckon?

'Probably, most of you are dumb arses.'

Racism wasn't an issue with any of us, no matter where we came from, the colour of our skin or our nationality. It was more about who you were rather than what you were.

The big passing-out ceremony the next morning was more about shuffling us along like sheep from one pen into another. After church service, we had a special morning tea out on the lawns of the convent garden, a location set aside for festive events.

After that, we were marched off to the big boy's section for the next endurance test. Here, we had more significant challenges, with the slight advantage of having some mates. Before my last brother left, he told me a few things never to forget around here. Don't volunteer to be an altar boy. Be wary of laymen who come bearing gifts; watch your back. These characters went by a variety of names; they sure had touchy-feely hands and had many tricks to con you into thinking they were your friend.

Some Sunday afternoons, they'd arrive all cheerful and smiling with little gifts of lollies and join in our cricket game or be the helpful pushers of our tyres. Inside these tyres, we'd sit, and off we roll down the back of the little boy's section. Going round and round and upside down made us dizzy, and it's a wonder none of us broke a bone. Occasionally, the friendly pushers would get over-friendly, helping the boys get up from falling on the ground. For a joke, they would pull our shorts down to tuck the shirt back in. If you objected, they'd flick you in the ear and laugh it off. Sometimes, in the brick toilet block, they did a lot more than that from the stories I was told. One time, one of them grabbed hold of me while I was standing at the urinal. I turned in fright, and his trousers got all wet, so I received a clip to the ear. I took off outside before he got hold of me. It was not a good idea to go there if they were about. Pee on the wall outside, even if it meant getting a belting for it. Stories were circulating about the actions of some of these so-called pious people and reporting them got the victim in a world of trouble. If you want to stay safe, never accept a gift or invitation to a special private event. My trust in others dwindled by the day, and life rolled along a bumpy path. My remaining brother told me of a few of his remaining mates that might be handy to know.

'Rickie, you'll need to find your own way; none of us will be around to support you.'

'Ahh Elan, can't you find some reason to stay? I've had a gutful of being on my own, you guys always seem to stick together, and I deal with crap from slimeballs on my own.'

'Sorry, Rickie. I don't have a choice. You'll be okay; just don't give up.'

Our new digs were in the lower dormitory, a useful spot of sorts. Our little gang slept near each other, prevailing the allusion of fortitude. We were close to the nun's cubicle, which extruded a small sense of security. This was subjectively effective as nighttime bullying was a form of entertainment; any newbie small fry was a popular target. Still, any night that I could sleep undisturbed was crucial to my chances of balancing the books during daylight.

The undercurrent of this life was an illusion of normality; I had to use my brain to defeat the brawn of some of these ratbags. One extremely slow day, I went up to sit in the shade and read a comic I'd found. Being distracted, I walked straight into some big kid who whacked me across the left side of my head. It was about the same spot by others on occasion.

'Watch where you're going, you little shit.'

'Stuff you,' I ran at him, managing to tackle him over. Some other kid pulled me off, lifting me up by the shirt.

'Calm down, who the hell are you anyway? You want the crap beaten out of you.'

'Rickie Battler.'

'Elan's little brother?'

'What of it?'

'Llewyn, this is Elan's little brother; he asked us to keep an eye out for him.'

'Really, George, this little firecracker? Well, I'll be buggered.'

'Listen, Rickie, don't make a habit of attacking bigger kids; some of them will beat the living daylights out of you.'

'What am I supposed to do then, run away?'

'Yeah, that'd be a good idea.'

44

Forgotten

In 1966, Australia changed from imperial to metric measurements and our currency from pounds to dollars and cents; not long after my eleventh Birthday. Hooray! Our generation got to learn two systems at the same time. We became walking, talking calculators.

Religion played a big part in our daily lives; every child here became a Roman Catholic. This gave us a sense of belonging with Baptism and Confirmation. Prayers are given in the morning and evening, and before all meals, mass is given on Sundays and special saint's days. We would go on religious retreats and attend public celebrations of Christ, especially at Lent, Pentecost, Easter, and Christmas time. We were all filled with love and belief in God. The comings and goings of the catholic hierarchy always remained a mystery and would have a significant impact on all our lives. Sadly, commercialism has derailed the importance of these events, which in turn affected the prominence of God. Unfortunately, the reverence for the religions of mankind has been derailed by those who seek to divide us all.

The elation of moving up to the big boy's section soon lost its appeal as we are now at the bottom of the pecking order. Our small group was often targeted, and we distrusted everyone outside our group. Once again, my world shrunk, and I disconnected from my surroundings and almost everyone in it. We developed a wary profile to protect what little dignity we could in our crawl up another dung heap. A new game plan was needed, something drastic to take the attention off us. In eighty per cent of our playground fights, we lost collectively or individually. When we won, we were the champions of the hour, slowly climbing the pecking order. Jai proved to be the best fighter of us all and gained respect from the older boys.

'Hey Rickie, who decorated your face?'

'Hi Jai, must be my turn to be the punching bag for the Provroff brothers,'

'Yeah, those three are total pricks; fight one, they all sink the boot into you.'

'Something needs to happen to them; they target the other kids separately too.'

'Rickie, those brainless bastards need payback. They're not as smart as they like to think they are. How about we get the boys together tonight to come up with something?' Jai had joined our justice league.

'No worries. The big table in the rec room gives us a good excuse to sit around doing puzzles while everyone else is watching TV,' I suggested.

Dinnertime was as tasteful as usual. Fortunately, none of us were on wash-up duty tonight. We sat in pairs doing different puzzles, slightly apart from each other but within hearing distance. Smaller groups are less obvious to nosy parkers or other ratbags looking for an angle to gain favour with the nuns. There's always someone wondering what you're up to.

'Hey Rickie, Bobbie, Petra.'

'Hi Jai, we all replied.'

'Guess what? I found something that might help us get even. Those three pricks sneak over to the girl's section after choir practice on Thursday nights. There might be an opportunity for us.'

'What're they doing there? Those three are more like mongrel dogs,' I asked.

'They're probably just perving at the girls through a knothole in the wall?' laughed Petra.

'Yeah, they're too ugly for anything else.' Bobbie grinned.

'What'd you think, Rickie, we get the drop on them and even the score?'

'Good idea, Jai, the darkness on that verandah will come in handy. We'll have to keep a lookout for the nuns.'

Our Game Plan

'If we get the Provroffs to chase us into a secluded area, we'll sort them out,' Petra said, sounding enthused.

'Yep, that'd work. We'll need a good plan. Something suitable to educate them would be helpful. It would be handy if we had a decoy, too.'

'I know just the person. I'll talk to Nigel; him they'd certainly chase.'

'Nah, he'd freak out and drop us right in it,' the guys replied.

'Leave it with me; there's one thing you don't know about him. I'll tell him it's a game of chasey; he loves that bloody game. If I can convince him, it's a secret night game, he'll be in it. There is nothing he loves more than a big secret,' I replied.

'It's worth a try, as you're the only one he'll know about.' offered Jai.

'More likely, he'll run all the way back to his bed. Hopefully, he's clueless as to what the real game is. He'll be too afraid to look back.' Bobbie laughed.

'Ok, we'd better move before someone takes too much notice of us. Don't all get up at once. Monkey magic ends in about twenty minutes,' I suggested.

'Catch up tomorrow, Rickie?'

'Ok, at lunch break, Jai.'

Most mornings were a bun fight for all concerned. The nuns, being punctual, ran a tight schedule, so there was no time to gossip or navel gaze. The devil was a busy fellow who deviously found work for idle hands, or so the story went. I caught up with Nigel during the morning break over a mini bottle of cool milk. This was a tasty blessing bestowed upon us by the State Health Department, provided it wasn't left out in the sun too long.

'Hey Nigel, what's happening?'

'Hi Rickie, I've been busy with my special school lessons and our "chasey game" in the afternoons. I haven't seen you around much; why don't you like the game?'

'Yeah, well, things to deal with, never a dull moment around here. Hey, have you heard there's a night chasey game next week?'

'No way, there can't be. The nuns won't let us play at night-time!'

'It's a secret game, Nigel. Invitations only. The nuns don't know, so don't say a word to anyone. OK!'

'Really, true, hey, and they'll let me play?'

'Well, I could probably get you an invitation, seeing as you're my special mate. One rule though, promise me you'll not tell anyone, not a soul!'

'I promise, cross my heart. Wow, how cool. I'll see you later. Thanks, Rickie.'

During lunch break, I caught up with Jai to discuss our next move. What we produced would depend on luck, courage, and the stupidity of our intended targets. Jai was going to find something we could use to educate our antagonists. He would also follow the Provroff brothers about after choir practice, as he was a natural at blending into the darkness. I scouted out a location for the ambush and planned our escape options. This was crucial research for a successful mission.

After that, I caught up with the other four members of the Justice League to bring them up to date. I had found the ideal spot, off to the side of the girls' lower verandah, hidden from view behind two classrooms. This area was generally used for daytime vigils, a sort of retreat. It was also suitable for this night-time clandestine activity. A high hedge of hibiscus shrubs enclosed the external perimeter on three sides, with the shrubs to cast shadows and a rose garden with thorns to direct anyone onto the one clear pathway. Aged cast iron bench seats and scattered statues partially hidden along the pebble walkways added ambience to the serenity of this courtyard. In the darkness, these bench seats would kneecap anyone who ran into them. There were three access points to consider, two being narrow gaps in the hedge and the other a locked back door to our classrooms. All would play a part in our payback plan. We'll soon see whether saints win out over devils.

I got old mate Nigel to do a track time from the verandah through the hedge and over to his dormitory after school to keep him occupied. Anyone seeing him running about would think it was his loopy nature. He loved the idea and almost pissed his pants with the excitement thinking of the night-time chasey race. I decided not to bother him with the extra details about the true purpose of our night-time entertainment. All our education equipment had been acquired to heal the souls of the evil boy brothers; our payback was planned for the following Thursday night. Anticipation and fear kept us on our toes, and the day couldn't come soon enough for us to deliver justice to our tormentors. Nigel was very keen to be the Chasey race starter.

'Hey, Petra, Bobbie, we're all set to go. Jai and I'll be hiding outside the hedge, and you two hide on the inside. Raga and Kris will stay near the rec area to cover our back in case anyone gets curious about where we are. When Nigel comes racing through, those pricks will be hot on his ass, be ready with your pamper pack. Aim for their legs; that should slow them up. Make sure you don't hit Nigel!'

'Yep, got it?'

'Ok, then throw the palings over in the garden and run. Just be careful to hold the right end, as the other might have bits of nails or splinters in it. We could do without any bleeding from any of us, as it'd be a dead giveaway.'

'No worries, if there are any rough bits, we will serve them up to that ratbag threesome.'

'Then Jai and I will come right behind them to drive the message home. This should give you guys time to escape; those bully boys won't know what hit them. The ruckus should bring the girls out, yelling and screaming. That'll be a good cover-up for us to get the hell out of there as well. Do you have any questions?'

'What if you and Jai get caught?'

'Then we'll be up shit creek. Anyway, that'll be our problem, Ok?'

'Ok, good luck,' and off we all went in different directions.

'Hi Rickie, am I still going to be in the race tonight?'

'Yes, of course, Nigel. I wouldn't leave you out of it, me old mate. Meet me after choir practice outside the hall, and I'll let you know what's happening.'

'Ok, see you then; I'll come over after *Monkey Magic*, is that right?'

'Yes, and don't let anyone see you leave. Now bugger off, and don't be late tonight.'

We all had our own preparations to make for the night-time rendezvous, and I'm not sure about the rest of them, but I'm a little edgy. If plan A goes pear-shaped, we will be in more crap than we bargained for. Still, someone had to stop these three buggers, and it'll be showtime shortly. This would prove if we're all talk. If we are caught, we'll be the ones most certainly on the receiving end of a whole lot of pain. Reality can bite you on the arse.

'Rickie?' Nigel whispered in the dark.

'Shoosh. No names, over here.'

'Sorry.'

'Good to see you, Nigel. Now pay attention, you wait quietly right here until you hear a whistle, then you jump up on that verandah and yell out loud, "Dickheads" to the three guys that'll be at the corner, then run like hell through the hedge and keep going over to the dormitory.'

'Make sure you don't call out anyone's name and don't look back. We'll follow close behind you, and most importantly, don't get caught. Got that?

'Yes, this is so much fun. I can do this, Rickie. I really can. Just watch me go.'

'I know, mate. You're a champion runner.'

The high-pitched whistle pierced the silence of the night, and quietly, I whispered in his ear, "Go, Nigel, Go!" He jumped up on the verandah and yelled out at the top of his voice.

'Hey, dickheads!'

Well, that's done it; his voice was so loud, the dead must've heard it. Then he ran like the devil was after him, which would be true if those swine got hold of him.

'Who the hell was that taking the piss out of us? Come on, you two; let's beat the crap out of him.'

The Provroffs came running in tight formation, straight into swinging pieces of palings. The boys inside clobbered the first one; the second one fell over him. We delivered the full pamper package to the last one, and he went down screaming. We all swung at the second guy getting up; he went down and stayed there.

Our payback was delivered in full measure for the pain they had inflicted on a lot of us over the last three months. Petra and Bobbie then took off through the gap in the hedge. Jai and I gave the ratbags a tune-up and then threw our palings. We heard them howling in the darkness as we escaped towards the classroom's rear door. Earlier that evening I had gained access into this room through an unlocked window. The key to the rear door was always left on the inside, so I had previously unlocked it and then headed off to dinner. Hopefully, it remained undiscovered as we quietly ran to the doorway.

Fortune smiled upon us; it was still unlocked. Slowly, we opened the door as old things had the tenacity to squeak; we went and relocked it.

Breathing a quick sigh of relief, we took off through the self-locking front door. The noise and bedlam the girls created covered our escape. Silently, we crept through the darkness, keeping to the shadows, we anxiously returned to our section. Raga and Kris had turned the outside security lights off and nervously waited for us.

'Quick, you two get inside; all hell is breaking loose. The nuns are not happy.'

'Thanks for waiting, guys!'

'As if we wouldn't. Here, take these.' They handed us wet washers and a towel.

'Get yourselves cleaned up quick; your PJs are over there and bloody good, hurry.'

One of them went and switched the security lights back on while the other kept a lookout. A minute later, we chucked our clothes and towels into the corner, and slipped past the end doors when Raga whispered, 'Nun coming.'

They went on ahead. Two were less suspicious than the four of us wandering about.

'What are you boys doing out here in the corridor?'

'There's a lot of noise going on, Sister,' Kris replied.

'But what're you doing out here?'

'We heard someone screaming. It sounded like it was coming from over there, Sister,' Raga informed her.

51

The Nun walked out to see what was happening, with Kris and Raga running ahead of her.

'Wait, you boys. Don't go running blindly into the darkness. Turn on those verandah lights down there.'

'Jai, you follow along behind her, and I'll move our dirty clothes and towels.'

'Bloody hurry, Rickie, we just got through by the skin of our arse.' He followed them, asking questions.

I threw the dirty clothes into one of the rear baskets, where they had come from earlier. The washers hung back on the taps, and towels were dumped on the floor. Some Nun would no doubt complain about untidiness the next morning. By now, the intrepid, nosey kids came streaming out onto the verandah, and I mingled with the crowd.

Some of them were hoping there would be a fight or a robbery. It was excitement plus.

Sliding up beside Jai, 'What's happening, bro?' I whispered.

'Shit Rickie, you're like a bloody ghost, scared the crap out of me. There seems to be some sort of trouble over there in the Girls section.'

'Really, wonder what's it all about?'

'I don't know, bro, but it certainly has got this lot stirred up. I haven't had this much fun in ages. If this keeps up, I might get to like this place a little, you know.'

'Well, don't get too carried away with the idea. We can't be expected to provide all the entertainment around here,' I replied.

We both laughed. Our tension slowly eased, and our thoughts were in victory mode.

Suspense

The girls' dormitories erupted into total chaos. They were shouting and running all over the place. Anxiety was spreading with the manic thrill of it all. The fear of being molested by scoundrels and thieves had enraged some and frightened others; the nuns struggled to control them.

While some tried to calm everyone down, two nuns went outside to do a precautionary search. Lights came on all over the place, and the bedlam escalated. This situation was favourable to the mysterious raiders at night. A few of the other kids decided it was a good excuse to escape and ran away. The nuns returned from their search and declared the area out of bounds, leaving it to be investigated by the police. The three injured boys were taken to the infirmary; though bruised and battered, they would survive. Their cuts were treated and bandaged where necessary. With a stern warning not to be running about at night, they were marched off to their dormitory.

The following day, a creative tale was told by the Provroff brothers, Ralph, Raster and Randal. Bless their cunning hearts; they'd spun a whopper of a story. Having found themselves in a real pickle, they were up the proverbial creek. True to their nature, they had concocted an imaginative story that was missing a few details. They were the heroes, returning to their dormitory after choir practice. It had been quite dark, the verandah lights being sparsely placed, when they heard noises in the retreat area and went to have a look. Spotting somebody who appeared to be breaking into the classrooms. They'd yelled out to them to stop, and these blokes attacked them. Their story was one of bravery in the face of overwhelming odds while they tried to defend the honour of our school.

This began their myth of extraordinary bravery. Never mind who beat the crap out of them, they'd embellished and rehearsed a story before their morning trial began. All of them were of an age that would get them relocated to other facilities. They'd heard horror stories of these other places. Facing the world and the many ratbags in it while being on their own wasn't something they wanted to experience personally.

Before school the following morning, I caught up with Nigel to see what he knew, as I could do without him adding to the story.

'Hi Nigel, do you know what happened last night?'

'Hi Rickie, no, I ran really fast like you told me.'

'That's good, Nigel. We were just behind you and got back before all the riots began.'

'Rickie, do you think those Provroff pricks were waiting for us?'

'That's what I thought. Maybe they set the whole thing up in the first place.'

'Well, someone got them, the bastards. They really deserved it, Rickie. They're always picking on me.'

'Nigel, maybe we shouldn't tell anyone that we were outside playing chasey last night.'

'I hadn't thought of that. Gee, we'll get in big trouble; you won't tell them, Rickie, are you?'

'Not me. I think it'd be a good idea if we said nothing to anyone. They may blame us. It'll be our secret, Nigel. Anyway, I was heading to bed when it all started.'

'Thanks, Rickie, you're a real mate. I didn't hear anything; I was in bed when all the shouting and screaming began.'

Later that morning, a Police Officer, accompanied by the mother's superior, entered our grade five classroom. Young Randal seemed nervous. His two older brothers had already attended the hearing. They were aiding police with their investigations into last night's events. The sounds of doom echoed throughout the orphanage. Depending on their tale, it might be our rear ends in the sling. Nervously, we waited for the drama to unfold as the in–house gossip mill churned out an unofficial version of what happened at the internal police investigation.

A nun remained with the boys should they become upset about their ordeal, which was just as well, as the coppers weren't known for their temperate disposition. Unfortunately, with the two-foot-thick walls, little chance of us eavesdropping.

'Now, boys, tell us exactly what happened last night; even the tiniest details could hold vital clues on the identity of your assailants.'

The eldest Ralph, the trio's spokesman, told the story while the other two confirmed things as the tale unfolded. 'We were returning from choir rehearsals, around 8.30-9 pm, Sir.'

'That would be correct; these boys often stay back to help with the packing up at night after choir practice,' the nun confirmed.

'Then tell me in your own words what happened outside last night?' asked the copper.

'Randal tripped over on the verandah,' he pointed to his youngest brother.

'I got a big splinter in my knee; it hurt like hell,' young Randal cried.

'While Raster and I were helping Randal, we heard noises over near the retreat area, behind the hedges,' continued Ralph.

'I called out, "Who's there?" Raster said.

'Then we all went over to see what was going on and were attacked by some ratbags,' continued Ralph.

'How many were there? Would you recognise any of them? asked the copper.

'There must've been a dozen of them,' quipped young Randal.

'Not that many, maybe six, but it was too dark to see anything; we certainly felt them, though,' replied Ralph.

'They beat the crap out of us with clubs and then run off, the bastards,' said Raster.

'That'll be enough of that language, young man,' the nun warned.

'Officers, this is mostly what they told us last night; I don't think they can be of any further help. The incident has left them very frightened. May I take them back to their classes, please?' asked the nun.

'Certainly, Sister. We'll continue to look around and catch up with you after recess if that's convenient.'

'Thank you, officer,' the nun replied, leading the boys to their classrooms. Over time, each of the brothers reported this story in different variations.

'Sister, this is all a rather strange turn of events. There's no damage to any property. Except for the boys' injuries, there are no signs of breaking and entering, and nothing to your knowledge is missing. Perhaps they were interrupted before they could gain access to the rooms?'

'Yes, I agree it is most unusual; we may never know what happened here last night, I'm afraid,' the sister replied.

'Except for the scuffle marks in the garden areas and the few broken fence pickets, there is little evidence to go on. Do you think a third party may have targeted the three boys?'

'Well, they're not the most popular of boys, as they bully about every one of the other kids whenever they get the chance. No one speaks, so little can be done about it.'

'Hmm, I see, there may be more to this matter than it seems.'

'I just don't know who'd be brazen enough to do something this dreadful.'

'It's possible that someone from outside may be our culprits; either that or the three boys got scared and ran into the fence themselves,' the copper commented.

'I'll see that a closer eye is kept on them in the future; thank you for your help in this matter; no point taking it any further if that's possible?'

'That's fine, Sister. I'll include the assailant's unknown minor injuries by misadventure in my report. A good day to you, Sister.'

'Thank you, Officer. I do pray that this dreadful business never happens again. God bless you.'

The seeds of discontent had been sown amongst the Provroff brothers, an unexpected benefit from our ruse. Over the coming months, they curtailed beating up on anyone. Justice had been served, and they were none the wiser. They became wary of shadows as they suspected everyone. The nuns told them that the police thought outside assailants may have targeted them. Knowing this undermined their self-esteem, a direct takedown had certainly put the wind up them. Their nature didn't improve with the rumour going around that a cat had scared them in the dark, and they must have run into the fence and tripped over. The junior classes continued to spread this around. Young Randal copped most of the flack. These brothers were no longer considered untouchables. Thanks to their dubious natures, the Justice League was safe from exposure. Still, we needed to lay low as any coincidence would attract minute scrutiny. There was not much that escaped our amateur in-house detectives, "The Penguins".

One of their many sayings was, *"The path to hell is paved with good intentions."* We certainly do not want to wander on to that path.

In the meantime, the Provroff brothers seemed a little jittery, which caused me to smile. The concept of the boot on the other foot was interesting to contemplate. The brothers counted down the days, anxiously waiting for the Easter holidays. Their nerves were fraying as others became bold and took any opportunity to enact their own revenge in small ways. This would be one story they'd forget to tell their father. He was a hard-nosed bugger who would not take lightly to his sons being attacked. He would be even less amused that the three of them lost a fight. The nuns told the boys that it was up to them what they reported to their father. Going home for Easter would be a mixed blessing. Fortunately, they looked uninjured from their recent encounter. Still, not all of us would be lucky enough to get out of here for the forthcoming holidays.

Yahoo the Holidays

On the other hand, I was looking forward to the Easter break of 1966. I'd recently been told that I was selected in this year's group of boys who would go to Chinchilla. This was like a rite of passage to us child inmates, going out to the wilds of the Australian bush. The generosity of heart and spirit in this country town, which was situated on the western downs of Southern Queensland, was amazing for a population of around 6,000. For years, their Rotary Club had been organising billets for kids from the multiple city orphanages to experience a country holiday. Many of the families in this district opened their homes and hearts to us unwanted children. What a holiday they gave us, far above my expectations and certainly beyond anything I had imagined. If there was a place that should be called Christmas, this was it.

Our drivers arrived in their own cars for an early morning departure. They chaperoned us on what was the longest road trip of my life. We travelled in a convoy through a city that I dimly remembered, out towards Ipswich, then vied onto the 1960s version of the Warrego Highway, which meandered on forever. The morning sunshine succumbed to the encroaching shadows of an approaching storm. This did little to dampen our spirits as we cruised past bushland forests, farms, and rustic towns. The rolling plains changed as we navigated the narrow, twisting roads that led to the Great Dividing Range, upon which nestled the city of Toowoomba. Population 57,799.

At the top of the range, we detoured off the main road to a popular local landmark named Picnic Point. This was shrouded in a lingering mist; the eerie atmosphere was exhilarating for us kids as we looked out over the scenery, a spectacular view of the valleys below, farms, and forests. Even the roads looked minute from this dizzying height. We dined on a buffet lunch that was prepared especially for us - what a wonderful feeling it was to feel exclusive. With our bellies full, we continued our journey further west along the

Warrego highway. Passing through Cecil Plains, Oakey, Jondaryan, Dalby, Warra, and other rural towns supporting their farming communities. Some had less than twenty houses. Most had a post office, church or two, general store, garage and if they were lucky, a local information centre called the Pub. Here, all manner of community news was discussed over a cool drink. Upcoming events are planned, and plenty of volunteers are ready to lend a hand. The personal lives of everyone in town were a suitable subject of gossip. Secrets were rare. A big glittering sign came into view, '*Welcome to Chinchilla.*' Obviously, they were there to welcome us - or so I thought at the time. After an eight-hour road trip, it was getting to late afternoon. We'd arrived in the wheat belt of the western downs and future watermelon capital of Australia, the shire of Chinchilla.

A sprinkle of rain dampened the parched earth as we were ushered into the Civic Centre Hall. Before an early supper, introductions were made to the various family billets. Some were townsfolk, only able to accommodate one child, while others on farms would take two or more.

It was here that Karma smiled upon me for the first time in a long time.

'You're a sign of good luck, young fellow,' said the largest man I had ever seen.

'Why's that, sir,'

'You've bought the rain; what's your name?'

'Rickie, sir'

'Well, Rickie, rain is always welcome in our district, and since you arrived with it, you've brought us good luck.'

'Really! Well, you are most welcome; I shall try to bring some more, Sir.'

'That'd be much appreciated, he chuckled. 'Call me Bill, Rickie.' as he extended his huge hand.

I, along with two older boys, Andy and Micheal [grade seven boys] and my Aboriginal mate Jai, went out to William and Gwyneth Mann's property, situated about fifteen miles outside of town. We drove over a low wooden bridge that spanned the Condamine River. Veering off the bitumen road was a long gravel boulevard snaking its way through the Hopelands mixed agricultural district. Soon, we arrived at their house, a huge Queenslander style sitting on low-set timber hardwood stumps. Trees grew on the eastern and western sides of the house, supplying fresh fruit and the occasional shady spot. Cool air [when there was some], blew under and throughout the home. The dry heat might pass forty degrees Celsius in the summertime and, in winter, drop down to minus four degrees, even lower with the wind chill factor. There was so much to see. The property had a huge hayshed, silos, holding yards, and a milking shed. Perched at the top of a large steel tower was a giant windmill that pumped water to storage tanks and troughs for all the farm animals.

It was mind-boggling trying to work out what all the tractors and farm machinery were used for. Being temporarily released from my life of isolation into the wide-open spaces of the bush was a spiritual awakening. My first impression was fun, fun, fun—well, at least from the viewpoint of an excitable, imaginative boy.

Every day, life was a treat on a real farm. Dairying was a consistent part; the property ran a herd of one hundred or so, mainly Illawarra Shorthorn dairy cows. Milking alone took about four hours, twice a day, seven days a week. Early morning and late afternoon, often starting well before sunrise. Breakfast was a monumental event; kids need a lot of fuel. We wanted to learn as much as possible about rural life, and eating was a popular subject. We tucked into a country breakfast of homemade cereal, bread, fresh cream, and milk. Steak or sausages with eggs and endless cups of real tea followed this. Most food was produced on the farm, unprocessed and delicious. We were used to our orphanage routine limited amount of food. This feast was like a king's ransom that might soon disappear if we did not eat faster.

'Slow down, boys; anyone would think you're starving,' Bill commented.

'There is plenty to go around, so eat slowly and take your time; there's no rush to go anywhere,' Gwyn laughed in delight.

We never told them that for most of our lives, we were starving. After breakfast, the household chores and washing up were done with the minimum amount of water; a scarce commodity out here, every drop was liquid gold. With the excess energy only the genuinely young possess, we fidgeted with excitement, listening to the day's plan of activities. First up, were going out to the back paddocks, in the open back of the Ute. For those of you who aren't aware, that's what a utility motor vehicle is called. Us kids all piled in the back, holding onto the roof rack. We headed off through the home paddock gates to inspect the crops, cattle, fences, windmills, and dams. This was time-consuming, the many gates needing to be opened and closed behind us, ensuring the animals wouldn't stray.

We pulled up beside the back holding yards, roughly in the centre of the property almost a mile from the front road. Here were fifty of the six hundred or so beef herd, mostly poll Herefords grazing in silent wonder at mini humans running around. Some of this unsuspecting group were headed for the sale yards and we pitched in with the mustering. That afternoon a cattle truck and trailer arrived to transport them. The flies, dust, and noise were all part of the spectacle, and we boys loved every minute of it.

After lunch we drove across the road into a neighbour's property. Passing through a few fence openings along a dirt track for about a mile, to the banks of the Condamine River where the water level was low at this time of the year. To our delight a tyre on a long rope hung down from a tree branch; an instant attraction for us, as we swung out and dropped into a deep chilly waterhole.

This was a sure-fire way to use up some of our boundless energy. Despite the temperature, we kept at it until it was time to head back for the afternoon milking session. The on-farm dairy equipment was driven by a series of long belt pulleys, coupled to a noisy diesel engine. This equipment consisted of a vacuum pump and a centrifugal separator with dual outlets for cream and separated milk. The cream went into ten-gallon cans, weighting arounds ninety pounds each and stored in a multi door refrigerator. Their dairy transported the separated whole cream into the local dairy co-op in town by courier, Clarrie. Where it was processed into cheese, butter, ice cream and a range of other dairy products.

The separated milk on the other hand was used on the farm and pumped through galvanised pipes to supplement the diets of the pigs and poddy calves. They were quite vocal, when kept waiting for their favourite drink. There were also the chooks to be fed their breakfast of vegetables scraps and a large jam tin of grain.

Clarrie was a local legend, his many services included Mail delivery and bulk fuel supplier. He arrived twice a week to pick up the cans of cream. Often, he'd linger for a cuppa, some of Gwyn's famous cakes and biscuits, and a chat. Obviously, the polite thing for us boys to do, was to join him and listen intently to his news. He was also a self-taught musician of multiple instruments and a bush mechanic and happy to share his humour with the scattered farming families.

The horses got a biscuit [a section of a bale] of hay each. We liked them, and they seemed to tolerate us, or at least they didn't bite us. Stock horses are not pets. They are extremely intelligent animals and know a good thing when they get it. Besides, we did not want them throwing us off their backs when we could ride the quieter ones around inside the holding yard. Just for variety, there were fences to be repaired and stick picking, which I mistakenly thought was a game. It turned out to be a tiring activity, trudging around paddocks and picking up sticks, which was part of the final process of clearing the paddock for cultivation. Trust the country boys for their creativity in naming this one. The rear windmill provided the bore water to the holding pens and back cattle troughs on the property. While we were here, we had a swim in the "Turkeys Nest," a big round water hole with mounded sides. With over two thousand acres of paddocks to cultivate, plant, and harvest crops, the list of chores was endless. It provided more entertainment from my personal point of view. Whenever we worked out in the back paddocks, lunch was a ritual beginning with parking our rear ends on a big log that lay under the shade of some gum trees. Gwyn would bring us out freshly made sandwiches and cakes, which we devoured with pleasure and washed down with lots of black sugared real tea. She would join us for lunch and listen patiently to our endless chatter. A billy was boiled on the open campfire for those needing a top-up. Talking certainly was thirsty work.

The smoke from the bottlebrush, gum and brigalow sticks gave off an aromatic scent reminiscent of the Australian bush. Throughout my life, the memory of this scent has always felt like home to me. Jai was sitting off to the side on the ground, so I wandered over.

'Hi Jai, you, ok? It sure is a beautiful place out here in the bush.'

'Yep, sure is. It reminds me of my country, back with my mob. Different tucker, though.'

'Was that a good time for you? Back where you come from?'

'Hell of a lot better than living in the orphanage with all you white fellas.'

'Hadn't thought of it like that. Your mob own a farm?'

'It's different; we owned the whole country for thousands of years.'

'Does it make you sad being out here with us?'

'Yes and no. I don't mind you, fellas.'

'Well, then come on. Let's make the most of it while we are here; what do you say?'

'Bloody oath, mate.'

So that's what we did, just like Bill said, 'You just have to make the best of what is.' Jai and I were nearer in age than Andy and Micheal, so we'd go off through the bush on our own little adventures. When time allowed, Jai would tell me about the different native animals and bush tucker. Sometimes, he took the mickey out of me, but what the hell? We had fun.

The variety of farm life enthralled me. I asked many questions: 'What crops do you grow? How do you grow them, and when? How do you know it's going to rain at the right time? What is too much soil moisture, and what is not enough? How do the cows know when it's time to come home for milking? Do they have a clock?'

One of the men asked me, 'Where is your off switch, young professor?'

'What's a professor?'

Shaking his head, he laughed, 'You sure are an inquisitive young fellow.'

My quest for knowledge may have created mental fatigue in those around me. I wasn't used to people answering my questions without receiving a belt in the ear. This was a world I'd easily live in and quite honestly love to lose myself in.

We went into town to the livestock sale yards the next morning after breakfast. Here, some of Bill's cattle, along with hundreds of others, were to be auctioned off. What a noise, cattle bellowing, men shouting, dust everywhere and millions of flies. If you were not careful, you could swallow them by mouthful; it was best to keep your trap shut. In this place, being tight-lipped was an enviable talent. Bill seemed to know everyone and introduced us to many people; I had no hope of remembering. All the cattle were sold by the auctioneers who had good, strong, loud voices; they talked so fast I wondered how anyone could keep track of things.

Halfway through the auctions, they stopped for a break, and Bill took us all over to the CWA kiosk for a cool drink and sandwiches. Most of the men seemed to prefer the bar area to wash the dust from their throats.

'You boys, wait here and help yourself with more sandwiches and drinks; the ladies will look after you. I need to talk to some fellows and will return in twenty minutes.'

'Ok, thank you,' I called after him. These women made delicious sandwiches and gave us each a slice of cake.

'If you boys want more, just come over and ask; don't be shy,' said a beautiful lady named Jodie. She made the best passionfruit cheesecake I had ever tasted—a little bit of heaven on my tongue.

Bill returned, 'You boys, Ok?' I raised my thumb as we all had our mouths stuffed with food.

'What do I owe you, Jodie?' I heard Bill ask.

'Don't you worry about that, it's our shout, Bill,'

'Thank you, boys. Please thank the kind ladies for your lunch.'

'Thank you very much for lunch; it was delicious,' we all called out.

'The auction restarts in about fifteen minutes. If you want to go to the toilet, they're over there; make sure you wash your hands. I'll meet you near the steps to the auctioneer's platform.'

'Where's that?' we all asked?'

'See the Green international truck parked near that loading ramp?' He pointed.

'Yes.' Then he walked off that way.

We thanked all the ladies at the kiosk again, hurried off to the toilets, and rushed back to meet Bill. He'd been arranging with the auctioneers for us all to stand up there with them to watch the action. *What a day out!* Bill sold all his cattle for a good price to another cattleman, a local fellow who was building up his breeding herd.

The Rotarians and their wives, on the first Saturday afternoon of our holiday, planned a social get-together with all their neighbours. In the bush, everyone was welcome. We were the guests of honour, a gratifying feeling bestowed upon us by these amazing people. The event took place on a nearby property. The community had prepared for a feast. This was country-style, a huge Bar-B-Q made from a half-inch thick steel plate mounted over the top of 44-gallon drums with a big fire trough in the centre. Sizzling on top were steaks an inch thick, meat patties, lamb chops and sausages by the score. You name it, it was there: a pig on a spit, salads, casseroles, pies, and desserts. These people worked hard, played hard, had big hearts and an appetite to match. We, being the young Christian fellows we were, did our best to do justice to the bountiful feast before us.

The heat from the flames kept us warm as we sat in the serenity of the bush and gazed at the resplendent sky of a country sunset. The smoky haze rising from the smouldering fires deterred the legions of insects, squadrons of whom had invited themselves to our twilight cathedral. Here the laughter and fellowship beckoned us all to join in. The bugs would have to find their dinner elsewhere. After a bit of a clean-up session, some of the local musicians started to tune up their instruments. Piano accordion, violin, guitar, saxophone, clarinet, and harmonica. They performed a two-hour rendition of classical, modern, pop, country and western music. accompanied by the rich vocals of both men and women, the music created a magical evening amongst the backdrop of the brilliantly clear star-studded night sky.

Every day was an adventure; the distance was no deterrence around this part of the world. Get-togethers were organised with the other kids from the home at various properties in the district. We exchanged stories of our adventures, sharing a rare feeling of trust. For once the loneliness lifted as we joined in the young country kids' lifestyle. They excelled at making us welcome and included us in everything they did. Here, out in the calmness of the outback, lived the men and woman who gave us a glimpse of the historic heart and soul of our nation, Australia! Some people can make you feel that you have always known them—these were those type of people.

Their generosity was both sincere and heartfelt. Maybe they might like me enough to invite me back sometime. The day we dreaded was not about the journey but the destination. To say we were sad to leave does not even touch the depth of our despair. The truth of this we had learnt to hide behind smiling faces. The joy of meeting these people was real, a treasure to remember for the rest of our lives. One that no one could steal from us. Having experienced life outside our isolation walls it was now time to harden our hearts and thoughts for sanity's sake. Suck it up was a way of life for us. Emotional desolation reared its ugly head, and my deep-rooted loss returned to its black hole of silence. I thank God for sending us these kind-hearted people to brighten our lives. The Rotarians had planned some exciting activities on our return journey. A surprise lunch at the historical Jondaryan woolshed, a trip into the mists of the past that included an actual shearing demonstration. It was a real eye-opener for us to experience the effort and endurance that rural people put into their livelihoods and, in doing so, nourished our nation. Their courage to continue wrestling with that fickle finger of fate.

The Lessons of Youth

Life in a children's home is bleak and seldom enjoyable, but to be fair, at times, well-meaning people improved it. They were hamstrung by minuscule support. The fault for this lay with the paucity of bureaucrats, who, to us, were part of an evil empire lurking in the shadows of the city.

I get that in life; we all must make the best of things and strive to move forward. What my recent holiday in the bush revealed was a different way of living. A life that highlighted just how bizarre my own was. The lack of nurturing would have long-term effects on each of us as functional human beings! A reality I had suspected was confirmed: we were indeed on our own. Without drastic changes, we were at risk of becoming debris, left adrift in the wake of our own society. For nearly four years, I've trudged the walkways of this Children's Home. There's a bit more than two to go before I'm released from this place. Never will I be able to relate to other kids about my school days. They wouldn't believe it. Freedom is a long way off. Someone once said to me after I had been knocked on my arse once too often.

'You can lay in the mud and cry or get up and fight, boy. This is a choice only you can make. Inside you is the strength to be whatever and be whoever you choose to be. Courage comes in many shapes and sizes; you must want it enough to make it work. Use your brains; that is your path to a better life.'

My only crime was being born a child of a dysfunctional World War Two veteran and a mother with Huntington's disease. They were disadvantaged by restrictive government policy at the time. My mother's condition was misdiagnosed. As a result, she was placed in a mental health institution. They told me I did not understand, and they were right. I didn't understand why one group of people felt they had the right to gain wealth and prestige by running experiments on those who did not voluntarily give up their rights. The truth will be what they say it is. Power and money talk; the rest of the masses can take a walk, which is the reality of life.

Possibly, this attitude has something to do with orphanages being renamed "children's homes". A convenience for Government and Religious Organizations to gain access to children. Was it their intent to abuse and use us for cheap labour under the guise of charity? This is a truth that is too hard for some to bear witness to.

My parents deserved better—certainly more than they received. They should not be allowed to go quietly into obscurity. Their lives meant something, especially to me. Such is my legacy; I seem to be an enigma to those around me, and most likely, this will always be so. I cannot wallow in the drudgery of this existence or bend to a preordained fate.

Grand thoughts slide into the realms of fantasy, depression, or inspiration. I am not equipped to win many physical battles by myself. The only advantage I have is that I'm smarter than the average bear, I hope. Some allies who aren't dingoes and won't run or turn on me when the going gets tough, and a tougher mental state would either get me into or out of trouble. You're what you think, and you can make it improve your life or not. I could change stuff all, really.

Keeping my mouth shut might be a good start. *Put brain in gear before mouth in motion; I vaguely remember someone saying.* Now that should not be too difficult for yours truly, little Mr Chatterbox! At the ripe old age of eleven, I've been thrust into early adulthood. I don't have a mentor or a protector, and really a shag on a rock has a better chance of survival than me. It's time for a different game plan. Fortunately, I did know one sleight-of-hand boy, Jai! We could be mutually beneficial to each other.

Grade five was sometimes tedious, with a shared classroom and a teacher with grade six. For my idle mind, their blackboard was often more interesting, so I watched what was going on over there. My problem began when the teacher asked questions, and I inadvertently called out the answer to the grade six question. This resulted in repercussions from several directions; the nun would give me three wacks with the blackboard ruler. One for not raising my hand, two for not minding my own business, and three for speaking out of turn. Highly informative learning style. Out in the playground, a couple of the older boys from grade six gave me a biffing at recess to congratulate me on my sheer brilliance. One of them decided to sink the boot in because a girl he was keen on in class smiled at me. As if I can control what girls smile at! Some guys have all the luck, and there is certainly truth in the fact that no gain comes without pain.

A few weeks later, the same girl snuck up, wrapped her arms around me and said, 'Got you, Rickie boy. Now try to run away.'

Then she planted a sloppy kiss right on my face 'Uhh.'

She laughed as she ran away, calling out over her shoulder. 'See you later, luscious lips.'

Not bloody likely if I see you first. What's the matter with that girl?

The end-of-year exams gave me an unexpected opportunity to stitch up one of those nasty buggers in grade six.

When we finished our final test papers, we all had to sit quietly, waiting for the bell. When it did, down went everyone's pencil and hands on our laps. If anyone continued to write it was met with a swift cut on the knuckles with a wooden ruler, most entertaining. Then we tidied our desks, put the exam paper in the top left-hand corner and waited some more. Following the teacher's instruction, we moved out in order of our class grade, starting with the left-hand side of the room, front to rear—except for those not-so-lucky individuals who were held back for special treatment.

'Rickie Battler, stay at your desk.'

Crap, what have I done now, my brain ticking over at a hundred miles an hour? Have they sprung me at something?

'Grade six, except for the following four names who are to remain, the rest of you stand and leave the room, no hanging about outside on the verandah.' Though this was quietly spoken, it was uttered with menace. When those four had been given extra information and left, I alone remained in the classroom.

'Now Rickie, I suppose you're curious why you alone remain?'

'Yes, sister. 'Well, for one thing, you're not in trouble. It's because you've shown yourself to be such a clever boy. I've decided you need to put that fine brain of yours to better use. You can take the grade six math exam as well. Isn't that nice of me?'

'Yes, very nice of you, Sister.'

'Good, well get started and remain in this room till I return.'

'Yes, sister.'

Hmm exciting thought; not the extra maths test, but the subject of the girls in our classes. I hadn't taken much notice of them before until I discovered I was juicy gossip. My disappearing act when the final school bell sounded intrigued them. What was I up to? A critical issue they wanted answers to, no doubt. The other boys would linger under some pretence, so they could pass notes to maybe meet their beaus for extra clandestine activities. Part of this covert practice of salacious rendezvous was shadowed by choir practice and dancing lessons. Social activities I had been avoiding for my own personal missions. Perhaps I was just shit scared of those female predators.

The nun returned about an hour later with a glass of milk, a sandwich and cake on a tray and sat down at her desk.

'How are you going with your new test, Rickie?'

'Oh, wonderful sister.' If a second maths test could be expressed so.

'Good, well, come up and sit at my desk and have some lunch.'

'Thank you, sister.'

'Bring what you've finished so far so I can see if you understand.'

'Yes, sister.'

'This a nice sandwich sister!'

'You're welcome, now be quiet and eat your lunch while I read.'

This food must come from the nun's kitchen, a rare occurrence.

'Why did you give this answer to question ten?' I almost jumped out of my skin.

'What do you mean?'

'There are no steps to your conclusion. These are needed to explain how you worked it out.

'I just thought about it for a while, and the answer came into my head.

'In your head?'

'Yes, kind of like a picture.'

'Well, now that you've finished your lunch, you can go back to your desk and write down the steps to get to your answer so that we can all see your big picture.'

'Is it right?'

'I shouldn't tell you, but yes, don't do this again; you may've just guessed the correct answer.'

'No Sister.'

'Now get a move on; you have one hour left.' So, I got back to it, with one eye on the clock. Why does she want me to make up steps just to arrive at the same answer? Now I must work backwards. What a dumb idea.

I finished with five minutes to spare. I'm not sure if the nun had even looked up, so I was left to sit in silence.

'Ok, time's up, bring your paper up here and park yourself in that chair.'

'Sister?'

'Be quiet!'

'Sister, I need to go to the toilet.'

'Come with me,' she said. Just outside was the nun's toilet, which she directed me into. 'Go inside and hurry; do not make any mess. I'll be waiting outside here.'

It wouldn't do for another nun to find me in their toilet, as there would be hell to pay. I whizzed for quite a while, too much milk. I washed my hands and headed back out the door. Two nuns were talking on the verandah. Quietly closing the door, I snuck back into the classroom, only to scrape my chair on the floor. The sound alerted the nuns. One departed, and the sister-teacher locked the toilet door and came back in.

'Okay, Rickie, before you go, there's something I'm going to tell you, and you must keep it secret.'

'Yes, sister.'

'This year, one of our lay teachers, Ms Smith, has organised a special day out for the best four students in grades five and six.'

'Wow, I hope I'll be one.'

'I'd be surprised if you weren't, but if I hear any rumours about this from anyone, I'll know that you cannot keep a secret and will be most disappointed.'

'Yes, sister, I'll not say a word to anyone.'

'Ok, mind you don't. Off you go then, not a word!'

Keep a secret! If only she knew I'm the master of secrets. I wonder what all this is about; it sounds interesting, a day out to what and where?

The noise from the dancing was a great cover for my own activity. No one would hear me as I crawled under the verandah to raid the kitchen pantry. My route took me under the main community hall and partially beneath the girls' verandah to traverse the area under the dining halls. This was a high-danger zone for me as those girls had the eyes of a hawk and a keen sense of hearing. One wrong move, and they'd be onto me like feral dogs. It was late afternoon, and their active imaginations saw demons everywhere.

Large tins of booty, fruit, baked beans, and powdered milk were in the kitchen pantry. This place was locked up tight, but there was an old access shute that'd been boarded up, and to gain entry, it made some noise. My collection of helpful contraband needed a resupply; this would be the last incursion for a while. I was about to slip the boards back into place when a voice called from inside the kitchen.

'Hello, is there anyone there? I am sure, sister, that I heard noises down here somewhere.'

'Really? I didn't hear anything.' Just then, one of those dammed cats must have jumped off the bench and frightened the pair of them.

'Sookie, what're you doing in here? The cat had run over near the pantry door; I could hear it scratching. Fortunately for me, the pantry door was still locked from their side.

'You come with me, Sookie. Okay, Cheryl, let's lock up and head over to the dancing.'

Good on you, Sookie saved my ass this time; there will be extra fish out the window for you and your mates tonight. It's time for me to get the hell out of here. I'd three tins in a hessian sack; it would have to do. One time I was in here, a bag with a small amount of flour fell off the shelf, I must have looked like *Casper* the ghost running through the dark. This time was too close for comfort, so I dropped my loot off in the storage hole beneath the classroom and called it a night. Getting cleaned up was a bit of a challenge, as I had to use an old outside tap.

The next day was Saturday, the boys' section washing day for towels and bed linen changeover. A good time to dispose of my slightly grubby sheets. As a regular volunteer, it was my job to collect the wash baskets, load them on a trolley and push them along the verandahs. For this service to our community, I received payment of a stick of barley sugar. If I kept this up, I may be on the way to sainthood or something. I've often heard that God helps those who help themselves. Who am I to disagree? Besides being on errands for one of the nuns, it was a good cover story most of the time. Might be a job outside waiting for just such a skill; appear to be busy while achieving nothing.

My favourite dalliance was at the bakery. We had our own baker on the premises, and I sort of had a chat-friendly acquaintance with the man. It was more of a one-sided conversation with his grunts and hmm's radiating from the cavernous room. He didn't seem to mind my litany of questions regarding the taste and crunchiness of his freshly made bread and buns, which he would leave some of out on the bench for us workers. Technically speaking, I was a worker, a dedicated trolley pusher and a Brodie taster, no less.

For the uninitiated, a Brodie was the top part cut off a high loaf of bread. When removed, the loaf could easily fit into the bread slicer. It was always fresh and crunchy, and with margarine and vegemite added on top was an excellent snack. Most of the workers down in this area were girls. When they took a break, they loved a delicious Brodie and a glass of cold milk. They would gossip endlessly while passing on secret messages for me to courier to some special boy on their behalf. When a nun came into view, it was best if we all scattered. The payment for a note courier varied. The girls seemed to think their attempts to practice kissing techniques on me were reward enough. My delivery service had a downside. Grumpy nun pulled me up one day, and I was told to empty out my pockets: one yo-yo, a tin whistle and a few rubber bands. Harmless enough items, she seemed disappointed. Earlier, I transferred the notes from my pockets to my penguin-designed underwear. This unfashionable garment was unique to the establishment, about as safe a hidey place as you could get. They were a battle to get off at the best of times.

Jacaranda Delights

A rare beauty came from nature in October when the jacaranda trees bloomed. Our playground was carpeted with blue/violet flowers from many trees. A little slice of heaven had fallen upon us, one of my early life's few good memories.

The end-of-year exams finished in late November, creating a break to our routine while waiting for the holidays to begin. We'd play fun ball games, school skits, dance lessons, and sometimes, an amateur play group from outside the orphanage would arrive to entertain us. These were brighter days as our thoughts would drift to the possibility of an outside Christmas. I wondered if I'd go out this year to a family or end up spending the time here.

The exam results were handed back to each of us to rejoice or not. I got a First in grade five and a fourth in grade six Mathematics. I had won two of the eight spots for the special day out. The teacher nun was quite pleased with my efforts when she told me.

'Congratulations, Rickie, I knew you'd do it. Now the problem is we're the only ones who can know about this, and you'll have to choose someone to take the spot you've created in grade six.' Which delivered to me a fait accompli in the process?

'Obviously, you only can have one of the eight spots Rickie.'

'Sister, who should I choose? I don't know any of them that well.'

'It'll have to be one of the girls, so we've equal numbers.'

'Who are the next three students in line?'

'Katie, Barney, and Wanda, in that order.'

'Well, it should really be Katie's win then, so I pick her.'

'Good, that's fair. This will have to be our little secret. Let's go and arrange some going-out clothes for you for tomorrow.'

Katie, the big smoocher, will have an interesting day out, minus Barnie, the boot boy, who won't be pleased. Isn't Karma wonderful?

This is a missed opportunity for him to be with Katie, his secret school crush, and will get right up his nose. It's not my fault the nuns chose the winners; he should have studied harder.

The next morning, with two teachers as chaperones, our cheery group headed off in separate cars. An EJ Holden Station wagon and a VW beetle drove to our newly opened Toombul Shopping Centre. The girls were eager to go window shopping. We boys had the opportunity to jump the queue for a few races on the in-house multi-lane slot car track. Even though it was a six-lane track, time was limited to fifteen minutes per driver. Still, it was just as exciting to watch the other kids race, some of whom were quite skilled. At lunchtime, we gathered at a fancy café for high tea and triple-tiered plates of delicious food. A visual feast for eyes and our tummies. The giggles and foot tickles under the table made me wonder which one of these girls was winding me up. They took great joy in my face going red.

Afterwards, we went to Bullen's circus, which was my first time. There were many exotic animals, and loud side shows to see. Waltzing amongst all of this were brightly painted clowns doing tricks and a few dwarves handing out free balloons. However, the main event was under the big top, a huge triple-peaked canvas tent with multi-coloured bunting all around. Inside were acrobats swinging on a high trapeze, Lion tamers in a round steel bar cage, with the lions giving us big toothy grins as they roared. Clowns in silly mini cars were being chased by dwarf police on foot who constantly tripped over their own oversized boots. Leading the parade were elephants trumpeting loudly, followed by horses with monkeys on their backs. A menagerie of animals followed, circling the main arena. With all their bling, tassels, and feathers came the performers dazzling the crowds. It was absolute bedlam as they twirled and danced their way past us.

Up in the tiered seating, another magic trick was going on. Katie ended up seated beside me. She had staked her claim and would not wait for some backward boy to make a move. I just sat there grinning and wondering what the hell to do. She would be one to watch in the future, a cougar in the making. Oh well Barnie boy. You have missed out on a kiss or two and a mischievous smile from the best-looking girl in your class. Steve and Harold were sidekicks of Barnie's in grade six, they had a sense of humour like mine. Which tended to be a bit on the dark side, but orphans can't be choosey. Steve was smitten with Charmaine, who was Katie's bestie and Wanda was Harold's daydream. It wouldn't end well for either of these guys to upset the apple cart with the girls. The trio stuck together like glue, in and out of class. They liked to have fun and schemed their own plans to a fine detail. If I'm not careful, I'd end up the jam in the roll here. I sensed a shit fight on the horizon. Life was starting to get slightly complicated. Sundays was Mass, the rest of the day adult visitors filtered into our lives, or we wandered about in circles. My options on Sundays were reading the adventures of superheroes in comic books, maybe an ad hoc cricket match or red rover/chasey game.

Gone Berserk

My day's entertainment was provided by a less-than-subtle third party for reasons not yet clear to me. I had stepped into the cool shadows of a building to find a few moments of peace from the rabble. Without warning, I got a punch in the face out of nowhere and not a nun in sight. I ended up sprawled out on the ground, and Barney's boots did a tap dance on my body. As I struggled to get back up, he knocked me arse over again. Grabbing hold of one of his legs, I managed to trip him over, and as he fell, I ran. Flight was the better part of valour at the time, as *Queensberry Rules* were not on his mind.

Getting in a biff up with someone taller, heavier, and stronger than myself had distinct disadvantages. He was in a rage and intended to impart a long-term memory that might put me in the hospital. The thumping on the floorboards told me he was catching up. I made a side exit for the nearest toilet block and shut myself in one of the cubicles. Barnie was pounding on the door, charging at it to break the lock. I went over the partition into the next cubicle just as the door crashed in.

He had slipped on the wet floor and went headfirst into the toilet bowl, knocking the old timber toilet seat onto the floor. The best form of defence around here is to be a berserker. I raced around to his cubicle, and with the only weapon available being the broken toilet seat, I beat the crap out of him. In the process, the lid completely broke in half, which was no longer useful. If he got up, I would be annihilated, so I grabbed the ancient wooden toilet brush and shoved it in his face a few times; it ended up partially in his mouth. *That should shut him up for a while, and it's high time I got the hell out of here.* I sprinted across the playground, where the other kids jeering spurred me on. I didn't want to come across the rest of his mates and have them gang up on me. Leaping onto the verandah, I bolted around the corner and ran smack into a nun. Of all the bloody places for her to be standing around it had to be right there in front of me. She stood looking dumbfounded as she leaned against the wall, staring at my appearance, bleeding, battered and bruised. It was a bit hard to hide the fact that I'd been fighting.

'Why are you running? Oh my God, what on earth has happened to you? What's your name, boy?'

'Rickie Battler, I stepped out on the verandah over there, and someone punched me in the face, then they started kicking me, I got up and ran away, sister.'

'Where are they?'

'They ran down towards the girls' section, I think, chasing after someone else, sister.'

'Who were they?'

'I don't know who they were; it all happened quickly, a hit and run sister.'

'Come with me to the infirmary, and then I'll find these hooligans.'

'Yes, sister, thank you, sister.'

Having been blessed once again, I got myself patched up and bandaged by one of the other nuns while fending off her many questions. Then I was given some Vincent's powder, a swine of stuff to swallow as it was so dry even with a small glass of water. Standard issue to help ease the pain as running off to the local doctor was not yet a custom. I spent the rest of the day and the following one recuperating in the sick bay. Laying down was a cure-all remedy for anything short of death. On Tuesday, I was judged to be fit enough to return to classes. My black eye patch, with other facial bruises, gave me the appearance of a pirate, and the rumour mill swung into action.

Old mate Barnie overnighted in the public children's hospital. He had a dislocated wrist, some nasty gashes, and a mysterious throat infection; he returned sporting a plaster cast on his forearm. His story was that some boys snuck up behind him and shoved a bag over his head, then dragged him into the toilets and beat him up. He'd heard one of them say we'll get your mates too, and then they ran away. So tough guy Barnie didn't want to admit that some little runt had got the drop on him. He might keep his shit to himself in future, and it's not my fault he was such a loser.

Our Christmas Holidays couldn't come quickly enough for me; it's a long time to spend ducking and diving from assailants. Surely, retribution won't visit me again so soon; hopefully, I can rest easily for a while. I had already concluded that if shit happened, I'm sure to be standing there. Over the following days, I spent my mornings in class. After lunch, there were no chores for me. I spent my time convalescing in the warmth of the sunshine out in the courtyard, away from the rest of the rabble. This was the exact same place the Provroff brothers got attacked by mysterious burglars a while ago. For the present, it was quite peaceful, idling away the hours of daydreaming in the retreat area below the girl's home economics section. The girls, on the other hand, seemed impressed with the image of me as the bad boy. This was a load of rubbish, but who was I to discourage their flights of fantasy? However, I accepted their offer of a cup of tea as it was the Christian thing to do.

They were dying of curiosity about the rumours of fighting and boys running amok all over the place. I couldn't enlighten them; I had a story to stick to, and loose lips could end up thickened by fist or stick. Katie, on the other hand, had cottoned on to what might've happened but kept mum on the subject. Sometimes, it felt uncanny, like the girls knew what you were thinking—that's scary stuff.

'Is there something else I could get you, Rickie?' she smiled so sweetly.

'Oh, a fan and something to read would be lovely, Katie.'

'Funny boy, I'll be right back.'

I wondered what she was up to. There was a mischievous gleam in her eyes. She disappeared for quite a while, and I had begun to nod off when she reappeared.

'Here, I got you a cordial drink and a slice of apple pie that I made. You must keep up your strength, and we wouldn't want your lips to dry out and crack.'

'Thank you, Katie.' I lifted the spoon and dropped it, along with some pie.

'Poor baby, here, let me help you.' She spoon-fed me the pie and held the glass while I sipped the cordial. This was turning into an agreeable pastime.

'This's kind of you, Katie.'

'Rickie, I can't help feeling that you know more about what has been going on. Is it possible I might be the reason behind your injuries?'

'No, Katie, just my bad luck, being in the wrong place at the wrong time.'

'Likely story. Is there anything else I can do for you? Just ask.'

'More pie?'

'Don't push your luck. Anyway, I'd better go before the others start to wonder where I am; those girls are such terrible gossip.

'Ok, Katie, your pie was mouth-watering.'

'You really are a cheeky boy; you have got an answer for everything, Rickie.'

Then she laid another one of her kisses on me, and the whistles and cries started from the small balcony above. Red-faced, she ran off to rouse her friends, who obviously had been spying on us. Oh, well, it was good while it lasted. I still had to deal with Barnie and his mates, which could get me in more strife than it was worth. There was no peace in my sanctuary, as one of the nuns had decided to pay me a visit.

'Rickie, I've something to tell you regarding the Christmas holidays; grab your crutches, and I will walk back with you to the dormitory.'

'Yes, sister. It's getting a bit warm out in the sun.'

'This recent fighting business has got me worried about what may happen if you went to a family for a long period like Christmas.'

'It wasn't my fault, sister; someone attacked me.'

'Yes, so you say, but it seems like it has to do with Barnie Russell. What I don't understand is the connection between the two of you.

'Neither can I, Sister; it's beyond all reasoning. I don't know who attacked me or that Barnie guy; it might be those outside kids who've got their noses out of joint again.'

'That's quite a stretch of the imagination, Rickie.'

'Well, just so you know, we've defeated quite a few of the local school teams since we've been allowed to play sports outside.'

'Be quiet. Now about Christmas break, some of the families at Chinchilla want to take a few boys that were out there for Easter holidays. Promise me you won't get into any fights.

'Of course, Sister, there's no one who starts fights on the farm, only the kangaroos and maybe the koalas, but they don't pay me any attention at all.'

'I'm sure that they keep a close eye on all you boys very well; this is what is going to happen. Six boys are going out there, two to each farm.'

'Am I going to Bill and Gwyn's place?'

'Mr Mann to you, Rickie.'

'But that's what they asked me to call them, Sister.'

'Well, mind your manners, and yes, they've asked for you.'

'Wow, that's great, as I really like them!'

'You must've been on your best behaviour out there to impress them, so you choose who goes with you.'

'Can I take Jai; he likes being out in the bush?'

'No, Jai's Aunty is coming to take him for the Christmas Holidays, which I think will be good for him to spend time with his own family.'

'How about Bobbie? I am sure he'd like to go?'

'Bobbie is fine; don't say anything to him; I need to confirm first.'

'No, Sister, Thank you.'

Wow, this is going to be the best Christmas ever. I never expected this would happen, as the bush holidays are only Easter events. They must have had a good season this year and need their lucky charm [me] to make it rain again. In the meantime, I must see what gives with Barney and his cronies.

The next day, I was back in my sunny respite area when Steve and Harold, Barney's mates, slipped through the gap in the hedges.

'Hey Rickie, how's it going?' This place is becoming like Central Station. There must be a sign outside saying, "Oracle in residence, do drop in."

'Hi guys, what's happening?'

'We just want to have a quiet word with you about Barney. He's been going off his brain about you stealing his girlfriend,' they said simultaneously.

'But,' I started to say. These guys took turns talking; when one stopped, the other started.

'We've spoken to our girls, Charmaine and Wanda, and their point of view doesn't jell with Barney's.' Steve interjected.

'He's got it in his head that Katie was keen on him, and as usual, he has got things backwards. Any girl smiles at him, and he is in love. She sees him as a classmate and nothing else, so she put him straight. He's got the shits something chronic, and you're his target,' continued Harold.

'You can say that again, but still not any of my doing, guys.'

'Yeah, well, no matter what his or your story is, Barney had something to do with your injuries, and we suspect that you gave him as good as you got. How you did it has us baffled. When it comes to fighting, he has you outweighed and outclassed.'

'What are you, seventy-pound wringing wet? Steve added.

'If that, still, it's got nothing to do with me, guys.'

'Have it your own way. What Katie decides to do with her spare time is none of our business.'

'Or mine either. That's what you guys don't seem to understand. Who any girl likes has nothing to do with me.'

'The thing is, we're not letting Barney's crap come between us and our girlfriends. We think you're ok and don't want to get in any fights over it, so as far as we're concerned, let sleeping dogs lie,' said Harold.

'What about Barney? I don't want to be looking over my shoulder every time that guy gets something up his nose., I replied.

'Leave him to us; we'll steer him in different directions. It'll be Christmas break in two weeks; try and stay out of his way in the meantime, OK?'

'Fair enough, see you guys around,' I replied.

It was going to be interesting to see how all this panned out. It's a tricky business trying to dodge anyone around here. We're all in one another's faces most of the time. The only redeeming feature might be the types of activities the nuns may find to keep us busy. It would be helpful if Barney and I were kept separated, as my chances in a second round would be nil. I got what I wished for; everyone got alternative work and sports/ leisure activities. Barney and his mates drew the cleaning duties on Tuesday over in the church area.

On Wednesday, Petra, Jai and I were far from thrilled to spring clean our classrooms. Floors, walls, and windows. A few girls would wander by occasionally and offer their advice. None of them volunteered to help. Fun was wherever you could find it with no adults about. We'd take turns sitting on top of the industrial polishing machine. Someone else would hold onto the handle and turn it on, a bit like riding a wild horse with a maniacal nature. It was nice to know that we weren't singled out. Everyone got a chance to show off their skills in getting things shipshape. Anything that didn't move got cleaned, waxed, polished, and shined. The odd thing during this time was that more opportunities became available to enjoy ourselves. With this short-lived sense of freedom, life didn't seem so draconian. The perennial cloud of depression slowly dissipated. Oh, what fun we had, being careful not to grin too much, as the nuns might get it in their heads that we love cleaning.

Extracurricular Activities

The days were counting down. After lunch, there were all free periods. Most of us senior boys [you grow up fast around here] went to an outside pool for basic swimming lessons. This included a breathing procedure underwater and kicking my feet while hanging onto the side of the pool. When we were shown the rudiments of freestyle swimming, I barely managed to stay afloat.

The Fortitude Valley public pool was fifty metres long; I often had to stop to catch my breath. Swimming was an activity I would have liked to improve on, but we only went twice before the holidays. The bus limit on each trip was fifty, including the driver and four adults, two of whom were nuns. They offered encouragement from the sides, with two laymen in the pool giving practical advice. I often wondered if we were drowning, would one of them jump in to save us? Their clothing design would make lifesaving difficult.

The senior girls managed to convince the nuns that dancing was another social grace that would be improved by regular practice with the boys as partners. Usually, they danced with each other. In the last week, most late afternoons were given over to combined dance practice. It was no small feat for them to get acceptance, allowing us all to associate. We clumsy young fellows were roped into the rudiments of dancing, quite a challenge for everyone involved. The girls persevered as their intent was focused on achieving more than dancing and adding to our 'education'. They had other extracurricular activities on their minds, as we innocent souls would soon find out.

'Hello girls, is Katie here by any chance?'

'Why do you want to know, Rickie? You're not up to mischief, are you?' they replied.

'Me! Mischief? Don't you recognise a saint when you see one? I've no idea what you mean. It was your idea to rope us into being your dancing partners.'

'Yeah, right! And we'll believe you, Rickie!' A few laughed.

'Katie is up in the canteen area; take these jugs with you; wandering boys doing nothing is suspect up there,' one of them offered a couple of jugs.

'Thank you, ladies.'

'Such a polite little mister mischief, aren't you?' one replied.

'What are you doing up here, Rickie Battler?' a bossy nun asked.

'I brought these dirty jugs up to be washed. The girls in the main hall sent me up with them, Sister.'

'Did they now? Well, don't stand about. The sink is over there. I assume you know how to wash dishes.'

'Yes, sister.' So, the girls had suckered me into doing their washing up, and I fell for it. Ah, well, I got my foot in the door, so to speak. *I best make it look like I'm useful.* These nuns are habitual spies.

'Don't make a mountain out of a molehill over there, Rickie. There are more dishes here that need cleaning.'

'Yes, Sister, I'm going as fast as possible.'

'You girls standing around over there, grab a towel, wipe up these dishes, and put them back in the cupboards. They won't get done by themselves. Also, wipe down all the benches, then get yourselves off and ready for dancing classes. We don't have all afternoon, so get a wiggle on.' A stern taskmaster this one was, so I had better make myself scarce soon.

'Oh, how wonderful, Katie and Maria. You girls have done a marvellous job with the sandwiches.'

'There are a few more trays outside on the trolley,' Maria replied.

'Rickie, could you go out and bring the rest of the food trays in?'

'Yes Sister.' Off I went to haul in four large trays of sandwiches, one after the other. On the way out to get the last one, I heard Maria call out to Katie, 'Where're the rest of the cordial jugs?'

'They're out on the other trolley, Maria. I'll get them.' This is a ruse for Katie to sidle up to me.

'Hello Rickie, would you like a hand?'

This girl just loved winding me up. The feel of her hand sliding up and down on the back of my shorts nearly made me drop the tray.

'Katie, you're very cheeky. That's not helping me much.'

'Really, and here I was thinking you needed a little push in the right direction.' Luckily, I made it back inside without any mishaps.

'Thank you, Rickie. Put it on the table over there and have a cordial and a sandwich before you leave.'

'Yes, Sister, Thank you.'

Katie came in, holding two other metal jugs, and called out to me, 'Hey Rickie, there're two more of these jugs out on the trolley. Could you go out and bring them in, please? Is that all right, Sister?'

'Yes, off you go, Rickie. Be quick before these girls turn you into their slave.'

'Thanks, Rickie, put them over on that far bench. Give him a hand, Katie.'

'Certainly, sister,' as she gave me a sly wink and set about her mission.

'All right, Rickie. Finish your snack and head back to the hall. You two girls lock the doors before leaving. Bring the key to me upstairs. Don't dawdle.'

'Yes, sister,' we all said.

I swallowed my sandwich and washed it down with the cordial. Placing the glass in the sink, I headed off down the back steps to the hall.

'Just a second, Rickie, I'll need to lock that back door after you go out,' Katie said.

Her breathing down my neck gave me goosebumps. When I turned to say goodbye, she startled me with a big kiss, and I turned bright red, looking at her twinkling eyes. A gentle push from her left me stranded outside the locked door. *What was that little pixie girl up to?* Slowly, I descended the stairs and sat on the bench seat outside the community hall to catch my breath.

Out of the blue, Nigel rocks up. 'Are you okay, Rickie? Your face is red.'

I took a moment to swallow before replying, 'Hi Nigel, yeah, I'm ok, I almost choked on a gumball.'

'I've done that. Got stuck in my throat till someone gave me a whack on the back.'

'What're you boys doing down there?' Katie and her mischievous mates, Charmaine and Wanda, were hanging out the window above us.

'Hi girls, Rickie is just having a drink; he almost choked on a gumball.'

'Really! A gumball. It must've been a big one?' Charmaine gave Katie a curious look.

'Yes, I found him red-faced and breathless, sitting on the steps.' Nigel volunteered.

'Really, oh poor Rickie,' cried Wanda. 'Don't you think so, Katie?'

'We've got to get ready, you lot. Leave Rickie alone.' Giving her mates a stern look, she turned and gave me a big wink.

Dancing Daze

'So, Nigel, you've been doing this for a while, are any of the girls your favourite?'

'Helga, I like her. She's fun to dance with.'

'Where does she tell you to sit usually?'

'Over there on the other side.'

Well, you should go and sit there. You don't want someone else to interrupt you and Helga.'

'Yeah! Thanks, Rickie. Will you be okay here?'

'I'm ok, Nigel.'

The dance instructor nun and her sidekicks appeared out of the shadows.

'All right, everyone, Silence! today, we'll be learning the steps to the Pride of Erin, which some of you already know. The others will pick it up as we go. Ok?'

'Yes Sister.'

'There may be time for a progressive barn dance as well. Remember, if you're standing near the dance table when the music stops, boys stay where you are, and their partners will swap with the other girls on the bench seat; is that clear to everyone?'

'Yes, Sister,' came the loud reply.

'Right now, girls form two lines and walk quietly down the side steps; your partner will be the next boy in line on the dance floor. Politely ask the boy to dance and then proceed to the middle of the hall and form a circle. You should all know the drill by now.'

'We certainly do! Sister.'

They had already checked out where their intended prey stood and assembled themselves in the same order in the line. I wonder who I will end up with. At least Barney isn't around; he seems to have lost interest in dancing lately.

'You're not picking out a hat, girls; get a move on,' Sister called.

'Hello Rickie, would you like to dance,' asked Katie.

'Why, hello Katie. What's the go? Do we hold hands?'

'No way! That'll get us both dismissed. We walk separately out to the hall's centre and then stand across from one another. Make sure to keep your eyes focused on the floor and wait for instructions from the sister.'

'Really, can we talk, or is that a sin too?

'I'm not sure. Boys don't usually say much; for some stupid reason, they just look at the ground. So, a certain *mister chatterbox* better be careful. The nuns have lots of spies.'

'Ok, perhaps I can say a prayer?' I replied.

'Yeah, right. I heard that you had a choking episode this afternoon. Are you ok?'

'I'm fine now, thank you; it caught me quite by surprise, a gob-smacker of a gumball.'

'Oh, you poor thing. It must've been a mouthful. Was it delicious? Where did you score that from?' she casually asked.

'A girl gave it to me. It was a pink one with a soft centre. A reward for helping in the canteen today.'

'You're lucky.' She smirked.

'Sure am.'

'All right, enough chatter. Girls, raise your arms out to your sides and touch your fingers with the girl beside you. Keep this distance apart. You boys, step up to your partners and put your left arm out so your fingers rest lightly on your partner's shoulder. Girls, you know where your hands should be by now. Follow the steps, as I call them, without the music for the time being. You'll all have to focus, boys. You're supposed to be leading.'

What a schmozzle it was, our feet and arms going in different directions. The girls all thought it was a great laugh. Us guys had red faces; we would have a better chance with a game of Twister. The girls enjoyed it immensely. We would have to do better if we were to impress on nuns that we weren't all hopeless. Stomp, stomp, take time to breathe, spin around and around, then stomp all over again. We twirled our hands together and stepped forward, then back. Our arms crossed over behind each other's heads and then back again, hopefully not choking our partners in the process. Eventually, we got the idea, though finesse was elusive. What an exhausting workout dancing turned out to be.

Every time the music stopped, some boys ended up with a different partner. Katie timed her moves seamlessly and remained my partner until the music stopped when we were right in front of the table, and she had to bow out. A new girl I didn't know took her place; she was almost as good a dancer as Katie.

This gave me the false impression that I was getting the hang of things. The reality check came when this girl moved on. The next girl was as nervous as me, so we didn't do so well, but we laughed all the same. Then, we started on a progressive barn dance, which was a little easier. Two hours went by quickly, and soon, it was a refreshment break. The boys shuffled past the serving table; amongst them were the femme fatale musketeers. Katie, Charmaine, and Wanda commanded activities. They condescendingly directed all and sundry where to sit. I had just finished my sandwiches and drink and was walking up to put my glass on the table when one of the nuns called me over.

'Rickie, would you please stay behind with one of the other boys and help pack these tables up? The girls will give the floor a quick sweep.' This statement sounded like I had a choice, but option B would certainly be less to my liking. It was best not to inquire.

'Yes, Sister, can I get Nigel to help?'

'That's good. He's such a kind boy.'

'Now listen up, everyone, you're all doing well, so we'll have dancing lessons three afternoons this week and two next week. Most of you will be leaving for the Christmas holidays by then. I hope you've all enjoyed this afternoon's lesson.'

'Yes, Sister, Thank you.' The volume of our reply rattled her a little.

'Ok, when you've finished your afternoon tea, everyone returns their own plates and glasses to the tables.'

'You boys on the bench seats near the side doors, pick them up and stack them in a tidy manner over in the far end corner. Thank you all for your assistance.' She pointed in the general direction.

The hall was emptied in under fifteen minutes, and the kids knew what had happened to their idle hands. Nigel and I weren't in any rush, and our work details lasted longer than one might've thought. He was a habitable gossip, and being around Helga made conversation more enjoyable for him. I, being of a quiet disposition, went to inquire if others might need my assistance.

'Rickie, could you help me with the stereo and speakers? Then we can stack the last table.' Katie asked inquisitively.

'No worries, Nigel, we're just about finished; you can get going if you want to.'

'Ok then. Well, bye Helga, thank you for the dance.'

'Yes, I'd better go as well. Bye Nigel, see you tomorrow.'

Katie and I finished rolling up the leads and packing the speakers and the stereo into their boxes. We carried them up the stage stairs and into the storage room, which had multiple timber shelves. Everything had a place.

'Did you like the music and dancing, Rickie?'

'I did, Katie. It took me a while to get the hang of it, though changing partners was quite distracting. I seemed to move better dancing with you, and I was pleased that the music stopped mostly when we were on the far side of the hall. That certainly was a bit of luck.'

'Wasn't it just, is that all you liked?'

'Well, now that you mention it, dancing made me a little nervous, but I enjoyed it.'

'Really prove it.'

'What?' Grabbing the front of my shirt, she pulled me back into the storeroom and closed the door.

'You're a distracting boy and maybe a little dense. Kiss me, Rickie.' The kissing and octopus meandering of hands lasted only a brief period. Our tete-a-tete was interrupted by a loud bang in the main hall. We both looked at one another and then I quietly opened the door to see what was happening. It was Bloody Nigel stuffing about.

'What're you doing wrecking the place, Nigel?

'Sorry, Rickie. I saw the door still open and snuck in to get my lucky scarf. I left it on that microphone stand, and then the whole thing fell over as I pulled it off. I hope it's not broken. Can you check it?'

'Yeah, ok, I'll sort it out for you. Give me a hand with this last table, then bugger off before you break something,' I replied.

My heart was pounding something chronic as Katie and I were almost sprung. Between Nigel and Katie, I'll end up going prematurely grey. *What is her game anyway? Is her interest in me just messing with my head?* I wondered as I went back to the storage room.

No Katie around anymore, she must've disappeared when she heard Nigel talking. The microphone equipment looked ok, so I stacked it all away. She had the keys; all I could do was close the doors and disappear myself. This Katie business was becoming a perplexing problem. I'd heard other boys say that girls could mess with your head. Also, they'd only go out with older boys, so what gives with me? Not that any of us could go out anywhere with a girl. She was the same height as me, but she must be close to fourteen. A teenager, no less, and I am just shy of twelve. Is she playing games, or maybe she is a stalker?

For the next two dance lessons, Katie and her mates were a no-show, and I ended up partnering with several of the girls. This was good practice as all of them had varying levels of expertise. One, however, had no patience at all. Now, wouldn't I like to see her go flying as she twirled around, and her hand came close to slipping out of mine? As the male was supposed to lead, any mishaps would be considered my fault, which would suit her cranky ladyship.

Dancing with different partners was a learning curve, not always an improvement. A lot of effort without much reward. I might miss this gig next week. Some of the more graceful dancers won't miss me.

What has happened to the mischievous Katie, Charmaine, and Wanda. They seemed to have done a disappearing act without a word. That's not unusual around here, especially at this time of the year. None of us wanted to spend Christmas wandering the halls, not so jolly; nothing could make you feel lonelier. The other girls in the dance class were either clueless or deliberately keeping mum about the whereabouts of the mysterious trio. Those merry band of girls did manage to light up my life, that's for sure. I've only just realised it, and now they're gone.

Lazy Days

On Saturday, Bobbie and I'd be off to the Mann's farm on the outskirts of Chinchilla. I should catch up with him and find out if he knows.

The next morning, Bobbie called out, 'Hey Rickie, wait up.' I haven't seen him much lately, so he might have an update.

'What's up, Bobbie? These end-of-year activities certainly keep us all on the move.'

'I'll say, less kids, more space, more options. I've been trying out with a new soccer team for next year's season. Guess what else has happened? I'm going to a farm in Chinchilla for the Christmas holidays.'

'Wow, do you know who you'll be staying with? I'm going out there also.'

'Not yet. The sister said we'll be given our places on Friday afternoon and then heading off early the next morning. Hey, with luck, we might end up at the same one. What do you reckon?'

'Wouldn't that be great? I'll catch up with you tonight, and we can talk about the place.'

'Righto, I've never been to a country town. Catch you later; I've got to shove off to soccer practice now.'

That's interesting, though. How come I didn't hear about this outside soccer team? Probably messing about with those girls dancing stuffed up my chances. There is always some secret business going on around here. But if I give up the dancing, what will I do sitting about the place for the next few days? Idle boys get jobs to do. It's best to look like I'm on a mission somewhere, even if I'm not.

There was a tunnel ball game in full swing over near the old cricket pitch. I appeared to be an interested bystander, waiting for a turn. As I got closer, Raga signalled me to the back of one line: 'I got to get out of here. Take my spot mate, that busted-up bastard Barney is annoying me.'

'Good on ya, just what I needed to cheer up my day.'

93

The game continued for ten minutes or so, and our team was ahead by one point till someone went arse over. This curious event gave Barney's team the chance to tie with us, and then they beat us. We all stood grousing at whoever stuffed up while waiting for the next game to start. This would be a tag game; it should be called "Belt the Bastard."

Barney still had his cast on his arm. He and his two mates drifted over for a chinwag. My danger buzzer was starting to sound louder.

'What've you been up to lately, Rickie?' Harold asked.

'Not much. I've been roped into this dancing malarky for a few afternoons, playing a little footy and trying to steer clear of the nun's never-ending work details,' I replied.

'Who's at dancing, any good sorts?' Steve inquired.

'Wanda and her mates were there once; I haven't seen them since. There are quite a few other girls keen on it as well. The progressive dance moves everyone onto a new partner every couple of minutes, so you don't get the chance to talk to anyone.'

'So how come you go dancing? I didn't know you danced,' mumbled Barney.

'Well, I don't usually. I got suckered in by the nuns. I spend more of my time setting up tables, chairs, and doing other crap than actual dancing. Most of the time, I've no idea what's going on, as I can't hear what they're saying over the music and general noise.'

'Sounds like fun, doesn't it, boys?' Barney was spoiling for something.

'Anyway, you guys used to go there, so you'd know the drill. With changing partners all the time, you learn bugger all about dancing.

'Yeah, the girls like to stand and gossip about God knows what,' Steve added.

'So why aren't you there?'

'Our girls seemed to have disappeared, so we can't be bothered,' moaned Harold.

'Well, we'll get out of here shortly for Christmas. Do you know where you're going for the holidays?'

'I'm going home to my family on Friday. Barney and Harold are leaving sometime tomorrow. I heard that Katie and her mates have already left for theirs,' Steve said.

'Well, good luck to them. Look out here comes that tall nun, who thinks she is my personal slave driver.' All heads turned to look.

Barnie said, 'Holy crap, it's Gigantor. We don't want to run into her. Let's bugger off.'

'Good on you bunch of dingoes. Thanks for the support.'

They left me stranded like a kangaroo caught in a spotlight. These nuns ensured that the devil didn't find work for idle hands. The days became a grind on my nerves. We were creating history for future counselling services in awe of our resilience and perseverance. Dawdling along aimlessly can sometimes have its advantages, as I was grabbed from a doorway and drawn into the dimness of a chilly room. This type of activity usually resulted in a face full of knuckles, except for the scent of a cougar girl and her whispering in my ear.

'Scared the crap out of you, didn't I, Rickie?'

'No, you didn't, I knew it was you.'

'Oh, you little fibber, did you miss me?'

'Katie, I've been heartbroken.'

'Hmmm, good answer; not sure I believe you, though.'

'We've been staying at a private school in the city to practice for our Christmas pageant. Isn't that right, girls!'

'Yes, Rickie, it's been a big secret, days of practice and a little shopping so we could finish making our own costumes,' Wanda added.

'Anyway, don't be a nosey parker. You'll have to wait until tomorrow night to find out,' Charmaine primly advised me. 'Barney and his mates told me that you'd all left for your holidays.'

'What! Don't listen to him; he'll say anything to wind you up. He can be such a little shit. Anyway, follow me, Rickie. I've something to show you.' Katie steered me into a temporary prop room. There was a gallimaufry of costumes, hats, and face masks, along with other gaudy stuff, hidden away in the cavernous shadows.

'So, what's up? I asked.

'Wait here, Rickie. I'll be back in a tic. Stay out of sight, and don't make a sound.'

I closed the door to the outside verandah and stood quietly behind a tree prop, hidden from unexpected visitors. *What is that girl up to now. For such an angelic face, she sure thrives on creating mischief.*

'Close your eyes, cheeky boy, I'm coming out, Taha! now open your eyes, what do you think?' She stood in the subdued light, adorned with a feathered sparkly mask. Her top half was clad in a skin-hugging multi-coloured outfit that outlined her breasts and barely reached her upper thighs. Beneath that was a lot of legs adorned in silky stockings. My eyes wandered all the way down to her calf-high white boots. Twirling and dancing, kicking her legs up as she approached me.

'Well, have you been struck dumb? say something.'

With a dry throat and a racing heart, I stuttered, 'You're not dressed like that on the stage, are you?' I am sure my face was bright red as it felt on fire.

'Never mind that this is my little preview dance just for you, Rickie. Do you like my shoes? Do you like my dress? What about my new stockings? These are the first ones I have ever bought. Don't you love my outfit?' She fired endless questions at me. Then the spider came even closer to the fly, and now I was pinned to that spot, shocked and breathless.

'You look beautiful, and the costume is "uhm" stunning,' I gasped. With that, she grabbed my hands, placed them on her rear end and slid her hands around my neck. We began to kiss. Well, I should say she kissed me, and I stood there like a stunned mullet. Slowly, through my fogged brain, it dawned on me that she had exceedingly small knickers on. My halo was sinking around my neck; this isn't a subject for confession, as some things should remain a secret. This is one of those times that fits that description.

'What're you doing for Christmas, Rickie? Are there any girlfriends waiting out there in the countryside for you?' she asked, giving me that dreamy smile of hers.

'I'm going out to a farm at Chinchilla, and the only girls out there are four-legged ones with big brown eyes who just love gazing at me. How about you? Where're you off to with your new stockings?' I asked.

'Ooh! You like my stockings, don't you? What a stirrer you're becoming. For your information, I've been holidaying with my Aunty Karen and Granddad for the last two years. It is about time we talked about our families; don't you think?'

'Ok, if you want, tell me about yours?' I asked.

'Well, to be brief, they now take me out on the last weekend of each month and every holiday.'

'My parents died in a car accident five years ago; I lived with my grandad and aunty for about three years. They're the only family I have, and they live over in the western suburbs of Graceville. Grandad works at a bakery, doing split shifts and working 7 days a week. My aunty Karen has worked for the Main Roads Department since she finished high school. She also does night school 3 nights a week as she wants to get into university. They're saving to buy their own house over in a suburb called Fairfield, which is where my granddad works. Children's services got involved, and here I am for the time being. So, what about you? How did you end up in this delightful place?'

'To cut a long story even shorter, both my parents ended up in hospital with long-term illness, and I was staying with one of my brothers and his wife for about a year. Thanks to Child Services, I came here almost four years ago. Three of my brothers were here when I first came, and they've all left. I did have family visitors for a while, but then that stopped. According to what the nuns said, it appears that nobody wants me to be part of their family. I've not seen any of my relations for years,' I replied.

Katie just stared at me while a tear streaked down her cheeks.

'Oh Rickie, that just can't be true. You're such a beautiful person, and I pray that things will improve for you in the future, she whispered.'

'Well, *Que Sera, Sera,* we'll see. I know what the future will be for you and me if we don't get out of here,' I replied. I was a little short on suitable, clever answers for her.

Playgirls Pageant

On the night of the Girls' Christmas Gala performance, we seniors had more space to spread out, as the juniors had all fled for their holidays. We all sat whispering in anticipation, with the standard demarcation of genders. There was no chance of any hanky-panky, as the nuns ensured that never the twain shall meet. Grade five sat on the four front benches, then a spare row and the other grades spread out behind us. I had sat my royal self on the front bench, with a good view of all the action. No doubt this performance would be tame compared to Katie's frisky prelude. According to the A-frame blackboard's colourful chalk notices, tonight's Christmas spectacular started at 7 pm sharp; be seated by 6.45 pm. Mixed student groups from all the senior grades will perform the show.

This confirms that I have not shown any noticeable creative talent to date. The black-and-white stencilled flyer was printed by yours truly on a hand-operated mimeograph. This contribution to the talented Drama group was placed in a neat stack on each row of seats.

TONIGHT'S SHOW

Act 1 - Little Red Riding Hood pantomime.

Act 2 – The School Choir – Songs of the Seekers

Intermission 8.00 to 8.20 pm -Cake and cordial will be served on the front verandah - Boys left, Girls right.

Act 3 - Dancing with the Stars.

Final Act - Nativity Play

10 pm – Finish, pack up your seats and go off to your dormitories- Lights out at 10.30 pm.

N.B 1. Our cast hasn't been identified for a good reason; the audience can decide who is whom and make a note on the flyer. Please add a name and place your completed flyer in the big pink boxes near the exits.

N.B 2 - Prizes to be awarded in the new year for the most correct entries. - Good luck. A red herring was thrown in at the end.

The show began on time, and the first question was a no-brainer. Little Red Riding Hood, aka the diminutive Katie, came swirling out in a bright red dress with petticoats and a facemask that I recognised. She daintily skipped along through the forest of moving trees and scrubs, inside which human manipulators swayed. They weren't easily identified.

The stage sound effects created a menacing atmosphere for the tale. This rendition was quite entertaining, with old granny being a boy in women's clothes who kept slipping over. The climactic part when the wolf appeared, changed somewhat when Red Riding Hood accidentally stood on its paw. The wolf jumped up and let out a howl, then stumbled and knocked one of the trees over. This had a hilarious domino effect on the other props. Little Miss Red Riding Hood decided it was a good time to exit the stage while the wolf struggled to get up from the shambles. Intended or not, the show ended with lots of clapping and laughter, which was an entertaining finale of a familiar fairy tale.

As the curtains were drawn to close, a nun appeared to engage us all in singing along with Bing Crosby's, *"I'm dreaming of a white Christmas."*

'Now I want everyone to join in,' and she started singing in a surprisingly melodic voice. This allowed time for the props to be removed and the stage set up for Act 2 - Songs of the Seekers, our favourite Australian pop group of the 1960s. The choir had three solo vocalists in front, playing guitars, with a mixed-gender choral group in the background.

"A world of our own."
"Hey there, Georgy Girl."
"I'll never find another you."
"Blowing in the wind."
"The carnival is over."

We all joined in on the last song, and the volume shook the dust loose from the timber floorboards above our heads. The audience added to the din with appreciative applause.

'Quiet, please, settle down, everyone,' bellowed the nun at the rear of the room. We all shooshed each other, wondering what new entertainment might be in store for us.

'Interval refreshments are being served out on the verandah. Girls first move quietly out through the right-hand side door. Boys stay seated and be quiet. When the last girl exits, the front row of boys moves out in an orderly manner,' this voice came from another nun hidden in the wings.

The mention of food was all the boys needed to be told. Good manners were one thing, but we hustled along for our portion of the goodies. Cordial and cake were not to be missed out on. With a little supervision, a few of the girls had the catering under control; none of the cast was to be seen.

'Wipe that spill up, girl,' instructed one of the nuns.

Intentional or otherwise, this gave a girl named Julie, a protégé of the Katie troupe, the opportunity to pass something extra with my cordial and cake. It was a shame magic was not part of tonight's show, as her sleight of hand at passing messages was amazing. I found a spot to sit and have a snack in peace. The extra napkin contained a secret message. *The morning shine would be fine if stocking glimmers were mine at nine this Christmas time. They last but once, so it's up to you to search and find or be left to pine.* This coded rhyme came from a certain somebody. If I don't figure it out, I might have something to whine about. Wiping the glass out with the napkin blurred the script. I returned the glass and plate and tossed the soggy napkin in the bin. Now, where have I seen shiny stockings? It would be best to be there by nine in the morning.

Wandering about came with challenges, and if I walked boldly, few would take much notice. The area I was in was eerily quiet at this time of year, a blessing and a curse depending on vocation or intent. I walked along silent verandahs, past a few boys kicking a ball out on the field. To my right, a group of girls were sitting on the grass in the sunshine, platting each other hair. None seemed to notice or comment on my passage, which under normal circumstances would be odd. Everyone seemed to be happy to chill out for a change. The temporary prop room was just ahead, and the sanctuary was within my grasp. I had less than thirty feet to go before trouble appeared further along at the verandah T-intersection. Here stood two nuns chatting, and I must surely be within their peripheral vision. Holding my breath, I stood perfectly still as if it would make me invisible.

'Good morning, sisters; how are you?' Katie called out suddenly.

'Good morning to you, Katie,' they both replied as they turned in her direction.

I do not know if it was perfect timing or good fortune, but I never let a chance go by. I silently slinked into the shadows of the doorway. Katie, ever handy with a prop, was pushing a trolley loaded with some of the costumes from last night's performances.

'These need to be put away in the storeroom. Is it open Sister?' Katie inquired while she casually looked in my direction.

'Well, that's kind of you, one less thing on my list this afternoon,' the elder of the two nuns replied.

'Here's the key: Could you ensure the other costumes have been put away while you're there? Some of those girls dump things anywhere,' inquired the younger nun, a kindred spirit of Katie's.

Being the consummate actress, she no doubt beamed her brightest smile as the words flowed from her lips: 'Of course, Sister. I'm only too happy to help. Where will I find you to return the key?'

'Well, we're on our way down to the kindergarten. After that, we'll be over in the kitchen. Why don't you join us there, and we can have morning tea together?'

'It should take me about an hour to tidy up the storeroom, so would 10.30 be OK? 'That sounds perfect. Thank you for your help, Katie. You are such a lovely girl.'

The nuns headed down to the kindergarten. The rattle of the approaching trolley confirmed Katie had combined her generosity and sweet nature to please all in her wake. Multitasking would undoubtedly be her forte in all she strived to achieve in her life. That creative mind of hers leapt over hurdles regardless of purpose or direction.

'Well, Rickie, what a pleasant surprise. Fancy meeting you here. So, the rumours are true: you are a good code breaker. Don't stand around doing nothing; give me a hand to hang this lot up.' With a wink and a smile, she opened the door.

'No worries, Katie, always ready to lend a hand to a fellow saint. As the nuns always say, "Many hands make light work."'

'What interesting thoughts you have.'

'Well, it's a cross to bear in life.'

'Hmm, it's who those saints are, that continues to be a big mystery around this place, wouldn't you agree?'

'Yep, that pretty much sums it up.'

'Here, grab hold of these coats and make yourself useful. Hang them on that rack over there. We must tidy this room up so that I can get back to those two nuns you almost got caught by. I saved your ass, so you owe me big time.' Her beguiling smile hid her possible intentions.

What eager beavers we were! With a flurry of activity, clothes were hung neatly, large props were stacked along the back wall, and small props went into the boxes on the shelves. I'm all done with time to spare for a chat and a special Christmas greeting.

'When do you leave for holidays, Rickie?'

'Tomorrow morning around nine. Why?'

'I leave about the same time and have morning tea with the nuns in about half an hour, so you'd better get over here and pay your dues.'

'So soon, we've got so much to talk about.'

'Talking can wait. Save your breath and come over here sweet lips.'

Kissing was what she had in mind, which scrambled my thoughts and left me short of breath. I think I may be developing some breathing problem; my heart certainly was racing. It might be all the fluff in the air in this stuffy room. It was fortunate that the dress dummy was standing so close to the inside of the door. The sound of it falling over would bring us both back to reality quickly, innovative if someone else tried to enter the room.

'Look at the time, we must get out of here. Guess what?'

'What?' I replied.

'Last week, I received a letter from my Aunty Karen, who said she had a big surprise for me when I got home. Maybe it's something for my fifteenth birthday in February?'

'What date? Mine is the 11th.'

'Really, so is mine; we are both *Aquarians,* ' she exclaimed.

'I wonder what your aunt's surprise is?' I asked.

'I've no idea; no doubt it'll be something special. She loves surprises. We'd better get going.'

'Yes, you won't want to miss your morning tea. Have a great Christmas, Katie. Can you check to see if the coast is clear?'

'The Coast is clear, safe as houses for all good boys not to be seen, especially the saintly ones. Enjoy your holiday in the bush and take care around those country girls. I have heard they are highly adventurous. I wouldn't put it past them to wrangle you in. Don't forget to remember me till we meet again,' she whispered.

Unbeknown to both of us, we would never meet again.

Christmas on the Farm

Robbie now knew we would spend Christmas at the same place. We were awake at sunrise, watching the early morning beams of light shimmering through the airborne particles of dust. With few nuns about, we talked endlessly about the adventures we would have. Breakfast was two hours away, and there was plenty of time to muck about. Then, we would wait for departure at nine.

The nuns kept our ears buzzing with the dire warnings of dos and don'ts. We were chaffing at the bit to get out of here and onto our road trip. The journey westward was peppered with exciting pit stops, but I was more focused on our destination, the open blue skies of Chinchilla. It was a dry, balmy 36 degrees, beautiful weather as we pulled up on Heeney Street. This was the main street of uptown, which was lined with fifty-year-old camphor laurel trees. Under the shade of one of these gnarled giants stood Bill & Gwyn waving. It felt like coming home. Hugs and handshakes of welcome weren't something to which I was accustomed. Still, a big grin did the trick when facing unfamiliar feelings.

'Rickie, Bobbie, it's so lovely to see you both,' Gwyn smiled.

'Hello Bill, Gwyn, Thank you.'

'I don't suppose either of you is hungry by any chance?'

'Well, now that you mentioned it, we could probably fit in a sandwich. '

'Okay, then it's my shout. We'll head over to Melegons Café for afternoon tea,' Bill joked in a rather posh-sounding voice.

This place was in the old part of town, where the Warrego Highway passed through and headed west. Unfortunately, during the "occasional big wet season," this low-lying section of the town flooded. Melegons was a 1950s-style café with vinyl bench seating and central tables stationed along the walls. In front of the milk bar were round vinyl-covered stools mounted on chrome posts. The stainless-steel and glass servery displayed scrumptious treats. On the top were large jars of lollies to tempt our gobsmacked eyeballs. The food was magnificent, and the Greek owners were friendly and knew everyone's name. It felt just like they were all one big happy family. It is a relaxing, comfortable establishment for everyone to dine in.

Milking time was later in the afternoon during the warmer months, so we had time to dawdle in town before heading out to the farm. While eating and talking simultaneously, we bombarded them with questions. Bill took the rare opportunity to get a word in while I was catching my breath.

'Well, boys, we have a few groceries to pick up before we head home, so you'd better finish up.'

Stopping at Luscombe's Cordial factory, we parked in the shade, so the car was cooler for Gwyn. Then Bill, Bobbie, and I headed into the factory to select a dozen of the locally made delicious soft drinks.

'That's strange. There's no one here. How do we pay for the soft drinks, Bill?' I asked.

'Don't you worry about that; people are more trusting out in the country. I've already told them we'd be stopping by this afternoon, and I'm certain they'll send me an account at the end of the month. Then we'll head over to the hardware store before they close, and lastly, we'll get some groceries from Harris's Foodland on our way home.' Bill informed us.

We buzzed about from place to place; there was so much to see in this country town. Some of the streets we went down were still gravel, but I suppose it would cost a lot of money to seal them. Anyhow, the dust added to the rural charm of the place, although the locals have probably had a gut full of it already. The houses all had wood stoves, and the burning of split timber blocks gave the town an aromatic scent.

'Well, look at those bags hanging over there in the shade under that shop awning.' I pointed.

'It's a wonder somebody doesn't steal them now that the shops are all closing,' Bobbie replied.

'They're perfectly safe up there. Check the name on the outside of the bags, Rickie, please,' asked Gwyn.

'Yes, those three have your name on them. Is there a ladder around?'

Gwyn laughed. 'Wait till Bill comes back; the groceries aren't going anywhere. So, while we're waiting, tell me how you've been doing at school?'

'Rickie and I came in at the top of our class this year. Cathy must've been feeling generous as she is usually in first place. Rickie, I, and another boy, Petra, battle for the next three spots,' replied Bobbie.

'Religious instruction isn't officially graded, except if you count the number of whacks you get for being unable to answer the questions,' I volunteered.

'Well, God is always important in our lives. What are your favourite subjects?'

'Maths and English,' we both replied.

'Here's Bill now,' Gwyn informed us. We jumped out the car door to sit in the back of the utility, aka "Tilly."

'You sure you want to sit back there in the hot sun? There is plenty of room in the front for us all.'

'Bobbie and I like it back here, and we can keep an eye on the soft drinks and groceries if you'd pass them down from those hooks to us,' I replied.

'Someone has to keep an eye on our ports, so they don't fly out the back,' Bobbie said.

'Well, we will not be going that fast for you to be concerned about anything flying out the back. The roads are dusty, so tie a hanky over your mouth and nose.' Bill replied.

Off we went with hankies covering our faces like two bandits, as we headed out of town, driving over a cattle grate out along Chinchilla-Tara Road towards the Condamine River.

The surrounding countryside was dry as a bone on both sides of the narrow bitumen road. Drooping crops looked in such a sorry state that they might not be worth the cost of harvesting. A weir over the Condamine River was still in the planning stage. The only crossing was a low timber bridge that, in heavy rain, was often submerged. As we passed over its rattling timbers, the steady stream that meandered below had fallen well short of what was termed a river. When we got to Pharaoh's corner, we turned off Tara Road onto the Avenue, a tree-lined gravel road. The dust cloud followed us all the way home. A couple of miles further, we turned left onto another long gravel road that led eventually to the Hopelands School. When approaching any oncoming vehicles, both drivers had to give up some of the road to pass each other. If you saw dust in front of you, it was advisable to stay way back so that you didn't swallow more than your fair share. Everyone was blessed with a polite nature out here and would wave and toot their horn in passing. We slowed to a crawl and turned into the timber-gated entry to "Apsley Meadows." Here the vista opened to reveal their resplendent white weatherboard farmhouse shimmering in the dry heat. It stood on low timber stumps, far enough away from the road to allow for the dust to settle. As was the custom whenever visitors arrived, a cup of tea and homemade biscuits were in order.

'There are a few social engagements for us all. Your popularity precedes you,' Bill announced.

'That sounds wonderful. What are social engagements? 'We both asked.

Hopelands Community Welcome!

'Well now, on Friday, the local school has invited us all to their Christmas party. All the ladies in the local area bring a plate of goodies. It's the men's job to crank up the bar-b-q and serve the hot food. The students, some of whom you already know, are organising games. Then, after lunch, there is a musical recital and a pantomime. They certainly have a lot of talent for a small school,' Gwyn informed us.

'Is there anything we can do to help? Robbie asked.'

'Well, I'm driving into town to pick up some eskies for the drinks and ice cream early Monday morning. The men at the ice works will load them on the back of the tilly for us as they're rather heavy. You two can come in and help if you like?' asked Gwyn.

'We can certainly do that.'

'At this time of year, I have a few odds and ends to do about the place. It's a good opportunity to take a break and socialize,' said Bill.

'Wow, You two must be popular around the district,' I quipped.

'Right then! I'll leave you boys to finish your afternoon tea; I'd better get the cows into the yards. The milking won't get started on its own,' Bill replied.

'These are delicious biscuits, Gwyn; I could eat them all day.'

'You're most welcome, Rickie. I'm glad you enjoy them, but don't eat any more; leave some room for your supper tonight.'

'Would you like me to wash up Gwyn?'

'Thank you, Bobbie. If Rickie can wipe up, I'll put things away, and we'll be done in no time.'

Us boys then changed clothes, pulled on gum boots, and charged over to help Bill at the dairy. From my previous holiday. I had a fair idea of what small jobs needed doing, so I informed Robbie as we went. Please fill up the old copper, and then we can light a fire under it to boil the water to sterilize the dairy equipment. A jam tin of crushed grain in each stall hopper made the cows happy to come into the milking bails. We put washcloths in each of the cleaning buckets, then we climbed over the fence to open the big gate to the main holding yard, so the cows would come straight into the yards.

'Now pay attention, Bobbie. When the cows come in, we stand over there so as not to frighten them.'

'Really? They're afraid of us kids?'

'No, it's just until they get used to us being around, unusual smells spook some of the cows, which upset them for milking.' I told him.

'Wow! You know a lot about this dairying business, Rickie!'

'Yep, you'll get the hang of it after a while. Once Bill gets back, there are other things we can do to help; let's go check on the fire.'

'Ok'

'The trick here, Bobbie, is not to put too much wood under the copper. If the flames get too high, sparks could blow into the grass and start a bushfire.'

'That's a bit of a worry. We're here all alone.'

'Fire safety is a big thing in the bush, and Bill is the local fire warden, so you can ask him all about it. In the meantime, pay attention, and we'll be okay.'

'Hey Rickie, there are a lot of cows coming down towards us. Should we move?'

'Nah, that part of the fence is closed off. This fire is stacked right, so it'll be okay for a while. Let's sit on the top rail and watch Bill put the cows in the yard. Then we can close the big gate behind him.'

'Righto, let's go.' Bobbie yelled.

'Thanks, boys, I see you got the water heater going.'

'Yes, and Bobbie and I put the feed in the bails and the water buckets,' I replied.

'Keep this up, and I'll think I'm the one on holiday,' Bill laughed.

Gwyn called out to us in the dairy. 'If you boys help Bill finish up, I'll prepare supper.'

'No worries, we'll get the job done.'

She laughed on her way out.

Dinner that night was roast beef and vegetables, followed by baked rice with ice cream for dessert. Robbie's eyes bulged at so much food. Our empty bones would appreciate some extra fat on them. Mealtime on the farm was a gourmet feast compared to our usual daily fare. Washing dishes and cleaning up after meals was no longer a chore, as we were happy to help. Nighttime entertainment was a friendly game of cards or a board game while we listened to a radio show or vinyl records played on a portable record player. The electric powerlines hadn't reached our neck of the woods. Any device that required power used batteries. Most available household utensils and appliances were hand-operated; exercise was always close at hand.

The lighting was supplied by a central battery system outside and was switched off around 9 pm. After that, it was a kerosene lantern or a candle for lighting, should a call of nature encourage you to venture out to the '*thunderbox*'. This was a traditional timber, non-flushing toilet. Generally, they were built away from the house so a breeze could disperse the occasional odour. Anytime, day or night, it was a popular haunt for snakes, spiders, and other bush creatures. It paid to be vigilant if you didn't want unexpected surprises. Such was the charm of rural living in the daily lives of country folk.

On Sundays, after a quick breakfast, we would drive into town for church services. Bill and Gwyn were Presbyterian, and Bobbie and I were Catholic. After services, everyone would take the time to chat and share news and goodwill. Sometimes, we'd get a lift into church with neighbouring families, which helped us feel more included in the community. We soon made many new friends who would invite us over for fun times. The Hart family often invited us over. At their property, we learned how to ride ponies and rope poddy calves. Milking the dairy cows still had to be done early morning and late afternoon, rain or shine.

The Hopelands School Christmas was lots of fun. There was plenty of food and new games to participate in, outside in the sports paddock. The kids were very friendly and interested in our city life. From their point of view, the big smoke was a place of wonder. We didn't dampen their spirits by telling them our own reality. The games they played always had a prize for the winner, runner-up and most improved. Quoits involved hurling horseshoes at a wicket set in the ground. Knocking tins off the fence, using a slug gun, was a bit of a challenge for us city boys. Bobbing in a big water-filled drum for apples kept us entertained with a bit of splashing about involved. Bobbie and I won a few of the runners-up prizes. The students held an outstanding academic record. A few had topped the state in their end-of-year exams. They were all talented young people who were generous in accepting us outsiders. I made some lifetime friends out here in the country.

It didn't matter about the time or distance that separated us. I was always made welcome on my return visits. Over the weeks that preceded Christmas day, we had a lot of outings to other farms and families in town. Relatives of Bill & Gwyn's. Barry & Silvia Mann treated Bobbie and me as part of the family. Here we would have delightful lunches and unexpectantly given presents which could only be opened on Christmas day. We were invited to many of the local neighbours' properties, and the level of acceptance made us feel like part of their extended family. Here, we never felt that a door would suddenly slam in our faces. For a change, the feeling of being a burden to society disappeared.

Not to be outdone, the townies put on quite a show with their colourful street lighting. The shop fronts had frosting on their glass panels and Christmas decorations all around. The local ambulance centre put on carols by candlelight on the main street. Bill was an active member of the centre and part of the choir; all appreciated his strong baritone voice. The local council organised a social dance in the community centre, and the upcoming New Year's Ball gave the ladies a good excuse to don their gowns and menfolk to polish themselves up

It'd been a good year financially, and the weather had been kind to the farmers during sowing and harvesting times. This also meant the town did well, with the extra revenue spreading out through the community. It was probably in a town like this that the saying, *"What goes around, comes around"*, originated. Everyone should benefit from the good times. The many service clubs sponsored local events, often with a raffle to aid those in need in the community. With extra Christmas cheer for all, their giving spirit amazed and humbled Bobbie and me. A full social calendar, both night and day, included almost everyone in the shire one way or another. There was no real reason why anyone had to feel left out unless by illness or choice.

Gifts were made to be delivered to those who found themselves in hospital over Christmas. The aged care centre was entertained with music and gifts for all residents, and to the best of my knowledge, I hope nobody was forgotten.

We kids had the privilege of handing out the gifts and wishing all a Merry Christmas. This was the most caring thing I have ever had the privilege to be involved in. Between all the social activities, the farm still needed our attention. Four poddy calves were born that week, and we got to name and enter their details in the livestock register. Bill also played in a couple of cricket matches, and Gwyn was in a local ladies' tennis competition, they were all serious contenders. One day, it was tennis matches, the next, cricket or something completely different. Depending on the teams, some games were held at Hopelands and some in the town.

The tennis matches were an extra attraction for me, as the ladies were all great cooks and served up a delicious variety of snacks for players, including ball boys. An extra bonus was that the ladies gave us a lesson on the correct handling of a tennis racket, as well as footwork and ball control. The latter however was short-lived as several of our balls went over the fence, and it took us some time to find them. In doing so, we provided them with some light entertainment as they pointed the different directions the lost balls went. Bobbie and I were looking for the balls while the ladies started laying out lunch. This motivated us to search diligently; fear of missing out was a thing.

Cricket is also a fine game, but during the men's games, I discovered early in life that I'm not a conscientious observer for any length of time. I've never been content to sit on the sidelines. I went over to help in the canteen with the preparation for the refreshment break. Part of my job was as a food taster to ensure the quality was up to standard. Bobbie, on the other hand, seemed satisfied, sitting on the bench watching the game, so I didn't bother him with this extra chore. He thoroughly enjoyed bringing me up to date with the score, run rate and other details that I'd missed whilst I was assisting at the canteen. He asked if I needed a hand to give him a whistle. Who was I to spoil his fun day out?

After Saturday breakfast, Gwyn told us she was heading into town to shop and catch up with the church ladies' floral group; we were welcome to join her. Bill also mentioned going up the road to help the Rodgers, who were mustering and branding about fifty beef cattle. It was a tough choice. Bill had a bigger need for our experience, so how could we decline? With the dishes done, Bobbie and I sat in the back of the Tilly for the ten-minute drive up the road to the closest neighbours.

'I'm off now and will be back early this afternoon to pick you up,' Gwyn informed us.

'Thank you, Gwyn. Have a nice time in town,' we replied.

'Alright. Well, we better get cracking. You young fellows need to take care around these cattle. They can get a little cantankerous. We have an essential job for you both to do, controlling when and where the cattle go. Open and close those two gates,' Mr Rodgers informed us.

'Ok, we can do that,' we both replied, and each chose our spot as gatekeepers. Life on a farm was casual, but one shouldn't assume it was easy or safe all the time. These cattle would bowl us clean out of their way and most likely knock us on our rear ends quick and smartly if we didn't keep our wits about us. It was a hot day, which soon tired us boys.

Before long, we're covered in flies, dust, and cow manure, much to the amusement of all. Amongst the light-hearted encouragement of the adults, it paid to have a sense of humour.

'Lunchtime boys,' the homestead ladies had arrived. The morning went so quickly, not that I was complaining about taking a break.

'Bobbie, Rickie! Close those gates off and get yourselves cleaned up. There's a bucket of water and a towel beside the tank stand. We'll finish up here and join you shortly,' Bill called out as he took another branding iron from the fire.

Getting cleaned up was a challenge as we'd managed to get coated in manure and animal blood. The cattle in the holding yard weren't too keen on the situation either. Watching the spectacle did little for their dispositions as they were roped and dropped to the ground to be inoculated, castrated, and branded. The scent of burnt hair and scorched flesh permeated everyone's nostrils. This was not a sport but a necessity of life on a farm.

The most relaxed spot was near the tank stand. In the shade, you could sit on large slabs of seasoned wood. These surrounded an aged, knotted timber-planked table. The ladies spread a tablecloth over it and held it down with vintage biscuit tins filled with goodies from country kitchens. With enamelled plates and mugs in hand, we helped ourselves to lunch. A mug of hot black tea on a hot day was most refreshing. The conversation turned to current wheat and cattle prices. When the ladies joined in, the discussion turned to upcoming social events in the town. Gwyn had returned in time to join us for a cuppa.

Once we finished here, there was no time to dally about due to an important event that evening. Well, at least as far as us young boys were concerned. We're going into the local picture theatre. By the time the cows were brought into the milking yards, we'd have everything ready to roll. After a light dinner, we were heading into town by 6.30 pm. The main movie was *"The Creature from the Black Lagoon."* This was a scary movie to us, though Bill thought it all rubbish. At intermission, we were treated to popcorn, a cordial drink and ice cream by the cinema owners. It must've been after 10 pm when we left, and a light misty rain did little to quell our imaginations to the sounds of the darkness. The countryside was pitch black.

Our six-week Christmas holiday in the bush was a wonderful time spent among caring people. They enriched our lives, and every day was a new memory to cherish. Time blinked as the morning sun shimmered on our final day, and we greeted it with cheery goodbyes. Our return road trip would never be long enough, where we were concerned.

Reality Bites

Who knows, maybe this year will be different. Dreams can sometimes change the world, but not today. Dong, ding, dong, ding. *What the hell was that racket?* My eyes opened, startled as reality sunk in. I watched other kids rushing about the place.

'You ok there, Your Majesty? Would you like breakfast in bed today?' Petra joked as he sat on the end of my bed.

'You bloody peasant, move off with you,' I replied. He started bowing and scraping, then jumped up and whacked me with a pillow.

'Rickie, get a move on before the dragon nun catches you lounging about. She's had a good long rest and is in fine form.'

'Bugger. She's already started on the newbies down the end of the dormitory. Let's go, Petra.'

'Ok, but how're ya going to talk our way past her? She is on the warpath.'

'Watch and learn young fellow.'

'Happy New Year, Sister. Did you have a nice break?' I called out then I stepped in front of Petra so he could pass behind me.

'Thank you, Rickie. Why are you still in your pyjamas?'

'Well, Sister, it's been a while since I last saw you, and I was waiting to say hello before you got too busy,' I replied. This gave the unfortunate newbies a chance to disappear if they had any sense.

'That's nice; now you better get moving unless you'd like me to help speed your day up.'

'Yes, Sister. Thank you.'

'Bloody hell, Rickie, you're pushing your luck. She will wake up to your crap one day,' Petra whispered to me.

'Saved your arse, didn't I?' I replied.

'Yeah, well, stuff that, let's get out of here before our day goes down the dunny. I'd rather start the new year without getting my arse flogged. Come on, we've got about twenty minutes to be in line.' He reminded me.

Such is life. Rush, hurry up and don't be late. Punctuality and good manners are taught with a stick, no carrot involved.

Was it only yesterday that I awoke to the baying of cattle waiting to be milked, the loud squawking of cockatoos and galahs stealing an easy feed of grain, the reminiscent smell of woodsmoke from the kitchen stove, and the acquaintance of congenial people with quiet dispositions? Here was a worthwhile memory to temper the current conflicts of this large-scale mayhem of lost souls.

Having been thrown together without thought for our mental well-being, we would never know what the closeness of a family truly felt like. This would instil a permanent lack of belonging, which became an elusive lifetime feeling. How quickly we all fell back into the routine of our existence. We were on autopilot most of the time, putting one foot in front of the other. Keep breathing and walking, two of life's necessities were the main thoughts forever in my mind. My mantra began sounding off in my head. *Trudge, Trudge along the walkway, keep on moving. It's what we do. Stop to dither and you're in the shit. Trudge, Trudge, do it their way, always do what they say. Oh, what a wonderful day. There is no point in complaining; it will bring you pain. Best to shut up and keep moving till there's something to gain.* The positive reinforcement of resilience in silence: one day, it will be my turn.

1967 rang in a change to our lives in more ways than one. This year, we had a different classroom with more light and fresh air, a nice change from the odious smells that, on occasion, infused the atmosphere of the other gloomy classrooms. Our Stern nun was in attendance on this first day back in school. How delightfully encouraging. I wonder why she didn't take the opportunity to relocate her good self over the holidays. Surely, there was another school that had attentive, adoring children who would be more suited to her disposition. Obviously, God had other plans for her, which I hoped didn't include me. What was that she just said? Something about a new teacher for English class, with my luck, she would turn out to be related to Attila the Hun. Still, one must be positive; a change is as good as a holiday, according to some complete moron. Oh, I wonder what joys will be in store for us precious little saints now. When class resumed from morning break, I was surprised not to see a matronly drab person. Here stood a stylishly dressed woman writing on the blackboard. Then, my daydream of a beautiful young princess coming to save me was shattered. The voice of Stern nun boomed throughout the room. Accompanied by the rat ta tat of the cane whacking the timber desktop.

'Attention, class. I'd like to introduce your new teacher, Mrs Jones. Please make her welcome.'

'Welcome to our school, Mrs Jones,' we all parroted.

'Thank you, children. I'm happy to be here. Now, I'd like to tell you a little about myself so we can all get to know each other better.'

The New Teacher

Mrs Jones had quite an impressive background in teaching at several private and public schools. Not that it mattered to us, as we were clueless about what a support teacher was anyway. As she droned on for quite a while, I erroneously assumed she'd be gone within a couple of weeks. Turned out she had a gift for connecting with disadvantaged children, so she remained with us until the end of my primary school education.

'On your desks, you'll find a white folded name tag; please print your name clearly.'

'Can we put our nicknames on them?' one of the girls asked.

'No, I'd prefer your real name. Once you've finished, stand up and hold your card before you.'

'Okay, all done. Now, when I ask you, tell me your name and one thing you like either in or out of class. Then, sit back down. Starting with the girl in the front on the left-hand side, then onto the next person in line.'

'Sandra Blaine. My favourite subject is English, Mrs Jones.'

With luck, this was going to take up the whole period. There was a new girl named Sharyn who sat at the only spare desk. She loved maths and spoke very clearly in a soft voice. All I could see of her from back here was long black hair. The next row at the back was Cassie. She loved English and would later become a journalist. Up and down the rows, the students told their details and finally came round to me, daydreaming in the far-right rear corner.

'Rickie Battler! Mrs Jones and my favourite pastime is horse riding,' so as not to be outdone by all these kids.

'Well, thank you. You've all given interesting answers. English is about expressing yourself so others can understand what you mean. Rickie, how are you able to ride horses here?'

'It is a rather long story, but the only time I've any chance is on the school holidays out at a farm in Chinchilla, Mrs Jones,' I replied.

'That sounds like a good place for us to start; I'd like you all to take out your notepads and draft a short story of three hundred words about your Christmas Holidays. What was it you most enjoyed doing? Hand them in by the end of tomorrow's class.'

Bugger, that'll teach me to open my big mouth.

English class was one that we began to enjoy, as it relieved the monotony of our lives. Little by little, her tales of the everyday antics of her husband and children gave us the allusion that we were part of the family. While doing so, we got an insight into a society that was primarily alien to us. I enjoyed the interaction with the stories as she invited us to engage in discussing the issues involved and thinking outside our sheltered lives. This was a means to an end, as each part came with both an insight into normal family life and writing homework on grammar; the descriptive particles of our language started to mean more than boredom.

It would become a tricky situation if I asked about Katie's whereabouts. Her girlfriends, Charmaine and Wanda, told me they weren't sure if she was returning. They had caught up with her two weeks ago in the city, and she'd been excited about some big secret. The nuns would know, though a boy inquiring about a missing girl was asking for trouble. My problem was how to get an answer to a dubious question. I was delighted when Mrs Jones informed our class that we'd be using our own ideas for short stories. There was the answer staring me right in the face. She wrote all the topics on the blackboard. Chalk was the preferred writing material at the time. Three columns with ten titles in each, ranging from sports, space travel, clothing styles, pop stars, holidays, and decimal currency. Hmm…go figure that one. Lastly, there was my own contribution: *mysteries*. It was a show of hands for each one, and the most popular five would be the subject titles for the term. Having more girls than boys in our class, the choices were biased. Mystery got voted into the top five. Obviously, quite a few of us found the subject intriguing.

That's how I began to unravel the whereabouts of the disappearing girl, known as Katie. We formed two mixed-gender groups for each subject and five students for each group. Our discussion groups were limited to Fridays, and there was a lot of English to learn before we began creating stories. All of us made contributions to our own group's storyline and elected one person to write the story and a different person to do the presentation. This group concept was new; teamwork was fun and a hit-and-miss process. Our closed existence had caused our imaginations to stymie. Time dragged towards the end of our term when we got to present our mystery subject.

Each of the writer's groups created their own story based on an actual event that in some way had influenced either life, school, or our class. The story started with a brief overview. And might include a twist in the conclusion. Our creative team had elected Cassie as the lead writer and, without any discussion, nominated me, the dubious honour of standing up at the front of the class to present our group story.

Typical behaviour in this school is that everyone appears to want to be involved but bows out before their face is in the spotlight. Our team's female amateur sleuths worked magic to uncover what happened to *Katie*. Separating the facts from the fiction was a twisted, murky task for which they are well suited. Our tale grew, skilfully blending gossip intertwined with the scarcity of facts.

On a more personal note, another mystery developed when a scrawled message on the back of a card appeared in one of my books. *"I know what you're up to, Rickie."* 'Bloody hell, who wrote this?' Someone in this class is winding me up. The gauntlet had been thrown down. This was a personal challenge, and I'd have better be careful. It had to be someone in this class, but who? That girl over there, maybe, the cross-eyed Sandra. She often appears to be looking at me; maybe it was her. Then again, it could be Cassie winding me up; she is intriguingly mischievous at times. What about the new girl? Is she a saint or a sinner?

Our story was taking shape nicely, primarily due to the girls doing the snooping. The following week, I was able to move on to this covert note business. I put a mischievous note card of my own on the desks of Sandra, Cassie, and the new girl. Fortunately, no one saw me going into the classroom that day. Now, if it isn't any of these three? It'll at least throw a cat amongst the pigeons. If nothing else, it narrows the field. In the meantime, this note conspiracy has caused quite a stir amongst the other kids, one of whom reported the drama to Mrs Jones. Then it became a serious topic for discussion of the who, how and why, as some had thought it a joke of our new English teacher.

'Well, class, this might be amusing to some of you; it's most intriguing to have a mystery within a class writing about mystery stories. Please stop passing any more of these cards around. Otherwise, I may have to report the incident to the sisters,' she informed us. We certainly didn't want "stern nun" waving her cane or blackboard ruler around our hands and rear ends.

'Ok, who's our nominated presenter with the final Mystery storyline today?'

'I am! Mrs Jones,' I replied.

'Well, now, how appropriate, come up to the front and stand on our bard's stage.' This stage consisted of two apple crates covered with cloth.

'Okay, Rickie, speak loudly and clearly so we all can hear your group's mysterious story.'

'Yes, Mrs Jones, the title of our story is *The Disappearing Kid*. It was compiled by our group writer, Cassie, with the aid of our team of in-house detectives.'

'As it was a subject you suggested, we're all most intrigued, Rickie. You've twelve minutes for your presentation. Please continue.'

'I'm sure that the more astute amongst you have noticed one of our students is missing. Now, this person was highly active in plays and sporting events and added a melodious voice to our choir. It's odd that the whereabouts of this student, who was well-liked, are unknown. There've been rumours of possible beaus. Maybe they have run off together?' This got a few laughs from the class; I was skating on thin ice here.

Under the guidance of Cassie, our story read like a who dun- it, with many turns and twists. There were several false leads and more than a few possible outcomes. The tale unfolded into a myriad of trials, which finally led us to be able to locate our missing student. She wasn't coming back and was now free to happily live her life with her Aunty and Granddad. Address unknown.

'In conclusion, we ask the class, have you figured out who our missing person is.?'

'Oh well done and within time,' Mrs Jones clapped in appreciation.

'Thank you, Mrs Jones and a special thanks to the creative members of Team Rickie.'

That certainly got applause and a few cheers all around. Stirring the pot sometimes can have positive results.

'Ok, Class, I've thoroughly enjoyed all your stories, so over the weekend, I want you all to think over which one was your favourite. 'I've spoken to the teacher's board, who will vote on the five most popular stories. These will be decided by you in a secret ballot, like the recent State Election system. I will tell you more about it on Monday.'

The school was becoming more interesting than it had been in previous years. Was it a sign of the times, or was Mrs Jones's teaching style aligning us with the modern world outside? She cast a new light on delivering education without constant threats and beatings. Maybe the Children's Services Department was loosening its parsimonious purse strings. The resulting atmosphere created a positive element in our daily lives. Previously, we'd only received schooling in line with the State Education Board, excluding extracurricular activities. Monday dawned on a class of kids keen to be at school. We had an election to attend this afternoon, as we were the VIPs.

'Right class, are all voters in attendance?'

'Yes Mrs Jones!'

'Petra, please proceed with the roll call. Sharyn, would you hand out one of these printed voting cards to each student as their name is called? Everyone else remains seated and is quiet. Each of you print the story you liked on your card; add your name and the writer's name. You have five minutes to complete your card, so think carefully and no talking. If you cannot remember the writer's name, raise your hand. That cheeky girl Sharyn sashayed past my desk with a card and a wink.

'Wow, that was quick, Sharyn. Have you decided already?'

'Yes, Mrs Jones, I decided on Saturday.'

'Sandra, as you are our temporary electoral officer, come up and retrieve the ballot box and keep it on your desk. Everyone, when you're finished, place your vote in the ballot box. Then quietly return to your seat as we don't want to disturb the next-door class.' Mrs Jones said. Then she quietly ducked outside.

When she returned, Sandra informed her. 'Everyone has finished voting Mrs Jones.'

'Well done, Sandra. Would you bring the ballot box up here? We will do the official count together. The rest of you can take out your assignment books and start on page thirty-two.'

It doesn't look like we'll get to goof off today, but it has been quite a buzz for us all. Mrs Jones began writing the results on the blackboard.

'In case you have glanced up here, these names aren't in any order. Five stories will be short-listed for the teacher's Literary award. The winners will be announced on Friday.'

When the vote score returned, Team Rickie's story had won first prize, Yay. The other four received a small gift. The first prize group scored a day out in the city botanical gardens with a picnic lunch.

Katie has left the home; I hope life will be good for her.

Sedition

Even the best of us can go astray as we travel through life, and yours truly is no exception. The new girl in our class, the one with the long black hair, nicknamed Shazza, had a mesmerising presence. Not that I was staring or anything so grossly rude like that. There were the odd occasions when these girls became touchy-feely people. Her imperceptible caress, along my side was quite a neat trick to perform in a crowd. Our new English teacher didn't appear overly observant, which was a nice change from the nuns. Was she just more subtle in her perceptions? *Something was not right here; how did she do that?* Maybe there is something wrong with my head. I've been whacked too often. I wondered, *What the hell did these girls get up to in their section? Gossip being the order of their day.*

They seemed to have endless subjects to dwell on, such as movie stars, fashions, music idols, and romantic daydreams. Daring one another to kiss a boy or two. Us clueless young fellows were in for years of turmoil. If only we could read their minds, we might have some chance of survival. What skills has God blessed them with? I was at the stage of my life approaching the ripe old age of twelve, a senior in grade six in 1967.

Occasionally, I would wander down past the rusty tin and timber sheds with mild interest. My main concern was not being seen out in the long grass that surrounded the farming area. There was livestock to watch and, if no one was around, an odd truck or tractor to climb about on. This, being the forbidden zone, naturally held a particular fascination for me, as some days, there were farm workers who I could idly watch for a change. On this Sunday afternoon, fate being what it was, there was little of interest to attract my attention. I decided to go exploring down towards the tennis courts and beyond. Here I would watch the girls playing tennis, as they had little conscience about hogging the courts most of the time. Amongst them was an enthusiastic slogger who belted a ball right over the fence, either at me or to get my attention.

'Hey Rickie, can you throw that ball back over, please, please?' I dithered as the separation of gender was a golden rule. If the nuns heard her, I was up the creek.

'Alright, I suppose so.'

I wanted to shut them up, so I went past the rear of the fence and hurled it back over. Then, another one of them hit a ball over a little further down. Now, there were several balls for me to collect as they all got in on the act. I felt like a duck in a shooting match.

'Come on, get our balls too, Rickie.' Anything to wind me up. So, I retrieved all the balls and pushed them through a hole in the chain wire fencing.

'Give it a rest, girls. You will drop me in the can if you keep making a noise.' It was a worthless attempt to gain sympathy; boys were fair game for tormenting as far as they were concerned.

'What are you up to over here anyway? You're going to get in trouble,' two of them started off a chant.

Another called, 'Hey Cheryl, do you know this wandering boy?

'Yes, he's in my class. He used to be Katie's special friend.'

'Oooh! So, you're the mystery smoocher; Katie kept you close to her chest. We thought it all was a big fib.'

'What're you girls all doing over there? We'll never win the competition at this rate. Now move it. A nun is coming over,' One of the senior girls chided them.

'Rickie, what're you doing? Quick! Hide in those bushes over there. You girls, get back to your serving practice against the end board. You better keep your mouths shut if you know what's good for you.'

'Ahh…Come on, Charmaine, we're just having some fun with him; these boys are so easy to wind up,'and off they went to practice their serves.

Saved by a friend of Katie's, whew, that was close; arse beltings tended to be merciless on Sundays. Now, I need to sneak away from the girl's secret hidden spot in the bushes. With that nun being on the tennis court, more girls converged outside the wire, which made my current position precarious. That left me with nowhere to go except outside the timber boundary fence. The mob of girls became louder as they shouted encouragement to the on-court players. All their noise covered my escape as I crawled along the fence line to a spot where several palings swung loose. I could easily pass through, and the palings swung back into place. Nothing was noticeable from the outside; bless Charmaine's heart for pointing me in the right direction. These girls no doubt had more secret escape places than their innocent looks conveyed.

With as much guile as possible, I meandered down a dirt road, turning into the fields, a chance to breathe in the surroundings and be safe from discovery. I headed off in the general direction of the old sheds when I heard a faint squeal from inside. This might be interesting, so I crept around the back rather than chance passing the slightly askew timber doors. I heard a shuffling sound from amongst the hay and giggling. I peeped through a knot hole in the wall and almost tripped over. In the shadows, I could make out two people who were up to some form of mischief. Maybe this will be one of the less boring Sundays. Any change in social activity around here was worth a second look.

To remain undiscovered required moving silently till I came upon a knot hole lower on the wall. Here, I laid down unseen with a better view of what these two were up to. Surely, they weren't having a cigarette or two. Smoking in a hayshed wasn't a smart idea. As my eyes adjusted to the dim view, I could see two bodies. The legs of one led all the way up to the bare bum of a boy. Nothing interesting here until the other one jumped up, wearing nothing but a pair of knickers. *So, this is how the older kids spend their idle moments.*

'What was that noise?' the girl whispered.

'What noise? You must be hearing things; come back and relax with me.'

'I'm sure I just heard someone outside.'

'Probably one of the cows mooching about.'

'Are you sure? We don't want to be sprung in here; the nuns will have a fit.'

For the next ten minutes or so, I got an education that wasn't on the school curriculum. This sleight-of-hand business had more avenues than I had experienced. Truth be told, it began to dawn on me why some of the older boys seemed to disappear at times; playing this secret game with the girls. It must have been hot in the itchy hay as I was warm out in the sunshine. The sound of approaching voices made all our ears prick up. Holy crap, it was a group of nuns on the warpath. The fearsome five had arrived: nasty nun, grumpy nun, giant nun, and strict nun. Bringing up the rear was Hawkeye nun, our local Houdini. The big timber doors screeched open, and the nuns charged in with their straps and canes swinging wildly. The young couple's amorous *tete de tete* earned them a whopper flogging on their path to hell.

'Cover yourself up, boy. You're a disgrace,' said one of the nuns.

'Get your clothes on, you wicked disgusting creatures,' yelled another.

'Yes, sister, please stop hitting me. I'm trying to put my clothes on.'

'Don't you talk back to me, you little Jezebel?'

It was a perfect time to make myself scarce; there was no point in being another target. Nervously I retraced my steps back towards the tennis courts. On the way, I noticed another couple wandering where they should not be. The amorous performance down the back blocks certainly livened up the lazy afternoon. It galvanised all the girls into a frenzy of juicy gossip. Their natural curiosity was in full flight.

Nigel Saves My Ass

I breathed a sigh of relief as I escaped from the danger zone and collapsed under the large shady trees bordering the gender demarcation zone. This was a dubious spot to layabout; hopefully, those sticky-beak girls don't venture my way. Suddenly, from out of nowhere, a bloody soccer ball hit me fair in the guts.

'Rickie, what're you doing lying about over here?'

'Nigel, how the hell are you? I'm just having a quiet Sunday afternoon nap in the shade. What're you up to; do you want to play some footy?'

'Cool! I'll go further back; you kick the ball over to me.' Our little game lasted no more than five minutes before we were rudely interrupted.

'What're you boys doing over there?' One of the nuns called out.

'I'm just getting our ball, sister. Can we play here? It's hot running around in the sun,' I asked.

'Alright, but don't kick it past the tennis courts. We cannot have you boys running wildly all over the place.'

'Thank you, Sister,' we both replied.

Good old Nigel's obsession with kicking that ball had unknowingly saved my rear end. I hadn't had much opportunity to catch up with him lately, so I was glad to join him in one of his few enjoyments. It certainly would do me no harm to have a witness, just in case. The fallout from this afternoon's romp in the hay had a ripple effect throughout the home. It wasn't long before a few more of the boys came over to join in the game, and the bigger group made Nigel's day. Though they weren't his close mates, they were at least kind to him.

'Gidday Rickie, what have you been up to?'

'Hi Petra, bugger all, not a lot happening around here on a Sunday.'

'Hmm, I've been looking around for you for half an hour. You know Bobbie's right, you're like a ghost, popping up out of nowhere.'

'Well, seeing as you're the detective today, what's all that malarky going on over there in the girls' section?' I asked.

'Really, that's all you got to say. Sometimes, I swear you walk around with a bucket over your head. How could you not notice that the nuns have been going batshit? Some boys have been caught having an orgy with the older girls down the back sheds.' Petra informed me.

'Bullshit, Petra. The nuns have eyes in the back of their heads. No way anything like that could happen around here,' I replied.

'True, hey, they caught a dozen of them apparently; some ran away into the bush; there's absolute bedlam going on.'

'Yo, Chris! Come over here and tell Rickie what's happening over at the girls' section. Apparently, he's been in dreamland again.'

'Rickie, it's all over the place. It started about an hour ago. One of the nuns checked on some of the senior girls who were supposed to be having a high tea thingamajig in the laundry tearoom. Their table was all set out, but the girls were nowhere to be found. The nun must've freaked out and rallied her stormtroopers. There's been a group of nuns frantically searching all over the place. I overheard one of the nuns saying, 'This is an absolute disgrace; how can it possibly happen here? Then off she went in a mad rush,' Chris was getting quite excited with his storytelling.

'How'd you know all this, Chris? Were you down there with them?' I joked.

'It's true, Rickie. The girls who were helping the nuns told me there was a group party going on with the senior boys.'

'Yeah, right. That sounds like a lot of bull.' I didn't know what they were talking about and doubted they did either; best if I didn't say too much.

'You would've thought we might've known something about it. How can something like this be kept a secret?' Petra sounded quite put out.

'Well, guys, whatever the truth of the matter is, we better get back to our game before they assume we do know something about it all.'

'Good idea, no joy hanging around here like dipsticks. We'll only get whacked for the hell of it.' Then Petra took off.

This sorry saga turned into a proper royal witch hunt, and the proverbial hit the fan. The fallout from this questionable behaviour placed serious restrictions on our freedom of movement. All grades six and seven were questioned as to their exact whereabouts at the time. Karma smiled at our own group alibi, the ball game that was supported by several of the nuns, especially the one who confirmed we were playing soccer around the time in question.

Oh Yeah, when the saints come marching in, it's no wonder we're in that number. Any unfortunate soul who had not a clear recollection of their days' activity with supporting confirmation would fall under the grindstone of interrogation. Within the week, the most likely of the prime candidates were identified and extradited to unknown places. Keeping with tradition, floggings were an integral part of the relocation and rehabilitation process. The known culprits were those who'd completed their primary schooling and were waiting for work placements or relocation to a secondary school facility. Such is the price of love on a physical level.

The eyes of the hawks were keenly focused on the rest of us. A smile or an accidental brush against one of the opposite gender could be deemed the devil's work. Life goes down the same old path, mischief being the spice of life from another direction. Recently, there was a theft of disconnected items. Two twenty-pound bags of flour, a box of barley sugar, and a novice's habit. These couldn't be accounted for, and it's possible that they were mislaid. None of these things appeared to be connected, or were they? This did, however, concern the nuns over the escalating crime spree that has descended upon our saintly paradise. Still, that was not to be the end of it. This took some time to surface, all be it in a roundabout fashion, such is in the way that legends are born.

Shenanigans

A little birdie whispered the mystery of the stolen items a few months later. It seemed to be the perfect ruse—a daring escapade that delighted the minds and hearts of all resident young adventurous souls. However, I remain sceptical that the person in question had gotten away with it.

The bags of flour had been exchanged for a return train ticket to Bundaberg. The barley sugar provided travelling pocket money for the trip. The novice nun outfit became a perfect disguise. It was used as a cloak of respectability that encouraged assistance from others. No one was overly concerned about the missing girl's whereabouts as she would be out on an assignment. The tale of intrigue unfolded, starting with the bus trip to a local train station, a perfectly normal activity for some. The local train conductor stopped for a chat with her, then moved on checking other passengers' tickets. She had arrived at the local station a little late, so she intended to purchase a ticket on the train, but it had completely slipped her mind. At Roma Street station, she changed platforms.

There was an hour to fill in before her departure. Time enough to relax in the platform canteen, where she ordered a Devonshire tea. This was a girl as bold as brass. Just before the train departed, she quickly called her family from the station phone cubicle, telling them she had a big surprise. She would arrive that evening, so could they pick her up at the station? When she alighted from the train, still dressed in the novice's outfit, she must've spun them an exciting tale. Despite all their questions, she asked them to keep this a secret. She changed into civilian clothes, and no one in town was the wiser. From then on, everything went well during her family visit. I wondered what happened to her in the end or if it was a fable of some girl's imagination.

After the previous term's amorous tango saga, there came about a curious deviation to our education. It was one of the most obscure descriptions of the birds and the bees that I would ever hear in my life. I'm unsure what the official curriculum was meant to include, but ours was short on the details. This subject wasn't conducted in mixed-gender discussion. Probably, as it was feared, it may lead to our moral downfall. We were filled with dire warnings of fire and brimstone for any discretions. Thank you very much for such an enlightening topic. With this newfound knowledge, we were ill-prepared for the follies of society. No doubt we would all be soon on the road to hell due in part to this lack of academic enlightenment.

Another event of historical importance was occurring this year, a Referendum. This was to change our Australian Constitution, and our English teacher ensured our class was well informed of the process. As none of us were remotely aware of what a referendum was, we looked forward to the discussions on the subject. No doubt, written questionnaires would soon follow it. Unbeknownst to us naïve kids, racism was rife out beyond the closeted environment of our home.

It was akin to being locked in the darkness of a cupboard, a thing that happened more to some than others. Here, we were all treated the same; few faired any better than the rest. The colour of your skin or race was irrelevant, or so we thought. This referendum would open our eyes to the outside race-conscious segregation of our society. Another spoke in the wheel of divide-and-conquer conquest of societies throughout the ages.

The two questions proposed to be voted on by older Australians, oddly Aboriginal people were excluded, even though they had the right to vote. The first question was to increase the number of House of Representatives members and not increase the number of senators. This failed to pass with a Three to Two majority, resulting in a No result. Obviously, the voters felt that they already supported too many *"Gunna"* individuals, the pollies who talked a lot and achieved bugger all.

With question two, the result was overwhelming: Yes. Ninety-three per cent of the voted in favour of including Aboriginal and Torres Strait people in the national census, what a dog act not to include them. The stated intention was to improve the quality of their lives with changes to laws. This process was supposed to reconnect them with their culture and country. Still, this too, fell well short of balancing the scales of justice. Their battle for equal rights would continue into the next century. I asked a few of my Aboriginal mates what they thought of the whole thing.

'The same old crap, bro,' they replied.

Jai summed it up, 'Rickie, nothing will change. The white fellas who took our land will never return it. We're still stuck in this shithole, and when we're finally released, what have we got to be happy about? Stuff all!'

'Yep, you guys got a raw deal. We'd nothing much to start with about where I came from. You've lost your country, culture and language. It makes me wonder how God could let this happen.'

Even though this was likely a political stunt to address the growing discontent in society, it reinforced in us the cruelty of the haves to the have-nots. After all the hoo-hah of the referendum, the lives of all us kids continued without fanfare. There is no political revolution here, despite the culture evolving amongst the younger generation, born free outside the great dividing fence. They'd shake the established order with their radical behaviour, clothing, long hair, and sign-waving protests. Distrust of the police and political leaders of the current government led to yet another royal commission that brought a lot of hidden practices into the spotlight. This was a time for change that would soon bring some truth out into the open, or so we hoped. Like any other children waiting for an exciting future event, we were no different.

Doctor Jang

Perhaps it was a sign of the times. We had waited long enough for our lives to improve; being part of a forgotten/and stolen generation of children lacked enjoyment. A dubious generosity bestowed upon us was the endless vaccinations delivered by javelin-sized needles. These contained concoctions which no doubt would render us immune to any disease plaguing mankind. This became a weekly occurrence for an extended period, and my anatomy was relieved when it ceased. I was not amused by the thought that should a pestilence scour the country; we may be among the few survivors. What a bummer that would be, trapped in an endless penguin parade. No illness would dare enter these walls for fear of being wiped out from their own genetic history.

Not to be outdone by the medical fraternity, the dental profession decided that they, too, would grace us with their services. Every six months, a large silver van arrives and parks behind our classroom. A cacophony of sounds and screams would emanate from within, doing little to entice us. Inside the van, every surface gleamed with trays of sparkling instruments of pain. Bottles of coloured concoctions lined the shelves of locked glass cupboards. Cloaked in white gowns, their faces masked, they hovered over us, these devotees of a culture of pain. Many seemed obsessed with an almost manic intent, searching every crack and crevice in our pearly whites. Fillings, the latest craze, had now come of age; these they gleefully bestowed upon us. Should a tooth crack during this odious procedure, great care was taken to choose an appropriate filler, which would require extensive grinding and polishing. Oh, what fun they had.

Occasionally, I was unfortunate enough to receive the highest honour, the opportunity for multiple teeth extraction, and was rewarded with a day out in the city. This entailed an escorted trip by bus and train to attend the Brisbane Dental Hospital on Turbot Street in Brisbane CBD. Here stood a monumental two-story building of a neo-Georgian design, opened in 1941. It was the only building completed from this grand development, and was designed by Richard Clare Nowland, who was employed as chief architect by the Queensland government. This massive building was a design engineering marvel, but to me, it looked just scary. The vast ground floor reception was control central, the bastion of the owl people with their large spectacles. Long corridors led to treatment areas, and God only knew what fate lurked back there.

I developed a pain in my neck while looking up at the high, ornate plaster ceilings. The dark timber panelled walls and hard wooden bench seats did little to cheer me up. Amongst the gloom sat many sad faces, who, like me, were distressed and wishing they were someplace else. The little old lady with grey hair sprouting from a mole on her chin was my designated minder for the day. No doubt a regular visitor as she seemed quite at home, dressed in her bright flowery dress, artfully knitting some garment.

She was not blessed with a disposition inclined to conversation. I waited in silent boredom till my number was called out. I'm not idle by nature, so I continued checking my surroundings. I noticed a large sign with a painted hand pointing down one of the corridors to a dental training college. I dreaded having to go there; students do not always pay attention. After sitting in one spot for what seemed like forever, I needed to go to the toilet. My squirming about would no longer stem the flood waters. This attracted the attention of the minder lady.

'Don't dawdle down there. Come straight back.'
'Yes, Miss.'

While mildly interested in the quality of fixings and fixtures in the toilets and hallways, I came across a drink machine. If you had a penny to put into the slot, a paper cup would drop down and fill with ice-cold orange cordial. It was fascinating to watch it operate as several adults bought a drink.

'Would you like a cool drink, young man?' A beautiful black-haired woman asked me.

'Can I? I mean, yes, please.'
'Where are your parents?

'They died. I'm here from an orphanage, and they're going to pull my teeth out.'

'That's terrible; I'm so sorry. Would you let me buy you a drink?'

'Thank you. I'm rather thirsty, but I'm not supposed to dawdle!'

'Okay, well, drink up. I'll keep watch for you, and this can be our little secret.'

'Thank you, lady.

'Well, aren't you just the sweetest boy.'

I put my empty cup in the bin and waved her goodbye, then wandered back to my seat. A side door banged open, and a white, gowned woman walked past me as if I were invisible. The door remained ajar, and through the gap, I heard muffled screams. Finally, my number was called, and another woman cloaked in white appeared to lead me into the slaughter. My minder seemed gleeful as she palmed me off to her, most likely heading off to have a nice early lunch at the teahouse.

The dental assistant told me not to worry; all would be well, and if I was good, I could have a cup of tea and a biscuit when I woke up. *Hmm, just how long will I be here?* Will I get lunch or dinner, I wondered.

'Can I go to the toilet first?'

'Yes, straight over there,' she pointed.

On my return, I was taken into a small clinical room off the main corridor, where two other dental assistants waited.

'Now, please make yourself comfortable in this black leather chair.' Before long, the nurse placed a rubber mask over my face.

'Just breathe normally and count to ten. Can you do that?'

'Auh, Ok,' I mumbled as the drug took effect. That was the last thing I remembered. It felt like no time had passed before I opened my eyes to see busy people moving around me.

'When're you going to start?' I mumbled with rubbery lips.

'We're all finished.'

'Really?'

I was given a sweet cup of tea to drink and a biscuit. This was a challenge to swallow, due to non-stop drooling. On the tedious journey back to the orphanage. I was somewhat groggy; and the anaesthetic wore off. The increasing pain gave me endless grief.

Sports and Pastimes

We spent most of our time absorbing endless information in school or doing chores. Option three was loosely described as leisure activities. It didn't amount to a hell of a lot, with limited choices to entertain ourselves. Creativity was the mother of invention. We made toys out of cast-offs, rubbish, or broken bits of other things. There was one special game we played whenever sufficient supplies were acquired. A probable name for it might be *reel racing*.

These homemade toy racers consisted of one used timber cotton reel, a rubber band, and two slim whittled sticks, one about an inch long and the other approximately four inches long. This gadget was wound up by turning the longest stick only, taking care not to overwind the rubber band. If it broke, you were out of luck, as they weren't easy to come by. Once the rubber band was under tension, both sides of the reel had to be held firmly. Then, it was simply a matter of holding your reel racer at the starting line and letting it go. Some just spun on the spot; others did amazing flips like a jumping jack out of control. Those still in the game just took off, spinning all over the place. The racer that went the furthest forward from the starting point was the winner. Control of your racer was in the hands of the gods, as some of them would turn around. The prize was usually barley sugar sticks, the winner takes all.

You had to be there to appreciate the excitement of doing it quietly. The silence was a necessity as the nuns considered gambling the road to ruin. Our sporting activities were sporadic, and we dreamed they might be a regular event. The lucky ones, including me this time, had the opportunity to join a local junior Australian rules club. One of the hurdles was getting to the practice field, where we played in bare feet. Unfortunately, we never got enough opportunities to immerse ourselves in the culture to become fully-fledged members. I sat on the reserves bench too often for my liking. Come to think of it, maybe that was our purpose.

We made do with donated second-hand jerseys and boots. Most of these were ill-fitting, but beggars can't be choosers. Often, I had blisters on my feet from wearing incorrect boots, hoping they would heal before the next game It added spice to my life; a change of location for a short period was a blessing. Having an opportunity outside that fence was highly sought after by us all, regardless of where, what, or why.

Cricket was a game we all enjoyed. If we could find a ball, and the cricket bat and wickets were released from the lock-up, a game was on. Our cricket pitch had seen better days, the cracks were a challenge, even to the most nibble of feet. Shallow hollows formed at either end; would leave you arse up if you were not paying attention. With fifty boys on the field at times, the game got a little hectic. Many a time, the bat was used for more than its intended purpose.

That is probably why the priests mostly batted, or they could not be bothered chasing a ball. We only had one set of wickets, which occasionally were used to slow up runners. Some 'brown nose' boys bolted up and down the pitch for the priest. Whenever a ball was slogged off, a pack of braying boys, yelling out *"Mine"*, would charge after it like it was some form of prize. With the sun in our eyes, catching the ball had its dangers: if you missed, brain damage might occur from more directions than one. Only rudimentary instructions were given, so the finer points of the game escaped us. Even these were debated. Sometimes, being called in or out created a squabble or a right royal biff up.

I liked to play Tennis when the occasional chance presented itself. Getting on the courts was limited to one Sunday afternoon a month. If it rained on that day, tough luck. The girls hogged all the new balls and the best rackets. The boys inherited the dog-eared balls along with rackets needing tensioning. I had a tenancy to use a tennis racket like a club, which was great for belting the daylights out of the ball but useless for accuracy on the court.

Swimming was an event we rarely got to enjoy. During the summer months, temperatures could rise above 38c, and sun lotion and skin cancer were unknown. Our basic lessons consisted of mainly floating on our backs, seeing how long we could hold our breath underwater, and foot kicking exercises.

On the rare attendances at the public pool prior to the Christmas holidays. It was not an effective process to becoming a competent swimmer.

Rugby league wasn't a regular sport and, at best, more like a free-running form of brawling and mayhem. Possession of the ball lost its importance at times in consideration of other 'matters.' Scrums were an excuse to slow the opposition to a crawl or remove them from the field. We had not yet obtained the finesse to relish a fair game by all concerned.

Plagues have an Upside

Ill health descended upon the home; an entire boy's dormitory was placed in lockdown. There was little joy to be found in these situations; if you were sick, sad, and sorry with vomiting and diarrhoea. In my case, exhaustion from working my arse off assisting with cleaning up as I became a conscripted member of the Chuck Chunder clean-up brigade. Either I was blessed with a strong constitution or unlucky. I did my best to stay as far away from the next bug attack as possible.

Honestly, I don't know how the nuns keep going; they look worn out most of the time. Their Irish constitution must be bulletproof, or God truly did love them. I am not sure what concoction we mixed into these moping buckets. It seared my nostrils, and my eyes watered endlessly. Demolition stuff destroying germs and drying out floorboards. It was also effective at removing patches of my skin and creating blotches on my shoes. At these times, I gladly looked forward to the school bell ringing, when I could take off to class. At least here in a mainly deserted classroom, I was safe from those mongrel mops, and my sense of smell had a chance to recover. Hopefully, it won't improve too much. the sweet stench of sickness invaded my olfactory senses, and the pong influenced my appetite.

I prayed that the other plagues mentioned in the bible didn't descend upon us. Boils were on the increase, manifesting as carbuncles that were unsightly and painful. They sometimes lasted for weeks, usually relieved by draining or sometimes a drawing ointment. This was a smelly black salve applied with a gauze placed over the top. An alternative was a small incision with a scalpel to assist the boil to drain. Fishing knives were not recommended as they can lead to further skin infections. Of course, if you intend to be a scarred pirate in the future, little make-up will be required. These things left hideous scars.

The upside of all this pestilence was that I had few restrictions on my whereabouts. I could be seen anywhere with little enquiry from nosey third parties. This made the time-honoured pastime of mischief entertainingly possible. We were all regularly dosed with a variety of mysterious concoctions that would make us gag. If taste was any indication, it's no wonder the bugs took off. Our metabolism was evolving into a defensive shield, protecting us against many future diseases.

Lunchtime was enjoyable in the sense that it wasn't so crowded. The girls were more relaxed with less supervision, and we would help ourselves to more significant portions. In return, we assisted the girls with the clean-up detail, where we swapped gross stories of the unfortunate bedridden and other items of common interest. Vigilance was necessary to ensure we were not overheard by younger minds. They had the annoying habit of repeating everything verbatim to all and sundry.

During these relaxed times, we received other lessons. One was up the stairs to the top level in the girls' home economics section. Here, we learnt the benefits of food preparation and nutrition. Usually, we boys were considered ill-prepared to grasp such convoluted information. Dire times breed special circumstances for some of us to improve our current speciality of baked beans on toast. Girls were rather good at sticking up for themselves, and they pulled no punches if they were annoyed. This was my first foray into the mysteries of the culinary arts.

I received instructions delivered courtesy of a bombardment of information from these devilish girls. They all tended to tell me what to do with the finer points of baking scones. My first batch was a tooth breaker with the appearance and consistency of rock. They were useful for throwing at annoying persons or noisy coo-ca-choo birds. The next batch prepared the following day was edible, an improvement though rather salty. The consensus was they'd be better served up as hard tack with vegetable soup. My final trial was two days later when I presented unburnt fruit scones that were palatable. I am sure they were not impressed. The cheeky buggers didn't like competition. Being of a gregarious disposition, I wasn't offended. It was best to go with the flow.

Life settled back into a chronic boredom, grinding on towards Freedom Day. This long-held dream was just a relocation, as we would eventually learn. The system was geared towards passing the parcel; the primary purpose was garnishing the public purse. Our controlled existence benefitted others in society a lot more than we did. These support schemes were waiting to be actioned by those with the knowledge to decide what was needed. It was a shame that we were not informed what support was available. We would then have some idea as to whom we could contact to thank for nothing. Increased financial support may have delivered better food, housing, and trained staff. Nurturing of any description may have made a considerable difference to the paths our lives eventually took.

Another school year ended, and our final examinations were done and dusted. Our end-of-year celebrations were a mixed bag of entertainment. Some of it was provided by the senior girls, who managed to involve us, saintly young lads. After that, we were all off for outside holidays.

Grey Clouds were Gathering

Christmas on the farm was just the best. The harvesting had been done, and new summer crops were planted. A little rain now would benefit everyone in the local community. This year, the weather would be a blessing and a burden. The rain started to fall steadily on Boxing Day, a welcome relief from the heat after cleaning up from our lunch. We all adjourned to the front verandah to open presents, a tradition with the many family members visiting our house. Listening to the sound of rain on a tin roof was relaxing, and we all enjoyed the serenity of it. While the storm thundered on the horizon, some of us had a nap on a variety of vintage squatter chairs and cushioned wrought iron day beds that were scattered about the place.

'Anyone for afternoon tea?' I called out. Us boys had put the billy on filling two large teapots to the brim, which were placed on the table with an assortment of cake tins, cups, saucers, and a stack of side plates. We did not want any of the adults to miss out.

The adults stirred; Gwyn said,' I'm not sure if any of us are even up for it.'

'We've got it all ready for you, ladies.'

'Well, in that case, we'd better join you,' a few replied.

'You've done a fine job, boys. A cup of tea is just the thing before getting the dairying started. It doesn't look like this rain will pull up anytime soon,' Bill gazed up at the darkening skies. The weather had a big effect on their livelihoods and was often a topic of conversation. Too much rain could be devastating, especially at harvesting time. A whole season's crop could be destroyed in the paddock, which would have a big effect on bank balances and future planting.

'There was a rise in the river as I crossed the bridge. The news report was for heavy falls up in the northeast. We'll have a huge flow coming down the river in the next few days,' Jim informed us.

'A lot of the country is already saturated to the south and west, which will add to our problems if we've more heavy rain around here,' Bob added.

'The rain stopped long enough for us to return from church yesterday. We are all in good health and don't lack food, so let's pray the good lord will be kind to us and give us a fine and prosperous new year,' Gwyn added.

'Amen to that,' we all replied!

'How will we get the cows up from the dam paddock in all this rain, Bill?'

'I locked them out of the dam area yesterday, Rickie. Otherwise, we'd be pulling them out of the mud. I had the foresight to leave the big gate to the dairy holding yard open. Most likely, they'll come in on their own to get some grain and shelter,' he replied.

'That was lucky, what a good idea.'

'Yes, I have them from time to time.'

Everyone laughed.

Fortunately, I had stacked quite a pile of split logs under cover in the dairy generator shed the day before so it should remain high and dry. By the time the dairy clean-up was finished, the fire under the copper had burnt to ashes. The poddies and the pigs had been fed, so I went over to feed the chooks and collect the eggs. Usually, we get about six a day, sometimes more. The eggs had to be washed and stored in the old fridge on the rear balcony. After breakfast, I returned to check the dairy cast iron copper. The ashes were cold, so I stacked kindling underneath and threw an old tarp over the lot. Hopefully, it will still be dry enough to light this afternoon. With the extra hands about the place, short work was done on chores, including dairying. It's time to clean ourselves up and head to the house for dinner. The ladies had prepared an excellent meal, courtesy of the considerable leftovers from lunch. Our feasts on the farm spoiled me for the rest of my life; few cooks can hold a candle to country women.

The following day, I woke to the phone ringing loudly as extra bells had been installed. One is in the hallway, and the other is outside to attract the attention of anyone within earshot. A family cousin living further up the Condamine River called to deliver dire news. The floodwaters would be swirling around us within days. The river was lapping at the sides of local timber bridges. They would go under before the day was out. Even though we were above the highest known flood level, there was a countryside section between us and the Tara Road bridge to town, which was prone to flooding and bound to go under. An alternative escape route was a gravel back road over a bridge to the Warrego highway. There was a chance it might flood first, effectively cutting us off. If the Condamine River broke its banks, the water would spread for miles. Then, the only way out in an emergency would be by boat. Mayhem was the order of the day; it would affect all and sundry before it was over.

Appearing unconcerned, Bill, Gwyn, and the visiting family went about their usual activities. The dairying was completed quickly and smartly. Breakfast was set out on the eastern verandah's long table. The conversation was light-hearted during our meal. Over another cup of tea, discussions drifted onto the possibility of imminent widespread flooding.

'I will make a few calls after breakfast to see what the river situation is upstream and around the district. We better get the community boat fuelled up just in case,' said Bill.

'With that in mind we should change our travel plans to be on the safe side,' replied Bob.

'Perhaps we girls should take a quick trip into town and stock up on some necessities. You never know just how long a flood might last, and extra pantry items will come in handy,' Gwyn added.

'What can I help with, Bill?'

'My first port of call will be the boat shed, Rickie, so you can give me a hand.'

'I'll tag along with you as well, Bill.' Uncle Bob decided to join us.

'In that case, I had better assist the ladies in town, as there may be some heavy lifting required, and two vehicles will get the job done sooner,' Uncle Jim said.

The three of us headed off in the tilly down to the community boat shed. This structure had been built many years ago by the Hopelands community. It stood on the boundary of Mr Joe Pharaoh's property adjacent to the Condamine River. The spot was chosen for two reasons. Its high section was above previous flood levels, and it faced towards the T intersection of the Avenue and the Chinchilla-Tara Road, which allowed access from multiple directions.

Unlocking the heavy double timber doors, we swung them back out of the way. The faint morning sun enabled us to barely see inside. The boat was secured to a heavy-duty steel trailer; its length was ten metres. A four-cylinder diesel inboard motor powered the open-walled steel boat. A retractable canvas canopy over the bow section provided some protection from the weather. Over the years, the vessel has served the community well, and its scars of dents and scrapes have indicated some dramatic events. Bob backed the utility partially into the shed to attach the trailer, hauling it outside for a thorough inspection. A couple of the local mechanics regularly maintained it. The service card indicated that it was scheduled for a run soon. No better time than the present. Bill lifted the batteries off the charging bench and placed them in the boat, one to start, one for spare. The twin fuel tanks were topped up from a forty-four standard gallon drum [205 litres] with a hand pump attached. A quick start was made to check that all was well, and then we went down to the river to launch the vessel. These blokes had done this often, so it was a smooth operation, and we were soon cruising upriver. The boat cut smoothly through the rising water. Bill steered, Bob was the observer, and I was extra ballast.

'The flood water is getting muddier, Bill!' Bob remarked.

'Yes, it won't be long before it becomes a thick soup,' Bill replied. We cruised for a while, then came about to check the other side on the return trip.

'The river has a lot of broken branches lying about. Why doesn't someone clear them out? 'I asked.

'Feel free to volunteer anytime you like,' the men laughed.

We returned the *MV Hopeland* to its high and dry shelter, ready for a call to action should the need arise. No one knew what this flood might throw at us over the coming days. The visiting relatives decided that after lunch, they would pack up and start their journey home to be on the safe side. They had come from all over the country, so they'd have to drive a bit on their return trip to different places, Goondiwindi, Toowoomba, Bundaberg, or Brisbane.

Sometime during the wee hours of the following morning, our local bridge, the last avenue of escape, went underwater. The call came at daybreak. The sky was grey, and the rain continued its relentless deluge. Bill answered the phone; it was Cousin Barry calling to inform him that they were required today on the 10 am to 2 pm shift to man the emergency boat. Both being dairy farmers, this time slot allowed them to complete the morning and afternoon dairying requirements, which worked in well together with neighbours in supporting their community. All be it a soddy change to their usual workload.

Dairying was no fun in this weather, but I found it exciting until I became stuck in the mud. My boots refused to release their suction in the holding yard as a cranky cow charged me. This event gave the adults the best laugh they had in quite some time. They would remember it for decades to come and never tire of telling the tale. Hearing Bill tell the rest of the family about it sometime later was amusing and quite a performance.

'I've never seen anyone move so fast. One minute, Rickie was standing in the middle of the yard, giving the cow cheek, and the next, he was flying onto a fence rail. The poor old cow only had two muddy boots left to look at. All the cow did was shake her head at him.' Everyone found the whole thing very amusing.

'No, that's not right, the cow was charging at me.'

'The poor cow could hardly move in all the thick mud,' Bill laughingly added.

At this rate, I'd be chided about becoming the bovine wrangler of Hopelands for all the wrong reasons.

Devastation

While the men were off providing a river crossing ferry service, I had the job of rescuing my mud boots and cleaning out the milking bales. Usually, this was done at the end of milking, but the morning was a little rushed. There was a trailer load of mud and manure to shovel before any hosing and sweeping could be done. It took hours before I was finished. Being covered in God knows what, I needed a rinse myself. A cold shower in the dairy annexe with the rain blowing in was mind-numbing and I turned a lighter shade of blue in the process. My clothing was damp from the rain, so I pulled a torn canvas over me and ran barefoot across to the house.

'Rickie, what've you been doing over there? You're shivering,' Gwyn was alarmed.

'I got a little carried away cleaning up the dairy, then washed all the mud off myself before I came into the house.'

'I'll put some warm water in a basin in front of the stove for you to stand in. Remove your damp clothes and hang them on that drying rack. That towel there should be warm by now. I'll get you some dry clothes. Get a move on before you catch a cold,' and off she went. I didn't need to be told twice. It was a pleasant experience to be wrapped in a large, warm towel.

'Here, change into these, I've made a big pot of soup for lunch, which should warm you up. After we finish, we'll take lunch down to the men at the river. No doubt they'll be a little peckish. Let's use the small table in the kitchen, as it's much warmer here. What took you so long to shovel the mud off the concrete?'

'I hosed and swept it as well.'

'No wonder you look exhausted. Eat your soup, which should perk you up a bit.'

'This is delicious. What type of soup is it?'

'It's an old family recipe of blended pumpkin with cream, and I also added the leftover roasted potatoes & onions from last night's dinner to thicken it up a little.'

'Is this some of Mrs Roger's homemade crunchy bread?'

'Yes, it is. We've got some pudding, warm custard, and Christmas fruit cake. Can you fit it in?'

'Only too glad to help out.'

Gwyn smiled. 'That's very considerate of you, Rickie. After you finish, we'll wrap up the food to keep it warm for the men, then head down to the river. Perhaps a few thermoses of hot tea as well. I'm sure the men will appreciate them.'

Fortunately, the rain slowed to a light sprinkle as sunshine pieced the translucent grey sky from the general direction of the town. Gwyn and I remained relatively dry as we packed the food into the utility and tied down the tonneau cover. The muddy roads, slowed our drive to the campsite, which remained safe from the raging river.

A large canvas tarpaulin slung over a rope slung between two trees kept out most of the rain. Underneath the tarp, road gravel was used to make getting about less tiresome. The men had just returned from the ever-widening river while dodging tree branches and the occasional dead animal swept along by the raging torrent. It was tiring work; Bill, Barry and two shore support helpers were sitting on some drums under the tarp, having a bit of a yarn ready for lunch. They had a small fire burning to keep the chill at bay. A few old, rusted fuel drums covered by a large timber door made a usable table and served as a windbreak at one end.

'Thank you, Gwyn, this soup is delicious,' the men all said.

I now understood why Gwyn had packed such large metal pannikins and extra metal mugs. These guys made short work of the entire large pot of soup, two loaves of bread and most of a pound fruit cake. The additional two litres of premade tea in the thermos soon disappeared. It had been a busy morning, ferrying passengers, food supplies and some spare parts for farm machinery.

'I brought down a billy and some tea leaf, so you can make a cuppa whenever you need,' Gwyn offered.

'What have you been doing with yourself this morning, Rickie?' Bill asked.

'I've been busy, Bill, cleaning out the bails in the dairy, then taste-tested lunch to ensure it was top-notch.'

'Yes, he's quite proficient at that,' Gwyn confirmed.

'Would you like to give Barry and me a hand after lunch till the relief crew turn up?'

'Yes, can I drive the boat?'

'It's a bit of a handful now. Maybe if things calm down in a few days, you can pilot us across.'

The river had turned into a churning muddy beast of destruction, strewn with multiple tree branches. One had a possum water skiing on it. The occasional dead animal floated past, with a couple of river rats perched on top, obviously taking their tucker with them. It was a tricky business navigating against the current upstream. The ever-widening river was encroaching on more road sections, though a safe spot remained to disembark.

'Hi Clarrie, how're things in town?'

'They're holding up, Bill. The buildings around the old sections opposite the railway are partially submerged. The Warrego highway is cut out near Charlie's Creek, and the culvert on this side of Warra is flooded. We'll be isolated for a while, should be ok for supplies.'

'What is the water level in the culverts between here and town like? We'll need to ferry the cream cans across in the morning,' Barry suggested.

'At present, a few inches is running in the closest one to here; the rest are ok. The road is passable from here to the top part of town up past the hospital, so access to the Dairy Co-op buildings should be ok. I picked up some mail on the way out. If Gwyn would be so kind as to see it's passed on,' Clarrie replied.

'We may not be able to return to Brisbane for ages at this rate,' I inquired. The idea wasn't unpleasant.

'Don't worry, Rickie; the trains are getting through. We'll have you back to school on time.'

I liked the idea of being flooded in and stranded in the outback; it had a certain stoic feel. My excuse for a holiday extension was stuffed. As the flood waters receded, the smell assaulted our nostrils, and the sand flies had a feast of epic proportions. The most immediate remedy I found was rubbing mud over myself. Even the cows over at the dairy snorted at my appearance, Fussy buggers.

The following day, I went with Gwyn to do Clarrie's mail run. At each farmhouse we visited, there was a cup of tea, some cake, and an update on the local news. If there wasn't anyone about it, we left the mail on their kitchen table and continued our delivery route.

Devising

1968 was my last year of Primary School. Besides an occasional scuffle with some uppity wanker, there was not much happening. I had learnt my lessons well, shut this life out of my mind and started planning for a better one. The distraction of the girls occasionally derailed my focus on achieving high grades.

Shazza was in fine fettle with interests other than academic brilliance. Government funding increases provided training for the boys in cricket and football, swimming lessons and a cooking class. For the girls, hockey, softball, and marching bands, which they loved the spectacle of. We had old-time square- dancing, and occasional rock and roll that remained mixed-gender activities. I joined the choir, a necessity to catch up with the girls. My voice tone, whatever it was, had become bearable to most. The days drifted by, and I was unconcerned with the troubles of others; until an incident occurred in the boy's section, just before Easter break

'Holy crap Nigel, what's happened to you, mate?' Blood splayed across his shirt; someone had broken his nose.

'Rickie, those new boys in special class belted me up and laughed at me for being a dum-dum.'

'You're not dumb, Nigel; we're all different in some way. Don't listen to those wankers. Let's get you over to the infirmary.' *Not this crap again.* The bully-boy business might need intervention, no doubt a drama for another day.

'Hey Rickie, have you signed up for the Footy team? We start practice after the holiday break.'

'Hi Jai, all good. It's a bit of fun to get outside for a change. It looks like we have a new group of bully boys. I found Nigel beaten up yesterday.'

'Poor old Nigel, what's he fifteen? He's twice the size of most of us. I don't know why he doesn't just grab hold of their arms and sling them off the verandah.' Jai replied.

'Have you put down your name for the scholarships next year, Jai?'

'Me! I've got Buckley's chance for an academic scholarship; where are they anyway?'

'I've forgotten their names; there's a choice of three.'

'Do they have a sports scholarship? That's something I'd have a better chance of getting. I don't want to go to the coast, probably infested with more mosquitos. Toowoomba is too cold for me; the other one in the sticks might be ok. Can you find out where it is?'

'Will do; what're we going to do about Nigel?'

'We can't look out for him all his life; leave it with me, Rickie; I'll ask around.'

Jai had a point. What was Nigel going to do after we were gone? He'd need a plan that was best suited to his nature. He wouldn't harm a fly intentionally. Maybe he could find a way to catch them with honey.

***

Easter break was upon us. I'm off to Chinchilla. Where I'll be next year will no doubt be a topic of conversation. It's always like coming home when I got to the farm, just like other kids going home from boarding school. In some regards, my school is a bit like theirs. Similar academic subjects, varied sports, religious teachers and probably biff-ups with annoying students.

'Welcome home, Rickie,' Bill and Gwyn greeted me as I stepped down from the Greyhound bus outside Vince Cafferty's shoe store. This trip had been quicker: a car ride from the home to Toowoomba and then catching a bus out to Chinchilla.

'Hello, Gwyn and Bill. It's great to see you both. That bus bounces all over the place on the highway.'

'At least you got here in one piece. Barry and Sylvia have invited us to their place for a late lunch, and we better get cracking. Grab your port, and you can tell us some of your news on the way.'

I looked forward to creating more memories of the bush. These days, everyone seems to know about my arrival. The bush telegraph was in full swing. Sometimes, the phone calls were even for me.

I had become part of the community. The farm animals were happy to see me; remembering my scent, they came over for a rub or a scratch. The cows didn't even run away. The poddy calves were leaping about with joy, playing a game with each other. The horses, as usual, were sniffing about for their snack.

We went to Easter events all around the countryside. This Saturday night, a bush dance was held at Warra community hall. There was always a big turnout, as dancing was a popular social pastime. Clarrie Barr and his band played the music of the night, which was immensely enjoyed by many happy couples. Many a romance was born at community town halls such as this throughout the district. It was a fine line for me to trend, asking local girls for dances. The experience of Barney's dummy- spit over a schoolgirl crush was a memory I did not want to repeat. Not everyone here might appreciate my intentions. These families had a lot of history; I was Johnny- come -lately. It was best if I avoided personal dramas.

Another great holiday ended the following morning, and then I was back to reality. A couple of days later, a familiar voice called out.

'Hey Rickie, how was your bush holiday?' It was good old Nigel, thankfully looking in better shape than when I last saw him.

'Good Nigel, how've you been?

'I'm great, you know those ratbags that beat me up before the holidays. Well, someone gave them some medicine of their own last night.'

'What happened?

'They were chasing someone past the special class when something happened to the lights, and broken glass was all over the place, and they cut their feet.'

'Really! That's terrible.'

'And that's not all, they got hit with a hockey stick.'

'My God, the things that happen around here. Where did the hockey stick come from?'

'I don't know, but I think I caused it, as I've been praying that something would happen to them.'

'Well, Nigel, don't worry yourself about it. I'm sure it wasn't your fault. It was more likely the work of some Devil. If they leave you alone, that's the important thing. You take good care, hey.'

'Thanks, Rickie, you've always been my special friend.'

'Too right, mate, I've got to bugger off now and do some study. We've nighttime homework in grade seven.'

'Yuk, you can have that, see ya.'

The nighttime study wasn't all it was meant to be. We spent our free time four times a week improving our academic knowledge. Still, there were exceptions on occasion. When we were left unsupervised, our interests might stray. The girls were elsewhere doing assignments. How much trouble can four boys get into?

'Hey, Petra. What did Cathy and the girls say they're doing tonight?'

'They'd some dress-making assignment to finish; why Rickie?'

'Just wondering.'

'Yeah, right, I know you and your—just wondering, what're you scheming?'

'Bloody lovely, a guy can't just ask an innocent question?'

'Now you got me intrigued, Rickie,' Bobbie piped up.

'Well, if you guys are finished homework, we can have an early mark and go and have some supper.'

'Supper? Don't be daft! We'll all get in the shit. Where the hell are we going to get food from?' they replied.

'Okay, so you're not hungry, then? I was thinking that maybe the girls were in the sewing room. It's above our heads, and their cooking area is right beside it.'

'How're we going to get in, genius?' Petra inquired.

'Simple, we walk up the stairs very quietly.'

'The door at the bottom is most likely locked.' Bobbie informed us.

'Well, what if we go and check? If it's locked, then we'll forget about it and head over to the community room to watch some TV.'

'Oh No, here we go! I thought we might have a peaceful year without dramas,' Chris moaned.

I knew they would run over hot coals to get something extra to eat. It wasn't the most enthusiastic "Yes" for a dare I've heard from them. We packed our books up, lights off, doors locked. Anyone who came looking would assume we'd an early mark and were over in our section. A lack of lighting, was beneficial to covert causes. Walking confidently, we approached the deserted alcove. Placing my hand on the huge wooden doorknob, luck was with us. With a bit of a shoulder nudge, the heavy door swung silently inward, and we all held our breaths. The stairwell was in darkness, except for a dim light on the first landing. Above us, faint voices could be heard.

'What if it's the nuns?' whispered Chris.

'Shoosh, I'll creep up the stairs and see if it's all clear. Wait for my signal, and then you guys follow. Stick to the right-hand side of the steps; there are fewer creaks.'

Luck Favours the Brave

My heart was pounding. This had better not turn out to be my most stupid idea to date. I had been up here a few times, but never at nighttime. I peeped over the last stair landing and saw two girls with their backs to me and two on the other side of the bench. None of them were directly looking my way. It didn't seem like they were doing too much dressmaking, as I could smell fresh scones. They had their own snack bar up here; hopefully, they would choose to share it with us.

"Psst, Psst," maybe they didn't hear me; the boys down the bottom were probably wondering what was happening. If I didn't wave back to them soon, they might decide to leave. I found a button on the floor and tossed it towards the nearest one, who looked like Shazza, but no reaction. It was time to see how good my underarm aim was. Crap missed her; the button went straight past her arm and back onto the floor. She must have seen it out of the corner of her eye as she casually went and picked it up. Turning around, she put her hand over her mouth with startled surprise as our eyes met.

'Rickie!'

'What about Rickie? The other girls asked; got him on your mind, have you?'

'I was just thinking that maybe he's still downstairs with the other boys studying. Why don't we invite them up for supper? It's only us here; no one else will know.'

'Oh, you're wicked, Shazza. What a good idea. What do you say, girls?' Cassie asked.

'We better not get sprung. Get some more cups out, we're going to have company,' one of the others joined in.

'I'll go get them, don't you lot make too much noise, I'll be back in a minute.' Shazza put her finger to her lips and winked as I waved back to the boys. She stomped down the stairs, and the boys were a little surprised. She shooshed them and went to the bottom, opened the door, and reclosed it. We all waited silently for a few minutes in the stairwell. Then she opened the door, closed it again, and turned the key in the lock. As she reached the top of the steps, she called out to the other girls.

'Look what I've found outside, these four little saints.'

'Well, isn't this a nice surprise? Hello Chris,' Marlene said.

'Hi Marlene, we were just locking up the classroom when we ran into Shazza. She invited us all up for supper. This is nice of the nuns.'

'The nuns don't know anything about it so keep this to yourselves,' Debbie grinned.

'What time are all saintly boys supposed to be in bed? Cassie chided.

'Probably the same as you girls.' Petra replied.

'Well, that's great. Tea boys?' The girls offered.

Pleasant conversation, tea & scones, what more could anyone ask for? An hour flew by. Then we all helped with the cleaning up. The girls gave us the push-off with a goodnight kiss, and we were on our way a little after nine p.m. All in all, it was an excellent study evening, and we had pleasant dreams for a change.

The following day, arriving in class with grins on our faces, we noticed the girls looked more cheerful as well. Nothing like a shared secret to brighten the day. Our first teacher that morning was smiley nun, who was also last night's study minder.

'Good morning, please be seated. I have a question before we start. I came by the classroom after eight last night; the study group of boys had departed.'

'You must've just missed us, Sister. We left early. Bobbie had a stomachache,' I replied.

'Oh! Are you ok this morning, Bobbie?'

'Yes, thank you, Sister. It must have been something that didn't agree with me,' Bobbie said, a little red-faced.

'And sewing group girls, I came to check on you as well. Why was the downstairs door locked?'

'It's my fault, sister. We feel safer up there with the door locked. I must've left the key in the lock,' Shazza apologized.

'I see. Well, that explains why my key didn't work, it's best to be on the safe side. I saw you walking back to your dormitory around quarter past nine, so I was no longer concerned. Now, let's get on with the history lesson for this morning.'

With that, she continued with tales of our early explorer's survival against the harsh environment of the Australian continent. Our own stories may well be recorded for posterity one day. Would they be believed? The facts and the truth may not necessarily be the same thing. Often, records are strangely lost in the mists of time. What is left are memories and redacted documents. Whatever the perceptions were of that person at that time. The choices we would make this year may make or break us for the rest of our lives. Soon, it'll be goodbye forever to a family of kids, formed in a cauldron of misfortune.

That Girl Rings a Bell

I had a change from the occasional mischief to scholarships, which left little time to wonder about things in general. I did notice something different the other day: a dark blonde-headed girl followed a nun around the verandah in the afternoons. Like clockwork every school day, they drifted past my classroom window. "Hmm, it was a mystery, a *subject of which I was fond. I'd not seen her around here before.*"

By chance, I was on the way to nowhere in particular when I came upon the girl with the big sad eyes. She stood on the verandah waiting; something about her seemed familiar.

'Hello, are you new here? Have we met before?' I asked.

'No, I'm waiting for that sister to come out; I help serve the nuns' afternoon tea.'

'I'm Rickie Battler. What's your name?'

'Gloria Davison, I'm not supposed to talk to boys.'

'I'm not supposed to talk to girls. How about we mumble instead?'

She smiled.

'So, how long have you been here? I see you with the nun every afternoon. Where do you go to?'

'Well, sticky beak, if you must know, I've been here about a month; I'm trying to catch up on lost school time. The nuns make me clean up things, and then I help serve their morning and afternoon tea.'

'Really, you do all that work; how can you catch up on your schooling?'

'Go away. You'll get me in trouble if that nun comes out.'

'I'll watch out for bossy nun through the other doorway. What does she look like?'

'A Nun.'

'Funny girl, what school did you go to last?'

'St Peters and Pauls, I missed a lot of schooling. Now go away, you pest.'

'Oooh spikey, I'll see you around Gloria, bye.'

'Only if you like scrubbing and polishing in the church.'

'Not Likely,'

'Yeah, right, smart arse.'.'

About three weeks later, I saw Gloria again. I had a feeling I had met her somewhere ages ago. Our class was in the chapel, at the stations of the cross, saying prayers, either in silence or quiet whispers. At the tenth station, slightly ahead of the class, I sidled up near the newbie, Gloria.

'You've done a nice job of the chapel.'

'What? Oh, it's you. Stick to your prayers and be quiet. Talking isn't allowed in church.' then she moved on to the next station.

'Who's that girl?' one of the other girls whispered as she crept up near me.

'A trainee nun. Shoosh, you're not supposed to talk in church.' I said cheekily.

'Ha, you're a fine one to talk.' Then I moved as two more girls came towards us.

'So, are you praying for me, oh gracious one?' I asked.

'Humph, the only prayer I have for you is to get lost,' Gloria hauntingly replied.

'Well, that's charming, sweet Gloria.' I glimpsed a little smile on her face as I moved to the last station of the cross. Perhaps a conversation for another time; my days were numbered around here, and other pressing matters took precedence.

Finally, I found out something about the scholarships. One was near the coast somewhere close by. One near Toowoomba would be good as I could go out to Chinchilla more often. The third was out in the bush somewhere south-west of Brisbane. I better pull my socks up if I don't want to fall behind. I wondered where the girls might be going to. I had heard that a few had been sent out as domestics to private households. Hopefully, it is somewhere nice; they all deserve so much more. In our final exams for grade seven, Cassie came top of our class, with Bobbie in second and me in third. Seems like I have been dragging my feet lately. I wonder if third place gets a chance of a scholarship. Time will tell.

***

Christmas break arrived; most of us kids would never see one another again. A bittersweet holiday as in the new year, we would all go our separate ways, disappearing from each other's lives. My train trip home to Chinchilla was also a nostalgic one; it might be the last. In the wee hours of the morning, the train stopped at what appeared to be a deserted platform. I took a moment to enjoy the starry night sky, breathing in the faint scent of woodsmoke still lingering in the air. In the shadow of the ticket office, Bill waited patiently chatting to the night porter.

'Hi Bill, how're you? It must be after midnight, and it's still warm out here.'

'Good evening, Rickie. Welcome home. It's closer to one a.m. We'd better get moving to catch some sleep before the sun's up.'

At this time of night, it took about half an hour to drive out to the farm and keep an eye out for wildlife and stray cattle. At home, we continued chatting over a hot cuppa and a biscuit, then said goodnight and went to bed. I had a bit of sleep-in that morning until about seven a.m. Bill had already gone to the dairy; he must have had only four hours of sleep. Gwyn was up and about as I strolled out to the kitchen.

'Good morning, sleepy head.'

'Good morning, Gwyn. How're you?' We hugged, something I seldom do with anyone else.

'I'm surprised you were so tired, I thought you'd have slept on the train.'

'Well, there were some awfully noisy people on the train.'

Gynn laughed, 'Hmm, I wonder who that might of been? Were there other boys you knew on the train?'

'Yes, there were five others going to different places; the last one was heading out to Charleville.' I thought it best not to elaborate on some of the hijinks the boys got up to.

'How'd you go in your final exams?'

'Good I hope I might be in the selection for a scholarship?' I'll go give Bill a hand before breakfast.

'I'm sure he wouldn't mind. It'll free me up. Would you please bring a jug of milk back with you?'

'No worries, I'll tell you all about it when we return.'

So that set the pace for the holidays. I gave Gwyn a break from the dairy and helped Bill with the jobs around the place. I thoroughly enjoyed life on the farm, no matter what there was to do. Whatever job I needed to do became second nature to me, although I still had a lot to learn. It was no mug game running a successful farm.

'Good morning, Bill; I thought you might like a hand, and Gwyn can take a break.'

'Thank you, Rickie. I'm sure she could. Can you hunt some cows up into the top yard and close the main gate down in the holding yard?' We were an effective team. Slowly, my knowledge of streamlining the process improved. Within two hours, we were back at the house, sitting down to a hearty breakfast.

'What's on the agenda for the day, Bill?'

'Well, Gwyn and I are going into the church. A few of us are attending to some minor repairs required in the hall, and the ladies are setting things up for tomorrow night's theatre group.'

'So, are either of you in any of the plays?'

'Gwyn will be playing the piano, and I'll be in two of the skits and sing a tune or two,' Bill replied.

'Would you be willing to help backstage with some props?' Gwyn asked.

'Love too.'

'What schools have you applied to next year?' It would be nice if you could get into a Toowoomba high school,' Bill inquired.

'Yes, it sure would.' We'd be able to catch up more often, seeing we go there regularly to visit relatives, do shopping, and other business Bill attends to,' Gwyn suggested.

'Do you have another business in Toowoomba as well, Bill?'

'No, Rickie, the farm has enough work to keep me busy. I go down to Toowoomba, sometimes Dalby and occasionally Ipswich, for meetings with various community groups and associations. Rotary Club, Cattlemen's, Masonic lodge, Dairymen's, and others. If time allows, also we like to catch up with family and friends.'

'A great deal depends on one of the neighbours volunteering to do the milking. I don't like to ask very often. Gwyn might stay down there for a week or so, occasionally. Other times, we are down and back on the same day. I'm sure we could extend that to visit you.'

'Wouldn't that be great?' I replied.

'We'll see what the new year brings. In the meantime, we have a busy social calendar planned.'

'Well, isn't that unusual,' I replied.

'Very,' they both laughed in turn.

We all enjoyed catching up with family and friends from far and near. It was nice feeling normal for a change, surrounded by smiling faces and sincere people. Time flew so rapidly. Too soon, I was back in my other reality. Nothing good ever seems to last long enough. I should have paid more attention to those forms. Not deciding is a decision that often does not end well.

Relocation -1969

Whatever else was happening in the world, its importance paled compared to the disastrous start of my new year. Scholarship options were off the table. I failed to note the applications closed at the end of November. Those in charge put in a request to children's services, which was a colloquial way of saying no. I'm not a form expert, but I knew applications took months to process as they shuffled back and forth courtesy of the PMG—post services. Why wasn't I aware of everything back then, or was my fate already sealed? I hope Bobbie went somewhere decent.

In the meantime, a few of us senior boys were heading to the city to acquire a new clothing kit. This was a first. To date, we only had second-hand clothing plus whatever the nuns could make out of donated rolls of cloth. We arrived at Barry and Roberts on Queens Street, Brisbane. They were a clothing outfitter business that had a contract with the government.

We received two of each: Shirts, Trousers, Shorts, T-shirts, and Pyjamas. Added to this was one dressing gown. one coat, one jumper, two pairs of shoes, six packs of singlets, underpants, and several pairs of socks. One grooming kit included a tin of black shoe polish, a brush, and a polishing cloth. A comb, toothbrush, a tube of toothpaste and a new thing called deodorant. We had a limited choice of the slow-selling range of colours. Our kit-out went into one large brown Masonite suitcase, sometimes called a port. These were delivered to the home and were available when we were relocated. A cardboard label with our full name was attached to the handle, that remained in place for a decade.

The most important bit of information missing was knowing where I am going.

Eight of us boys lingered for the remainder of January waiting to move on. Activities were created to keep us occupied, the major one being work detail. Jai was the only one of our brotherhood who remained.

165

'Hey Rickie, I thought you'd be off to one of those posh schools by now. What happened? Did you miss the bus?'

'Not sure Jai, something odd occurred. Do you know where you're going or where the other boys went to?'

'Not a clue bro, no one tells me jackshit. Don't worry wherever it is we'll sort them out.'

'Well, I'm going down to the old tool shed to clean up the place. Come and give me a hand Jai, before you end up with some crap job.'

'Aren't we supposed to tell someone? I don't want coppers chasing me around the paddocks.'

'No worries, there is a job list in the common room. My name is under "toolshed," add your name to it. Unless you'd like floor maintenance or window cleaning.'

'Who chooses?' Jai queried.

'Buggered if I know. Best if we decide first before the decision gets made for us.' So off we trundled, no point getting there too early. We passed down the verandahs without interference. Most nuns were about their duties, so we had a moment to stop outside the bakery to test some *Brodies*. Extra sustenance never goes astray, then off to the woodwork shed.

'Good morning, Mr Bobson, I've brought extra help this morning, this is Jai.'

'Huh, Good morning, Rickie, Jai. I wasn't too sure if any of you'd be back today. Still, many hands make light work. If you two can continue sorting out those piles of lumber, I can get started on the shelving.

'I will add you both to my crew list. At this rate, we'll have it all done in no time.'

Jai and I sorted the lumber according to the sizes Mr Bobson had written on some samples. The time flew by. The jumbled pile shrank, untreated split lumber was put aside to fuel the bakery ovens.

'Ok, boys, it's morning teatime. How about you go up to the kitchen and ask them to refill my flask with tea and get two extra mugs? See what's up there in the way of tucker.'

The kitchen staff obviously liked Mr Bobson. They refilled his flask, added another, and gave us extra mugs and three large slices of sponge cake. This was conveniently placed in a basket for us to carry back. I added a couple of brodies to the basket as we passed the bakery. You never know; this bloke might be a big eater. We don't want him to faint on us.

'Well, I'll have to have you pair down here more often; you certainly know how to rustle up smoko.'

'We tried to do our best; once we mentioned your name, the sky was the limit.' I replied.

'Yeah. Rickie is experienced at getting the best out of people,' Jai mumbled with a mouthful of cake.

After smoko, we assisted with the assembly of the timber shelving. The lumber was rather heavy, with us two on one end and Mr Bobson holding the other. With clamps, we drilled holes, then bolted each section together and smoothed the edges with a wood rasp to reduce splinters. The whole lot was coated with a smelly linseed oil. As gloves and a mask were required to apply this, we left it to Mr Bobson. We headed back outside to our sorting job until the lunch bells rang.

'You boys go and have your lunch. If you want to come back after that, I'll see you then.'

'Ok,' we both replied.

So, Jai and I avoided harm's way as Mr Bobson's trade assistants. He taught us to use some hand tools and how to sharpen them. All the shelving was finished, and the timber was stacked on it. He was getting the workshop shipshape ready for the new woodwork class and, thanks to us, was ahead of schedule.

'It's a shame this course wasn't available last year so that you could have attended. I would have been proud to have you both as my students. Thank you, and best wishes to both of you in the future,' we all said our goodbyes.

What a mess. In the first week of February, I got the news. Five boys, including me, were being sent to a rural high school.

'This school is very modern, with agriculture, trade, academic studies, and a wide variety of sports, art, and music included in the curriculum. You will have a lot to keep you busy,' the Bossy nun told us.

'Who are the other boys, Sister?'

'They are standing right behind you. Their school bus will be picking you up at the Greyhound depot in South Brisbane tomorrow afternoon. You boys should all get acquainted.'

'Hi Rickie, this is Red, Smithy, and my cousin Douggie.'

'Funny guy, Jai. How long have you known about this?'

'About thirty minutes more than you. Hey, the lunch bells are ringing. I hope they've got something special for us. Last Friday and all that,' Jai was hopeful.

'Yeah, delightful seafood buffet,' I suggested.

Off we all went to see what was for lunch. I had known Jai for years; the others were recent arrivals. We ended up with a light lunch in the lattice-lined walkway, a reminder of my first day here. A trainee nun and another girl arrived with trays of tiny sandwiches and jugs of cold cordial.

'Enjoy your lunch, boys. Take care of yourselves, and don't forget to include us in your prayers,' they both said.

'Thank you, lunch looks delicious,' we all replied. Well, at least we didn't have to have fish with the rest of the rabble. You would never guess who happened to walk by at that opportune moment.

'Hello Gloria, how're you going?'

'Oh God, not you again, pest; what've you boys done now?'

'We're being deported; this is our last meal,' Red answered her.

'Humph! should be peaceful here then.' And off she went. *As fate would have it, I would meet her again in about forty years or so.*

'Who's that?' Dougie asked.

'A trainee nun. She loves me.'

'Not bloody likely, Bro.'

Late Sunday morning, after mass and an early lunch, we headed off in a minibus to the city, our new gear stacked in the back. On the way out the big wrought iron gates, we received a bugger-off salute, the forks from the boys hanging over the fence. I supposed it counted as a farewell around here. The nun on the bus was giving us the pep talk on our new country home. There were six residential cottages with house parents, each containing twelve boys. *Hmm, sounds Ok, I wonder what they aren't telling us about; I guess we'll soon find out.*

New Challenges

Our new school bus met us at the South Brisbane Greyhound terminal. With our luggage stowed, we all piled aboard with half a dozen other boys from God knows where. Everyone looked at each other dubiously. *What shitholes are these other kids from.*

'Hey, where're you from?'

'Up north! you?'

'Swamps, me, Jai here and a few others.'

'What about that white fella?'

'You a white fella, Yao?'

'Stuff knows Samy, this is another fine mess you got me into.'

That summed up the introductions, such as they were. Watching the scenery, we all wondered what was in store for us, sure that joy would not be part of it. Our trip out to the country private estate lasted around two hours. The old Bedford bus groaned along narrow country roads, barely wide enough to pass any on-coming vehicle. The occasional white wooden sign identified landmarks along the way. We passed through a few small townships; I caught glimpses of a rail track. The idea it might be suitable for a getaway crossed my mind. For all we knew, we might have been sold off as slave labour.

The Brother driving the bus was not a talkative chap. He was focused on getting us to our destination, I hoped. The aged vehicle bumped, along lowland forest roads. As we crested a rise, a country town appeared; the streets were almost deserted. The bus cruised along the main thoroughfare before turning at a roundabout, exiting onto an undulating narrow highway.

Before long, we slowed down and turned in between two brick pillars. On the front was a sign, *visitors welcome*; I wondered how much truth there was in those two words. Then ascended a long-curved driveway. There were football ovals to the right and farm paddocks to the left. Later, I would find out they had over two hundred acres of loamy fertile land, with an extra three hundred acres further up the highway. We slowed to a crawl at the top of the driveway. There were old wooden buildings on the left and new brick low-set buildings to the front and on the right. The bus turned into a high carport alongside a double-storey- fibro building. We had arrived. Without exception, we kids came from a variety of melting pots of trauma and neglect. Survival just ratchets up a few notches.

'Everyone out, grab your ports from the back and wait in a line alongside that fence,' the bus driver informed us.'

While we newbies stood in a line, he strolled past, casting his eyes over us. The residential lads reminded me of a bunch of cows in a paddock, chewing gum instead of grass. They were bigger than I had expected, with faces devoid of emotion. It looked like they were sizing us up. A cold shiver went down my spine. *You're all alone.*

'Ok, pay attention, I'm Brother Shaven. Grab your gear, follow me.'

We all marched down to a long, low-set brick building; the end part had a big Administration sign plastered on it. Here, we stopped, and a large rotund fellow in a white gown appeared, slowly casting his eyes over the lot of us.

'I'm Brother Solemn. Welcome to your new home. We're pleased you have arrived safely. You'll be given a number that is your new cottage, and a house parent will welcome you. Like everywhere, we have rules and consequences. First, no fighting and no stealing. As you can see, we've no fences. If you choose to try running away, penalties will be severe.' There were six brothers and a group of other adults standing around us.

'The houseparents will advise you of their rules and any other information, which you'll need to remember. Lapses of memory are not tolerated. Sunday night is a free evening, so you'll have time to settle in. Uniforms for school, etc., will be issued in the morning. Now I'll hand you over to the care of your house parents. Thank you.'

That was the last time I ever heard him thank anyone. Most cottages had a husband-and-wife team. The one I was in had a woman with a stern disposition. She looked as if she smiled, her face would probably crack. I named her Mrs Bothersome, and over time, she lived up to her title. Jai, Yao, Red and I were to reside in cottage six, the last building. This house parent must be the 'new' kid expert as the other five cottages only have one extra kid each. There were older boys from multiple cultures and backgrounds. Our dormitory had twelve box-like rooms lined with stained panel board. This three-by-one-and-a-half-meter area had a single bed, a fixed cupboard, and a solid wooden chair. A wooden door with a glass panel and a small rear window. I put the suitcase in the cupboard and sat on the bed. *Hmm…at least I had my own space*: I had made my first mistake.

Miz B appeared, 'What're you doing sitting there, boy?'

'Nothing,' She glared at me as if I was some vermin.

'Stand up when I talk to you, and answer with respect; I'll not tolerate rudeness.'

'Yes, Mrs.'

'Now unpack your suitcase and store it on top of your wardrobe. There are hangers inside and drawers for your underwear. Shoes are to be placed neatly at the bottom, and your toiletries on the shelf. Nothing is to be left on the bed or floor. And hang your towel on the rail behind the door—have you got that?'

'Yes, Mrs.'

'No other items are allowed in your bedroom. Always keep it clean and tidy.'

'Yes, Mrs,' Same old story, with a slightly different tune, from another charming person.

'You're not to be in your bedroom outside bedtime are sleep or cleaning the room. Now get into the common room with the rest of the boys.'

'Yes, Mrs.'

I could hear someone whingeing down the other end of the dormitory; better stop it if you know what's good for you. Out in the common- room, I got the communal stare of non-welcome. There were four single spots left for us newbies in the seating rows. I chose the far end at the back. Here sat one of the Aboriginal boys, who chose to treat me with total disdain. I didn't blame him. Western movies were far more interesting. Red came out last; it looked like someone had slapped him across the face. He sat down in the only spot left, the middle of the front row. Most of the time, I didn't give a rat's arse what was going on. However, it was best to pay attention, if only to protect my hearing from further abuse, a cuffing around the ears.

'Smoko!' All heads turned towards her, who can't be ignored.

'Thank you, Mrs,' they mumbled. Then a bell tinkled, starting the movement of almost everyone towards the kitchen servery.

'You better get a move on if you want to eat,' the big boy beside me said.

'Yep, what about you?'

'I don't like her shit scones.'

'Thank you, Mrs,'

I took one of the scones and a cold drink. There were two scones left on the plate, and it would appear someone else declined her culinary efforts. She looked over at the two boys sitting in front of the TV, then closed the servery. I ate mine in five seconds, and the drink certainly helped me swallow it.

'You're right about the cook; they are survival rations.'

Side on, he appeared to smirk. He was not a big talker. I wondered what his name was. This place is a whole new kettle of fish. I doubted they like smartarses here. Ah, well, just another lot who don't appreciate my sheer genius.

Dinner was stew and dumplings, very nourishing and plenty of it. The flavour was improved with a liberal dose of Worchester sauce, and we got pudding every night. This place might have some possibilities. We were seated three to a table each with a newbie. I scored a spot with two chatty fellows hell-bent on drowning me with information. Top of the list were chores based on the theory that many hands made less work. The other tables seemed to have a good connection. The main topic was Football. The senior boys had a good chance of taking the trophy in the under-sixteen rugby league competition. I was not up to speed with the game's politics, but I soon discovered they were all sports mad.

On the surface, this was a grand country private school, attendance by invitation only. The reality of the place would taint the glamour over time. Week one was okay, and I began to understand the gist of the place. Don't argue, don't talk too much, don't annoy older boys. Fighting might be against the rules, but the odd smack in the head from some of these buggers would leave you dazed.

The program that became a constant in our lives for the next three years commenced. At precisely six am in the morning, it was time to rise and shine. Then, make your bed, throw water over your face, and dress. You were to be on the parade ground by 6.30 am. If you were late, it was at your peril. There were calisthenics for thirty minutes, and stopping at first drew verbal abuse. We had one week to get our act together or spend our spare time before and after school running around the oval as punishment. Penalties were also widespread, and you could accrue ten laps for every offence, served consecutively. In addition, there were performance motivators like the strap, a cane, or a swift boot in the rear end.

Each morning, we started with ten push-ups but were expected to get to thirty within one week. Add an extra two each day. Only ten minutes are allowed before moving on to other exercises. Working on the farm over the holidays improved my upper body strength. Still, I was buggered by the end of the first session. Failure to achieve the goal was not acceptable.

At seven o'clock, it was time to run back to your cottage.

A quick shower before breakfast, and don't be late. Thirty minutes was considered adequate to aid digestion. If you finished early, moving on to your roster job was a good idea. By 8.30 am, you were expected to be dressed for school, your room tidied, and wait for inspection. You might have thirty minutes free before school starts if you were efficient. If you weren't, your arse was going to be a sorry one. The job type was changed each Monday, and it was printed on cardboard signs and placed just about everywhere. Common sense suggests that you read it at least once for self-preservation. The roster wasn't a choice, it was do it or you are in for it. Eventually, we would go on a grid roster that never changed; you moved forward with the day of the week.

***

ROSTER NOTICE

    * 2-person job- sweep, clean & mop amenities,
   toilets, and sinks, including floors and walls.
    * 2-person job- wash/dry/put away breakfast
dishes/ pots/cutlery [no dishwasher].
    * 2- person job - Clean down tables, sweep and
          mop floors in all common areas.
    * 2 -person job- clean and hose down outside
patios and water gardens.

```
 * 1-person job- wash all towels and washers and
               hang them on the line.
  * 1-Person job - chop firewood; it's a wonder
      some of them, did not chop off toes.
  * 1-Person job - clean out the firebox, stack
      chopped firewood inside the cottage.
    * 1-Person job - peel vegetables
```

***

Our house mother took great interest in the slightest discrepancy. Around this time, my hearing began to deteriorate; she participated in the national sport of boxing our ears. Her high-pitched screeching contributed to many a headache; even the cockatoos took off. New boys especially received the benefit of her coaching style. For the first month, I was on the two-man detail, a different one each week to balance our experiences. Boys with precious personalities had short life expectancies; trauma knew no bounds around here.

'Pay attention and get a move on you little shits. You better not make me late.' Mrs B is an anal expert on cleanliness. She reports defective behaviour to Brother Shaven, who'll add it to his weekly flogging list. In this, he had a wholehearted attitude.

'What's the housemother's name? I asked.

'Don't know, don't care, it starts with a B. To most of us, it stands for Bitch. Ask Jonny if he is chummy with her; who knows what they get up to? You'll likely get a fat lip if you ask too many questions. Just shut up and get a bloody move on; I'm not waiting around here for your sorry arse.'

This Italian kid, Tony, was a polite fellow in comparison to some of the others. We made it to school with minutes to spare. I knew I had better move faster tomorrow; I didn't want to end up on this guy's shit list. There is a knack for everything, even cleaning out the amenities area. At least it wasn't covered in cow manure.

Orientation was brief. I didn't know what to expect, never having had one before. First up in grade eight, we had Rungee. A tall bloke, well over six feet, who had a tenancy to babble on. He wrote our class times for English Expression, General Maths and Level 1 science, on the board. The only thing that changed was the subject teacher rotation; a hooter sounded every hour or so. Technical subjects were in the other classroom blocks. We had two breaks, one twenty minutes for morning smoko and forty-five minutes for lunch. Washing up was included if you were on that detail for the week.

Rules, rules, what bunch of tools.

This lot must have a degree in rules and procedures. From my viewpoint, they are prepared to teach total morons. Maybe a dollar can be earned in this type of career choice. Or maybe that was the only career available for their intellect levels. As the saying goes, *you don't always get what you pay for.*

Bush Bootcamp

Let me tell you about a Kangaroo. Really, a few were hopping about the place; they had the good sense to move on? My new abode amongst the gum trees was unlike the previous place. I even saw a koala down in the back paddock one afternoon; its location remained my secret. This new internment camp had everything a private school could ask for, though I felt a nasty undertone lurking.

Still, on the surface, the place wasn't half bad; appearances can be deceiving. Money poured in like diarrhoea from an official's gob. The classrooms were of the latest design, constructed of raised concrete floors with brick walls and a tiled roof—a sensible design from a fire and maintenance perspective. The layout was as follows.

***

Block A—Three classrooms were for grades eight, nine, and ten. Brother Curly taught math, and he had a distinct aroma of alcohol. English and Sports were assigned to a local bloke called Rougee, who liked to test his pointy shoes on our rear ends. Brother Beagle taught science. Other small rooms housed a first aid room and a teacher's office /lunchroom.

Block B—Classrooms were technical drawing and metal work, Brother Shaven presiding. The woodwork class was taught by Brother Spiky, who also fancied himself as a hairdresser, using the round bowl style of haircut. Other small rooms at each end were for records and materials storeroom.

Block C—Contained a reasonably sized library and theatre, which was used for group meetings, choir practice, ad hoc music lessons, and, on occasion, the odd play or interrogation. Debating teams were dramatic. I tended to be on the wrong team, as I generally agreed with the opposing opinion. This was all overseen by Brother Shaven, a taciturn fellow with hidden talents.

Block D—Included chemistry and biology classes, including a laboratory where a small explosion occurred one day. A lay teacher taught these subjects; he was an opinionated mad scientist. Not the most empathic person, as he often informed us that we'd never amount to anything worthwhile in life.

***

According to in-house rumours, there were plans to build a gym and a swimming pool soon. In one of the top paddocks, the new horse stables and go-cart track were nearing completion. In the meantime, we made do with what we had. Our farm, dairy and machinery sheds, and mechanical workshop were out of bounds at present.

However, other activities were well catered for. We had Tennis, Basketball, and Volleyball courts, two sports ovals, and a small gym space under an old building, above which art and other advanced courses were held. For our spiritual well-being, we had a Chapel, where the faithful were led by pastor Brother Solemn, the administrator. Our days were spent constantly on the move. There were always chores, lessons, sports, or exercise programs.

Yes sir, no sir, three bags full sir was the modus operandi. Healthy bodies were a key to healthy minds, and if that failed, a swift kick in the rear end would motivate you. If you ran away, they would hunt you down. Then, seeing as you liked running so much, you'd spend every day after school doing laps around the oval for a month, rain, hail, or shine. Sometimes, there would be a dozen boys trudging along, creating a rut on the outside edge of the oval. To keep us entertained, some bugger would nudge you over on the high slope side, then you'd go arse up.

This led to a total shit fight one afternoon between two of the boys, who stood swinging haymakers at one another. While the rain continued to drizzle, the situation deteriorated, and they both ended up at the bottom of the ditch. This encouraged some idiot to slide down the embankment just for the fun of it. So, we all joined in, and it soon turned into a mud fight; within minutes, we were all covered in it.

'We're going to get into more shit for this,' one of the boys laughed.

'It's raining anyway, so why don't we continue running around the oval? That might wash some of the mud off,' I suggested. Off we all went, barely visible in the teeming rain. Pacing ourselves at a steady trot, slow and easy, a feint yell came from up near the cottages.

'Did you hear someone calling out to us, Rickie?' asked Red.

'Nah, Mate, I've got a hearing impairment.'

'A what?'

'Look it up in the dictionary.' Anyway, stuff them. They can bloody well come down here and tell us.

Ten minutes later, an older boy came running down the hill, slipping and sliding on the slope. He almost made it to us before he went over into the mud.

'You bloody idiots, why're you still running around in the rain?'

'It's only 4.30; we have to keep going till 5,' I replied.

'You morons, now I'm covered in mud as well; Brother Shaven said to go up and have your showers, so move your arses.'

'Ok, keep your shirt on.' Cowering never led to any good around here.

'Hey, smartarse, what's ya name? You're a newbie?' one of the older mud-splatted boys asked.

'Battler.'

'Thanks, you've saved our arses.'

'No worries,' I had to be careful not to appear a brown nose.

The house parents weren't too impressed with our intelligence either; we had to hose our clothes and boots off outside and hang everything up to dry in the laundry. A hot shower soon changed our blue complexions. We'd probably cop another earful afterwards. The upside of all this exercise was that our body strength increased rapidly, which they always put to good use.

Soon, we would be able to crash through brick walls, scale every mountain, and wade every stream. One way or another, they'd make you part of the team. On weekends, if sports games were not on, we had a change of scenery: cross country run, for possibly two hours. Then, another change of pace, an uphill scramble and back down the other side into a water hole. Just take off your boots and jump in; you will dry off on the run back. After a while, I began to enjoy the whole process.

Running about in the scrub, that is, gave me a sense of freedom. It beat the crap out of sitting in classrooms and getting bored. Not sure what the other kids had been taught before coming here, but it all sounded like a regurgitation of grade seven. A thought I kept to myself. The tech and science classes were interesting, though.

The Council of Bothersome Buggers

Well, what do you know, we have yet another level of annoying personages of privilege, interfering in our lives and generally stuffing us about. This student body consisted of an in-house drongo mayor and four dingo aldermen, envoys to a higher power.

What is their function? From the looks of things, dobbers when it suits them and standover merchants by choice. A person needs the skills of Houdini around here to find peace. *A friendly face can lead to disgrace when one's trust is misplaced.* You would think by now I would have learnt this lesson well. Life's a slippery slope whenever I stray to place faith in those who meddle in everything. Rattle the cage enough, and the rampart dogs surround you. The concept of divide and vanquish was a common denominator. Little wonder I preferred my own company to that of others. There are many good people in this world, just very few in mine.

These guys have perfected the art of injury under the guise of assistance in our mental and physical well-being. Nothing too obvious occurs, especially in the sight of the brothers and day teachers. Unseen biff-ups and trip-overs could be done on the run. It would appear to be just very clumsy kids. Misguided missiles might ricochet and cause *accidental* bruising. Volunteering to do someone else jobs or homework may alleviate situations. Alternatively, bashing the crap out of them tended to have a more permanent effect or not. Between the brothers and their support crew, there was no end to the mind games and underhanded subtlety of these charmers.

My eyesight was a little out of kilter. When playing cricket, I learnt to catch the ball with each hand due to double vision. If I only caught the thin air ball, the real one sometimes hit me in the head. Things were fine if I didn't drop it. If I did, the coach got upset for not using both hands and the result. A kick in the arse with his pointy shoes. I liked bowling best as the only thing I had to keep my eyes on was the person down the other end of the pitch. Even this took me a while to get the hang of; full tosses often got the batsman in the chest. Short, bouncy balls sometimes in the crutch. We were a little short on protective equipment.

Still, over time, I improved as I developed a spin to the ball. In the final game of the season, I eventually got the chance to be *the* bowler. Five out, for twenty runs, beginners' luck they reckoned. The two usual bowlers were related to the council of buggers, but one had the flu and the other had ankle injuries. Our cricket season ended on a high.

Soon, we'd be training in preparation for the footy season, a sport most of the boys liked. We could dissipate some aggression. The coach mostly focused on tackling and the occasional obtuse game plan.

Blind Freddy could work out where that ball was going next and just wait until it arrived. Of course, interception was always the fault of our players, and we received the penalties for not winning after the match. Because our coach had been a local lad, I sensed this was a deliberate attempt to jig the game. I mentioned it to a couple of the boys I had got to know a little bit. Two of them just shook their heads and their eyes looked over to my left. By the time I looked that way a fist connected with the side of my head.

'Keep your shit to yourself.'

'Who the hell is he, the coach's arse kisser?' I mumbled to the other two boys.

'Battler, it's best to keep your thoughts to yourself around here. You just found out the wrong person was listening, and the coach was looking elsewhere. Fall back down on the ground when the play restarts; you are probably concussed anyway. Sit the rest of the game out and pay attention to what happens,' the halfback advised me.

The whistle blew and it was a scrum down again. I ran up to the play and I fell over. I did feel a bit dizzy. The closest winger came in to take my position as the lock. The game went back and forth. The coach was waving his arms about; he was a highly excitable fellow at times. I heard a mention about some injury to the opposition's lock, the dipshit [me] should watch what he runs into.

So that is how it goes hey?

The game recommenced; disaster loomed, and the opposition team was now tied with us. Five minutes to go, we were scrummed down at the 10-meter line. The scrum collapses, our hooker lays on the ground with a badly tagged calf muscle. Now we are down two players and have no subs. The game stopped, and the injured player was removed; he was the same ratbag who sucker punched me. He is useless now, but who is going to replace him, we only have eleven players on the field. The half-back called out to me.

'Battler! Get your arse over here and take over as hooker. The front row will hold you up; just get that bloody ball, mate, no matter what!'

The game restarted and the hooker on the other team decided to kick me in the shins. The prick, I kicked him fair in the crutch, and our feet became entangled. The ball got caught behind my feet, and the second row moved it out. Our half-back retrieved it and passed it to the five-eight, and he kicked a field goal. Then, the scrum collapsed into a brawl. We won the game.

Unfortunately, any fights or disagreements on the field were always blamed on us. So, if we played an away game, we got ten laps of the oval to do when we returned home. If it was a home game, then the next day, a Sunday, we played a long game against one of our own teams for an hour each half. Certainly, it improved our temperament and character building, one might say. Did we care? Not if we won; so, it was winning at any cost! We just loved winning.

Our school choir was invited to join the local choral society, which was performing a pageant in the town community hall. We were first on after the intermission. The townspeople greatly appreciated our choir. Some of the girls from the local public high school took a special interest, as their applause was quite enthusiastic. I bet that wiped the smile on the dials of the local lads.

Soon after that, a positive change in our lifestyle occurred: interschool sports with mixed tennis and basketball teams. No doubt a goodwill gesture by the Christian Churches in the town. Previously, rumours had spread that didn't show us in a good light, and the girls seemed glad we weren't completely feral. In the games we played against the locals, either side won or lost on their own merits. The relationship between our school and the town had been strained in the past. It was probable that some of our boys who ran away got up to mischief. It might also be possible some of the town's younger people got up to mischief, and the finger was pointed in our direction. Let us face it: we are an obvious target.

We were the most likely suspects until proven otherwise. Undoubtedly, the town merchants appreciated our school. Our direct support of buying local produce and services benefited many. The year rolled by till the August holidays, gave us a break from the ever-present threat of violence or injury. Even the house parents could take it easy in our absence, I assumed. Strangely, our housemother didn't seem too joyful about it. Who would she have to pick on while we were away?

Rural Life Over the Ranges

I was glad to bugger off for holidays out to Chinchilla, even though it was the chilly time of the year. Temperatures could drop to below zero Celsius, even lower when the westerly winds blew. I boarded the Greyhound bus at South Brisbane, sitting down for long periods was not my forte. At least on a train, one could get up and walk about, even go to the dining carriage on board. I arrived in the early evening, a more convenient time for Bill or Gwyn to pick me up. The next morning, I leapt out of bed around six am. Bill was listening to the early weather report on the radio.

'Good morning, Rickie. Did you have a good sleep? I'm a bit slow starting today.'

'Good morning, Bill. If you'd like, I can saddle up Old Bess and fetch the cattle into the dairy yards.'

'Well, in that case, top up the teapot, and I'll join you in another cuppa. You had better wear an extra coat, though; it's cold outside. There's a frost on the ground, and the mist may take a while to lift,' he added.

'OK, care for some fruit cake with your cuppa, Bill?'

'I think a small piece won't do me much harm,' Bill was diabetic. The cuppa and cake had become a tradition with Bill and me in the mornings. Gwyn, no doubt, was aware it wasn't the mice making off with the cake.

Bill was right, and it was difficult to see past the head of the horse. At these times, the horse had better sense than me. I let her decide how to round up the dairy cows. I on the other hand, could lie on her back with a big overcoat over me. To keep the horse warm, mind you. It was fortunate that this horse liked me; otherwise, I'd have found myself tossed off into the cactus trees. It would be a cold walk home in the fog. That horse was smart enough to take the coat with it if I got too careless.

Bill and I finished the dairy jobs, in a timely fashion. Gwyn had a hot breakfast waiting for us. Sitting around the dining table, we had plenty of food and conversation. I hadn't been home for Easter, and my letter-writing was sporadic at best.

'How's the new school, Rickie?' Gwyn asked.

'Interesting, we play a lot more sports there.'

'How do you find the Christian brothers as teachers?'

'Entertaining.' I had to keep the details out of the conversation as I didn't want them to be concerned.

'In what way are they entertaining?' Gwyn inquired.

'Well, they have a different style of teaching to the nuns, and we have a wider variety of subjects. I like Science, Chemistry, Art, woodwork, metalwork, and technical drawing, as well as English and maths. We go swimming down at the local pool when it opens and play Rugby league, Cricket, Tennis, Basketball and sometimes Soccer,' I informed them.

'They certainly keep you all active with one thing or another,' Bill replied.

'We have a choir and are performing a play next term down in the town's community hall.

'Oh! What is it called?' They both asked.

'*Oliver Twist*, most of us are in the production. I didn't tell them that we got no choice in the matter. '

'That sounds wonderful.'

'Yes. So, what're we planning for today?' I asked. It was time to move this conversation to more local matters.

'Well, I'm going down to the river to check our water pump as it has been sluggish lately. This evening, we're all invited to a bar-b-que at McCafferty's place in town,' Bill replied.

'I'm making a woollen garment on my new knitting machine; it's rather complicated. Would you like to have a go? Gwyn offered.

'Thank you, Gwyn, but I think things would go better if I stayed away from your new machine.' They both laughed.

'That's a shame you might be able to knit a pair of woollen socks. That would impress the other boys.

'I am sure it would, but I don't want to make them jealous.' Gwyn smiled at the idea.

The river pump could be a cantankerous piece of equipment at times. We hauled in the suction hose, added an extra float, and cleaned out the foot valve. Then we gave the engine a grease and oil change and a bit of spit and polish. She started first go and settled into a slow rhythmic sound, which echoed throughout the bush. Wallabies seemed entranced by it, and a koala or two lounging in the surrounding trees watched on with droopy indifference, dreaming of some choice eucalyptus leaves, no doubt

Bill remarked, 'The fuel tank is half full; remind me to let Clarrie know this evening to top it up next time he's out this way with his tanker.' We shared the cost of the pump equipment with our neighbours, as the reticulation served both properties. There were plans to add an electric pump when money was available. We dropped into the Davis's house for a chat and cuppa on our way home. Bill updated them on the state of the pump and a little news about my new school.

'By the way, Ken, I turned the valve back over to your tanks. We have a few trough valves to repair up the back paddock, so I'll switch our line to the rear holding tank while we are up there. 'Would you shut the pump down this afternoon?'

'Will do. We'll catch up with you all at Vince's this evening. You'll be able to tell us a little more about your new school then, Rickie.'

The Davis's had kids away at boarding school and were looking forward to seeing them. They farewelled, and Bill and I headed home. I thought about sticking to some of the facts but not the whole truth. As far as the local community knew, my educational facility was top-notch. It had the backing of churches and government agencies. Any cracks in their façade had been *plastered* over well and truly. My holiday was always enjoyable. But then, I didn't have to deal with the hardships of running the farm continuously.

All is Not What it Seems

On my return to school, I heard that two of our boys from cottage six were missing. They had supposedly been charged with theft in Brisbane and sent to Wilson Youth Detention Centre. From all accounts, this was a jail for male and female juvenile offenders that were harsher than those in adult prisons. If those in authority chose to, a teenager could be shuffled along without notice. Possibly to Westbrook, another charming detention facility. Let's face it, if anyone disagreed with this lot, they would be tagged as a problem delinquent. Our local rumour mill differed in what preceded the theft. There were suggestions that this was the outcome of unwanted personal attention by older adults, resulting in a fight-or-flight situation. Facts versus fabrication. It's not my first time hearing whispers of this nature closer to home.

Brother Solemn, perched on his podium at the main roundabout, gave us a brief welcome home along with any items he deemed worthy of mention. A box of altar wine had disappeared from the chapel. Also, cigarette butts had been found on the property, so everyone's ports would be searched for contraband. I wondered if this lot got on the booze and made this crap up. It didn't make any sense, and there wasn't supposed to be any of the boys left here. Who else has been having a good time while we're away on our holiday break?

Two new boys joined our cottage family to fill the roster schedule. Some stay, some go. This revolving door syndrome must be a lucrative racket. One of the newbies was from Woodridge and the other from Inala, courtesy of the child welfare Department; they had stories to tell of wild escapades. The gangs from these two suburbs were antisocial and took a dislike to each other. Better not start their crap here, we have enough of our own to go around.

How much wood can a wood -chopper chop? Plenty, it turns out. The housemother seemed to like how I chopped wood, so it became my only job for the last term of the year. Chopping, chopping, and stacking was one of my daily activities; never has she had such a large reserve of wood for the stove. She found another job for the previous stacker position, cleaning the windows, inside and out, which was never-ending. What a devious mind this woman had. She never lets a chance go by to offload work to us boys. A lesson in life is what you know that is important, knowledge rules the roost. While I was out on the farm, Bill taught me the fine art of splitting blocks of wood and sharpening the axe. If done the right way, it was not such a challenging job. The other boys at the school thought chopping wood was a crap job, but that was fine with me. No more broken axe handles by the other boys, or injuries for that matter. Out here, I had a relatively peaceful time.

The house mother even occasionally brought me a mug of tea. Life was settling into an almost pleasant pattern of normality.

The football season being over did not stop the constant health and well-being programs enforced to strengthen our physical and psychological performances. The mind games continued; their ability at subterfuge was an art form. The person you were talking to may be either friend or foe, confident or betrayer. I hadn't yet gained enough experience in understanding the subtlety of body language. My conversations were minimalist at best. Not having an opinion or being vague had an upside. I saved all my talking for when I was out at Bill and Gwyn's place. They just loved listening to my endless chatter, I hope.

Even though the beginning of September still had a chill in the air, some of the brothers decided 6 am was a good time for grades eight and nine to use the local pool. It was not due to open to the public for another six weeks, so it was all ours for three mornings a week. Grade ten scored callisthenics in the morning and swimming in the late afternoon. This was character-building stuff; you either stood in the chilly wind or dived into the near-freezing water. The more you swam, the warmer you got. After an hour of swimming practice, it was off to the shower block to wash off the chlorine. There was cold water only, slightly better than the pool temperature. With no one else around, the brothers thought it necessary to watch us while showering. Fat chance of us escaping through the small vent holes at the top of the walls.

To reinforce their power trip, the last five boys to line up outside the bus, received an extra gift. The twenty-minute run back to our cottages, where you would arrive with a ruddy complexation. The extra exercise meant you'd probably be late for breakfast and your morning job. Luckily, I was ahead on woodchopping; I got a bowl of porridge and a mug of tea, which suited me fine. The eggs and toast were long gone. Mrs B waited for no one, you were on time, or you missed out. You wash your own dishes if you're late. Whatever you do, don't whine over anything, or you will cop more crap. Tears are only helpful for removing the dust from your eyes.

This weekend, in addition to our regular activities, we went cross country, running around the mountain range and surrounding bushland. I gathered that we had permission from the property owners. Brother Shaven was a very fit bloke who would probably give a drill sergeant a run for his money. He had a knack for discovering interesting places. We trotted along a dry creek bed that presented a challenge. Sometimes, we discovered multi-coloured agate and occasionally petrified wood. A hidden lagoon with a natural spring was at the end of one of the creeks. There were many hanging vines that dangled from the overhanging tree branches. They had a certain amount of elasticity, ideal for swinging out and drop into the freezing dark water below.

If lucky, you might catch a freshwater yabby on the end of your toes; and it paid to keep your speedos done up tight. I enjoyed being out in the countryside. The run back to the bus was another challenge. We had to run flat out, up and down small hills, then across open grasslands. If you were not back within fifteen minutes of the driver's arrival, the bus left. You got the three-hour run back home. If you weren't back at your cottage by dinnertime, you were reported as a runaway. Some days, there was no end to the *joy* in my life. At spasmodic intervals in the dead of the night, there would be bed checks for God knows what reason. A bright torch would be shone in your face. Was someone where they weren't supposed to be? There was some peculiar behaviour going on around here. Some boys seemed very friendly with one or two of our learned leaders.

Occasionally, on a Sunday afternoon, we had a free period; some of the boys would spend it in a friendly game of tennis or basketball, and others might watch the black and white TV. A few preferred not to be found, smoking outside the end of our cottage, including Red and Yao. They imagined themselves as supervisors doing bugger all, helping me dig up a garden bed. I decided to park my arse on the edge of a concrete flowerpot. There was little likelihood of getting this job done before Smoko.

'What are you two smart-arses grinning about? I asked.

'Us? Nothing really.'

'Come on, what's the joke?'

'Well, Rickie, it looks like you've grown small tits,' Red grinned.

I looked down at my chest; I could see his point; all this exercise had increased the size of my chest, shoulders, and arms. My T-shirt was stretched to its limits.

'Funny guys, come here, and I'll give you a big hug,'

'Piss off,' they both took off somewhere.

I had better get some oversized T-shirts, those pair of deviants had a point. The constant exercise and chopping of wood added muscles. I'd gained 13lbs, almost six kilograms, since being here one year. That's more than I gained in the previous five years. I certainly didn't have any fat on me. *This place was doing me some good physically despite its hidden agendas.* If I keep this up, I may be able to play in the senior league team.

A few of the boys occasionally disappeared during free periods; I would search around the place without appearing to do so. They weren't doing any sports or in the library/theatre building. *I wonder where the hell they get to.* I went past the chook sheds, then diverted towards a noise from the small workshop. They're hiding out in here, the sneaky buggers. I've got them. Big mistake!

'What are you doing down here, boy? You're out of bounds.' Crap, it was Brother Shaven, a hard taskmaster.

'Good afternoon, Brother. Would you like a hand?' Volunteering for work was not high on any of the boys' list of activities. He just stared at me for a few minutes.

'Do you know how to mix concrete by hand?'

'I could learn, Brother.'

That's how I became his garden pot apprentice. He was responsible for the large concrete pots in wedge-shaped designs that adorned the garden area outside cottage six. His moulds had both inner and outer sections. A threaded rod down the centre and clamps on the four outer sides. The inner part of the mould was screwed down by turning a handle above the top plate. Each section had recycled sump oil applied to it, so the concrete did not stick to the plywood. This all resulted in a pot about 600x 600mm in diameter at the top, tapering to 400 x 400mm at the bottom. The pots stood 800mm high, and the walls were 100mm thick with steel mesh reinforcement and remained in place wherever they were put. The pots weighed thirty to forty kilograms each; if you ran into one of them, you would come off second best. It took a week for them to dry, and we produced three more each weekend. A two-man assembly process, cleaning off one lot while the other three are cured.

Over the following months, we produced thirty-six concrete pots. Each cottage received six of them, with a few spares for the common areas. Once the brother's training level was completed, he passed the job over to me, and Yao became my assistant. It was a far better pastime than being at the beck and call of the bothersome ones. I sealed and painted Mrs B's pots in different colours; it improved her empathy towards me.

A shit fight started one Sunday afternoon; a tall kid tripped me over as I ran past him. A habitual pastime of his on all and sundry. As I got up off the bitumen, bleeding, I saw he was about to do it to someone else. While he was distracted, I ran up and jumped on him, unintendedly kneeing him in the groin. It was time to run. I needed to find somewhere to hide, my life expectancy somewhat reduced.

Ten minutes later, I heard his quiet voice calling, 'Where are you, whitey? Come out and play. Maybe this guy harboured race issues; playing with him was going to end very badly for me. I hid under several classrooms, then into the caged chook shed, and later moved behind the dairy bales.

He openly just wandered around everywhere, tracking me down. Once or twice, he nearly got me if it wasn't for some adult asking him why he wasn't where he was supposed to be. Finally, I thought I was safe. I heard the afternoon smoko hooter sound. I crept into the first aid room through an unlocked sliding window. I left a blood stain on the outside of the glass, as I was still bleeding from multiple skin grazes. Crap, I had been leaving a trail everywhere I went a smudge here, a streak there. No wonder this guy was always on my tail. I got some Dettol & cotton wool from a cupboard and cleaned myself up.

'Shit that sting,' I yelped. I thought I heard a sliding window and went to check in the other room, it was still closed. *I'd better get out of here.* I found some plaster to put over my wounds and cut it into patches with long-nosed sharp scissors.

'Got you,' a big hand grabbed my wrist.

'You bastard, how'd you get in here?' I struggled to escape him.

'Calm down, or I'll beat the shit out of you, and don't say a bloody word; there are two brothers outside, probably looking for both of us.'

'Stay on the floor and don't move; if we stand up, we'll be seen.'

'Ok, so what're you going to do while we wait? I had to ask, didn't I?'

'Well, I was going to beat the shit out of you an hour ago. You led me on such an entertaining chase. I haven't had this much fun for ages. I wanted to find out if you were a complete moron or just bloody nuts. I still can't make up my mind.'

'Really?'

'I've been here nearly three years, and you're only the second person stupid enough to take a swing at me. Besides, I'm out of here in a month and finally going home to my mob. I don't want to give them any excuse to send me anywhere else,' he replied.

'I get where you're coming from. By the time I'm free of this lot, it will be nine years since I've been locked up. After that, I suppose I'll have to wing it on my own.

'Don't try to poke someone with scissors; they might stick you with them,' he warned.

I said, 'So, you're not such an arse hole after all.' I was somewhat relieved I would end up with my bones broken.

He stared at me, 'Don't push your luck; if anyone asks, we ran into one another at the library.'

Silently he stepped back out through the window and disappeared. *Whew!* That was the close; the angels are working overtime today. I didn't even know the guy's name, although he wasn't hard to spot: seventeen, six foot tall, and as strong as a mallee bull. I saw him again two weeks later, or I should say a part of him. Three guys were shoving me around, and a fist came over my shoulder and connected with the head of one of them.

'Listen, you dipshits, leave him the hell alone if you know what's good for you,' then he just walked off.

'Sorry, Battler. We didn't know you were a mate of Bluebirds.'

So that's his bloody name. It's a shame he is leaving soon. It is cool to have a physical guardian angel around for a change. That is one good deed I never got the chance to repay. He left suddenly one day.

The cricket season was in full swing once more. We were playing a mid-week game against one of the district's junior teams. It was amazing how many teams were fielded in country areas. On this occasion, I got to bowl one over. When we went into field, I was delegated to the outer boundary. There was only a remote chance someone would slog a ball over here; and it was boring standing around in the hot afternoon sun. Finally, it was the last inning, and we were ahead by five runs. This was going to be a tight finish. Most of our team was close to the pitch, trying to stop any chance of a run. I was getting rather dizzy and decided to have a sit-down. Then the shout went up.

'Battler! Get up,' they all screamed.

'What?'

I jumped up and put both hands above my head to shield my eyes from the sun. I could see bugger all, everything was blurry. You couldn't have planned it better if you tried; the ball went smack into my hands, and then it fell past me. I reached blindly for it, getting my hand under the ball just before it hit the ground, clinging onto it like my life depended on it. Everyone started yelling, and I ran in with the ball. We had beaten them on the last ball. The bugger had slogged a six right in my direction. They would have beaten us by one run if I had not caught that ball. Rungee had something to say about it, though.

'What the hell do you think you're doing, lying about on the ground out there?'

'I was dizzy, sir,'

Jai ran up, 'Wasn't that the best catch you've ever seen? Sir.'

If there hadn't been witnesses, we both would have gotten his pointy shoes up our backsides. We had won, but I doubted Rungee would forget my last stand for quite a while. He still didn't believe I had eye problems and that my seeing double was just an excuse for poor performance.

On the other hand, Brother Shaven had heard of my unusual cricket style, and the following morning, I found out what his method for testing me would be. Our English teacher was off on other duties, and Brother Shaven took his place. When the hooter sounded, we all went into class. I as usual, was in the back row. The brother had been writing proverbs on the blackboard in different styles, and they appeared to shrink in size as he went down the board.

'Ok, starting in the back row on the left side, stand up and read the line I point to on the board.' When it got to me, I started and then stopped.

'What's wrong, Battler?'

'Some of the writing is blurry, Brother.'

'Come up the front and start again.'

I did this. I discovered I had less of a problem with reading if I shut one eye. He directed me to change desks with Smithy in the front row. I wondered what his game was—some sort of punishment for almost dropping the cricket ball yesterday, I suppose. The clock ticked on, and the hooter sounded for the change of class.

'Battler, remain seated; the rest of you keep moving.' We were all in his technical drawing class next, so whatever this was about, it would need to be sorted quickly.

'Why haven't you told anyone about your eyesight problem?'

'I didn't think anyone cared,' I replied. There was no point in me dobbing in Rungee; he thought my double vision story was an excuse.

'Find me after school this afternoon, now get a move on.'

One never knows if a summons is a trick, a diversion or an assault for hidden agendas. A few of the boys wanted to know what trouble I was in. I left them in suspense by saying I'd find out after school this afternoon. It was none of the above. Brother Shaven had arranged an appointment with an Optometrist in the local town for the following Monday morning at 10. am. I got a lift down there with one of the houseparents, and a few tests were done on my eyes.

'You have Monocular Diplopia in your left eye; do you suffer from headaches or dizziness?'

'Yes, both.'

'I'm surprised that you haven't had any serious falls. I'll order you a pair of prescription spectacles to help resolve the problem. In the meantime, I want you to wear these light-shaded sunglasses whenever you are outside.'

'Thank you, Sir.'

'Do you have any questions?'

'No, Thank you, Sir.'

'Ok, give this envelope to Brother Shaven. Do you require a lift back to school?'

'I'm all good, Thank you.'

Cool, I've got sunglasses! I checked them out as I passed by a shop window. *Looking good there Rickie!* As I strolled back alone; I bought a coca cola at a nearby service station. After all, no one said I couldn't walk back. It was almost lunchtime when I arrived at the administration building and rang the bell. Fortunately, Brother Solemn wasn't around. Their housekeeper came out.

'What can I do for you young man?'

'Hello, could you hand this envelope to Brother Shaven? The optometrist asked me to give it to him. Thank you.'

Mrs B must have been informed about my eyesight problem, as she didn't mention anything about the sunglasses as I wandered into our dining room. I doubt she feels remorseful about how she has harassed me about minor dish stains. My spectacles arrived in time for the Christmas holidays, although I was cool with wearing the sunglasses. Heading to Chinchilla would give me time to adapt to my new glasses. This time, I scored a train ride out home to enjoy the serenity of the bush for six weeks.

Time Flys

Enjoyable times are fleeting; far too soon, I was back to the grindstone of reality. On arrival, we began with the usual contraband inspection; the newbies looked like they were crapping their daks. Some of their faces showed the fear of facing the school of hard knocks. It's sink or swim time, boys; life wasn't meant to be easy, especially around here.

I was assigned to cottage four this year, along with Jai and his cousin Dougie. We must have passed the trials of cottage six. Half of the previous year's boys remained there, including Red. Mrs B would have to find herself another wood chopper. This year, it was the same process with a few more challenges. Our exercise regime didn't falter or alter; it was set in concrete. A few kids ran away the first week; they would learn that the grass only seemed greener elsewhere. The best advice I could give them was to deal with the crap you have. My new house parents were all right. They did more about the place than Mrs B ever had. Still, she had drummed into us how to look after the house and ourselves. I now had more free time, and the housemother got us involved in preparing some of the meals and taught us some basic cooking lessons. My favourite was caramel tarts.

The cottage 4 house-father chopped the firewood, one of his many jobs. He soon realised I could split the firewood safely and look after his axe properly. The woodchopping soon became my permanent job. He wasn't a bad bloke, a bit stern, ex-military, but we got along. I would accompany him down to the local town on Saturday mornings to deliver some of our farm fresh produce. Part of this job was for me to drive the old Ute around the property and down to our driveway boundary. He would take over at the main gate to drive on the public roads. Any outing provided a sense of freedom. These house parents proved decent people; respect was a two-way street with them.

This year's newly elected school council of bothersome buggers were an improvement on the last bunch. Maybe I was just getting used to the mind games and not sucked in as often. Still, trust is an elusive quality around here. Someone was always looking for an angle to mess with your head. Resilience and adaptation were the name of this game. Occasionally, on Saturday afternoons, we all piled into the 'old faithful' bus and went out to swim at nearby creeks. There was one place where we could jump off a cliff into the deep hole below; it was almost a rite of passage. One fool forgot to jump outwards one day and landed in the scrub. Spoiled it for everyone. The bloody wanker froze as he ran up to the cliff edge.

Brother Shaven has always been keen on team-building activities. My favourite was when we constructed temporary makeshift mini bridges across a narrow stream. This was an annual event that involved all grades divided into several teams. The water could be more than a metre deep and flowing swiftly depending on recent rainfall. The idea was to use local bush materials. Each team had a spade, axe, and hand saw. The result had to be sturdy enough for three boys to cross. It was a great challenge with four teams doing the actual building, backed up by their support crew. Each pylon post needed securing by piling rocks around the base; otherwise, kiss your bridge goodbye. We had more country boys in our team, who knew a thing or two about bush materials, which gave us a decided advantage. Some of the other teams' bridges were unstable and tended to wash away, so those boys wasted time chasing logs down the creek. It proved a disaster if the elected team leader had little common sense. Grand designs and limited materials didn't make for a good plan. Still, everyone enjoyed the challenge of creating a design, teamwork and utilising the materials that nature provided.

This year, the earthworks behind the science block commenced the foundations for the proposed new gymnasium. By the size of the base footprint, it was going to be massive. I dreamed of going on one of those front-end loaders. I didn't think they would be much different to driving a tractor with a bucket on the front and a blade on the rear. The building was designed to have a full basketball court that would alternate as two shuttlecock courts. A gymnastics area was included down the far end, with an observation gallery high on one side and a combo boxing gym area on the other. It is an all-weather place for various activities. They planned dual sets of showers and toilet areas for visiting teams. The walls were remarkably high, with small windows all around the top and long pulley ropes hanging down to open and close them. *These would come in handy in the future for clandestine activities.* The building project took eight months to complete, which was quite an accomplishment.

Brother Solemn was replaced by another brother who was more involved with our daily lives. Brother Fitbean is now the troubled youth's new administrator, teacher, psychologist, and mind manager. Under his authority, our lives became even more challenging. On the surface, it appeared outwardly positive, but something seemed off. Interaction with the local townspeople had improved. Often engaging with them in events like tennis, basketball, and swimming competitions. We also competed in gymkhanas and rural show displays, to name a few. Even our social interactions were taking a new direction, which showcased a productive and successful training facility for troubled youth. According to their mission statement, the idea was to help troubled boys fit back into mainstream society.

Brother Fitbean called me over one afternoon to where he sat on his observation bench talking to a couple of the younger boys.

'Battler, where are you off to in such a hurry?'

'Tennis Brother.'

'Well, the courts are occupied at present. You have time to stop for a little chat.'

'Yes Brother.'

'You're scheduled for a counselling session first thing Friday morning; we'll have plenty of time to discuss anything that might be bothering you. One thing that makes me curious is that I seldom see you smile. Why is that?'

'Don't know brother, never thought about it, I guess. Can I go now?'

'Hmm…interesting, off you go then.'

I wondered what his game was. I will no doubt find out on Friday. Jai was sitting on a seat outside the courts. He was my doubles partner. We were into the semi-finals. Win this one, and we will be in the finals. A first for me, I wasn't the best of players.

'Hey Rickie, I've been watching this pair on the right-side court. They will be hard to beat if we face them tomorrow.'

'Well, Jai, if there were two of you, it'd be a hands-down grand slam, but you're stuck with me.'

'Yeah, you've improved a bit since you got glasses, except when the sun is in your eyes, learn to look down. When you're on the net, do your deadly slice returns, which will annoy them and put them off their game. When you're at the back of the court, hit the return high and long, giving me time to sort it out. Don't try anything fancy! Ok?'

'No worries.'

Jai was a superb strategist, and he was fast. He could put that ball anywhere on the court he wanted to. A sliced ball from me just over the net caused the trajectory to fly off on a divergent angle or return to the net. The opposite player had to move fast to get anywhere near it. My serves were easy to read, always just inside the line far corner. They would be waiting; their problem was the speed of my delivery. Blink, you'd miss it. I followed Jai's advice, and we won the match.

There would be a lot of interest in tomorrow's game. The unofficial bets were on, and we were the underdogs who had slipped in on a wild card. If we won, I would give up competitions. I decided I might as well retire as a champion and collect my winnings.

'Good morning, brother.'

'Take a seat, Battler. You seemed to have fallen through the cracks regarding counselling sessions. Why is that?'

'Don't know, Brother never thought about it.'

'There is a file on every student here; yours is light on information. There is one small statement about your physical improvement, one about your eyesight, another about smoking, and a brief note stating that the student fudges his exams deliberately.'

'Smoking Brother? I don't smoke.

'You were caught with some other boys smoking in the back area of cottage one.'

'That may be so, Brother, but it still doesn't mean I smoke.'

'So, you were there, but you weren't smoking.'

'That's correct, Brother.'

'So why didn't you say something at the time.'

'What'd be the point, Brother.'

'Do you like it here?'

'Everyone has to be somewhere, so this is as good a place as anywhere, Brother.'

'What sort of things do you like doing? Don't keep saying brother at the end of each answer.'

'I like everything here; it's a wonderful place.'

He sighs; maybe he is getting annoyed.

'You go on holiday to a farm in Chinchilla. Would you like to work on the farm here? Our dairyman could use help. We've doubled our herd over the last year. You'd be excused from morning house chores and exercise class; would you like that?'

'Yes, Brother, that would be good.'

'Okay, I'll organise it for Monday week with Mr Stuggy. If all goes well, we can make it permanent.'

'Thank you, Brother.'

'Off you go then, and Battler…'

'Yes Brother.'

'You seem like a decent young fellow; do you ever get enthusiastic about anything?'

'All the time, brother.'

'Hard to tell with your facial expressions; try smiling. It helps people to like you.'

Yeah, it's how much they like me. That's what bothers me around here.

On this daily work detail, with time off for school, sports, and other social events, I became the dairy assistant, which had other benefits. We had an old Morris Minor that we customised to create a small utility with a rear timber tray. It was handy for cruising around and moving small items about the farm. There wasn't any payment mentioned. I suppose this is my extra contribution towards the cost of our new gym building. Or maybe the altar wine, who knows? Like the rest, I worked for room, board, and education. The roof over our heads did not come cheap. Doing chores was part of life, there was no such thing as a free lunch.

However, the grade ten class got a choice project: constructing the go-kart track. This was situated in one of the paddocks that doubled as an equestrian training facility. The horse stable and spelling yards were a few hundred meters further on. We welded the go-karts in our bottom workshop and fitted them with old lawn mower engines. The weight of a driver limited the forward motion speed.

Our new gymnasium was officially opened with great fanfare. Local dignitaries and officials from far and wide were invited. The lord mayor of Brisbane, Clem Jones, officiated and cut the opening ceremony ribbon. What a grand addition to our school. There is no doubt the local high school was envious. They were invited to use the facilities, and one of the first interschool functions was a dance evening. One of the local lads had a mobile DJ system with flashing colour lights, a strobe, and a mirror ball, he was at the top of the list. The basketball court became a dance floor for the evening. Attendance was by invitation only, which the local town and country high school girls accepted with good grace. Most likely keen on evaluating our dancing technique.

Who knows what the local gossip had conjured up to whet their appetites? I hope they will not be too disappointed; after all, we're mildly conditioned by our Gestapo overlords. Get caught putting a foot wrong around here, and you would get the gong. Two gongs, and you are gone.

Rock and Roll and Disco were popular choices, followed by Latin American and ballroom dancing. Not all the boys were up to speed on the finer points. It was an entertaining evening as the girls had the choice of partners. To them, it was a lolly shop. The DJ did a brilliant job of keeping us all on the move, with a few breaks for a drink or a snack. The safest place from prying eyes was on the dance floor.

In a couple of weeks, we would all be off for the Christmas holidays, a much-anticipated event. Going out to the country to see Bill, Gwyn, family, and the many friends I'd made over the years was a breath of fresh air to my mental well-being. I could not wait to see the back of this place. Six weeks of peace and enjoyment without being on guard against ratbags up to no good was my idea of heaven. Every day was a treasure, stored away for a mental escape from the reality of school days, which mainly were an endurance test, don't give up. Learn to adapt.

Wherever I go in my future life, people and places won't particularly bother me. With luck, a lost childhood will become a distant memory swirling in the murky fog of my school days.

Smoke and Mirrors

The school's rickety old bus usually arrived punctually at our marshalling point after our holidays. With any luck, it has broken down on the highway somewhere. A few of us were in the Greyhound Terminal Cafe, a rowdy bunch of storytellers. No one seemed to notice the bus was almost thirty minutes late. I thought I would take the opportunity to wind up a few boys.

'Well, you lot, I have to get going.'

'Where are you off to? We got to stay here,' a voice from the back called out.

'Nah, the rule is that if the bus is over thirty minutes late, we must return to our holiday locations and be picked up the following Sunday. They don't want us loitering around here on the streets.'

'What? No one told me. How am I supposed to get back to Rockie?' Poor young Bollo was counting his change. I knew at least one of them would bite.

'Bugger off. That's a load of crap, I've never heard of it. One of the cottage six smart-arse's replied.

'Don't you read our school paper; it was in the notice's section.'

'That rubbish! The only thing it's good for is hanging on the dunny wall.'

'Bloody hell, Rickie, you'll get us into trouble.' Red exclaimed.

'Mate, you don't need me for that.'

A big, shiny bus pulled in and tooted its horn just then. We took a little more interest when two brothers stepped out in their white habits. The shout to get aboard got us all out of the café quickly. I knew one of the brothers, the other with beady eyes, was new. Was there a changing of the guard? This new bus was a significant improvement on the *old, shaky model*. Almost twice as long, with high-backed seats and an air-cooling system. It had more grunt, and power steering was a vast improvement for dealing with the winding roads.

On arrival, I was glad to see that our old bus hadn't gone to the scrap heap. Our fearless leader, Brother FitBean, was standing on the large roundabout, tapping a cane on the side of his habit. No doubt, he was anxiously enthused to search our suitcases for contraband. We all trudged over for the standard search and decimate session. He looked at the rowdy mob and then homed in on me.

'Battler, come up here.' Brother FitBean's voice boomed. *What's his problem? Don't tell me he's missed our riveting conversations.*

'Pay attention, you boys; if more of you were like Battler here, we wouldn't have to waste time checking your luggage after every holiday.'

That got a groan from some of them; one or two nearly choked. The boys standing in a line were being searched by two of the other brothers. Oh well, in for a penny, in for a pound. Incidentally, my suitcase was half full of cigarettes. Three of my mates had paid for them, minus my haulage fee, as this was a valuable trading commodity. I had been elected the one most likely to succeed because I didn't smoke.

'So, Brother, did you have a relaxing holiday?'

'Yes, I did. Thank you. You have been relocated to cottage one for your final year. Go and introduce yourself to your new houseparents; they'll want to have a chat. We expect big things from you this year, Battler.'

'Yes, brother, do you want to check my suitcase before I go?' I was pushing my luck here while trying *not* to hold my breath.

He looked me up and down, 'Don't forget you're on dairy duty in the morning, so get a move on.'

Whew! That was close; I didn't need to be told twice. I jumped down to head off and noticed a few boys were watching me with a grin. Maybe we all learnt something about reverse psychology. After all, it was all about following the leader.

'Good afternoon, Sir, I'm Rickie Battler,' I introduced myself to the new house parents.

'Good afternoon, Rickie. Welcome to the historic cottage one. I'm Jim, and this is my wife Pam. You can drop the sir bit; we're not keen on formalities.'

'Thank you, sir, er um, Jim.' What a lovely accent they had. *These two must be from somewhere in the UK.*

'You're in the first section in the dormitory. Why don't you leave your luggage there and join us for afternoon tea? The rest of the boys will be here soon enough.'

He was a big bloke with a kind voice, and his wife seemed to be the caring type. The third member of their family was a cheeky little scotch terrier named Max, who came over to sniff me out. Having decided that I'd do, he parked his butt on my feet and waited for his ears to be scratched. The dog chucked a hissy fit when the rest of the mob trickled in. Barking at no one and everyone to let them know this was his territory. I reckon the dog had good instincts; all the same, Pam took old Max to his bed in their unit. Too much excitement for him.

What a surprise! I was good mates with most of this mob; it was like a family reunion. The houseparents were quite chuffed that we all got on so well. The newbies would fit in unless they were planted amongst us to spy for the brothers, a possibility. Time would tell, and if so, we'd give them hell. In the meantime, the choice was up to them. After our meet and greet, we unpacked and settled into our new digs. Sam, one of our in-house smuggler boys, went off to the toilet, while the rest of us scoffed delicious scones. He knew the best hidey holes in this old place. All the others left their suitcases out on the verandah, giving him ample opportunity to swap his case with mine.

He and Yao occupied the two beds at the back of the place, so they always had plenty of warning of approaching snoopers. I came in to find my unlocked suitcase sitting on top of my bed, without a name tag.

'Hey Rickie, we got our luggage mixed up; I think this might be yours; who's have you got?' Sam asked.

'Buggered if I know, the cases all look the same.'

'That's mine, you must've picked up the wrong one.'

Our lives slipped back into school mode. Life is shaped by the places you have been, the people you meet and your choices. Resilience and ingenuity are virtues, and coupled with sheer bloody-mindedness, you have a chance to succeed. The new house parents in Cottage One had a knack for connecting with teenage boys, so our life had a peaceful change. One of the new kids, Gerald, seemed a little odd; that could be the way he looked. If his personality matched his looks, he'd get short shrift from the rest of us. Most of the boys were used to a regimented life, they would be right at home in the army. The drill sergeant could save energy and put his feet up. We had already done three years of boot camp, and knew the program:

run, jump, and follow orders. No doubt he would still have given us the same response, move your arse!

There was a subtle change around here, but I could not put my finger on it. People who didn't seem to belong here came and went. I had an ill feeling something was brewing, and that wouldn't bode well for any of us. A chill rippled down my spine.

We loved our new indoor sports centre, including gymnastics. It had abundant equipment. Handstands, parallel bars, springboards, vaulting horse, weights, punching bag, speed ball, overhead trapeze rings, climbing ropes, and on it went. Our instructor was the new Brother Beady, who was agile for his size and weight. He started on a program of balance control and upper body strength training. I was like a monkey on speed, and I finally found a sport in which to excel. I could do somersaults from a standing position. Our trainer had a hissy fit one day. He turned up unexpectedly and caught me doing turns on the overhead rings. I'd build up speed by constantly turning, then letting go, grabbing the nearby ropes, and sliding upside down to the floor.

It took quite a lot of practice as I was ten metres off the ground, and there was no safety net. He banned me from the gym for a month. Still, I found something else to entertain myself by climbing up the outside block wall and sneaking in through the overhead windows, where I would abseil down with the window rope. One day, the rope broke, so I gave the idea a miss. A sprained ankle was difficult to hide.

Last Man Standing Wins

Biff-ups became non-curricular entertainment. The brother's decided boxing fitted the bill. No one received any official training. The equipment was there: a boxing ring and an assortment of gloves ranging from sparing to gorilla-sized battering rams. Weight, height, or age had no bearing. A Friday night event was born, a blood sport. The events were much anticipated by the brothers, who may have had a wine or two extra with their dinner.

The boys were encouraged to cheer on the sidelines enthusiastically. Those who were lucky enough to have the opportunity for boxing training outside of here appreciated that the practice might contribute to their survival. My brother Illy had given me a few pointers, but not enough to consider myself proficient. Some of the boys had been training under the old buildings; occasionally, I would join them. To become any good at this, constant practice was essential.

One evening, I was wandering around the back section of the gym and decided to climb up on the overhead trapeze to watch. Two opponents were reasonably matched, putting on a good show for their three rounds. The next match was plain cruel, some small kid set against a much bigger one with anger issues. It was a total slaughter, something I didn't appreciate. I should have stayed where I was.

'Battler, we haven't seen you in the ring lately.' Brother FitBean called over to me.

'The gym keeps me pretty well occupied, Brother.'

'Well, we can't have you missing out now, can we? We've another three fights to go, and you can be the last one for the evening. I'll find you a suitable opponent, so get ready.'

Brother Beady was standing off to the side. He was the first aid officer for the evening.

'Battler, how much boxing training have you had in the past?' He asked.

'Very little brother, and there's not much of that here either. I'm not in the habit of beating the crap out of someone for no good reason. This is not boxing, brother.'

'Well, keep your feet moving and your guard up. Don't stand still, this isn't wrestling.'

Three rounds of three minutes can seem like forever when you have heavyweight gorilla gloves on your hands. I noticed that my opponent sported a shiny red pair of lightweight gloves, stood a little over ten centimetres taller and had a weight advantage of around ten kilograms. We tied in the first round. My opponent won the second round. The bell sounded for round three.

He whispered. 'I got you now, Battler; you can barely lift your arms; I'm going to bash your bloody head in.'

What a charming bastard. He did his best to achieve his intended outcome. I was cut above one eye; my breathing was laboured, and my nose was slightly rearranged. Risking a further battering, I pushed both arms outwards, deflecting another jab to my face. His head momentarily came forward, and I held it in my humungous gloves. Then I did the only honourable thing to this pit dog; I head-butted him on the nose, followed by a knee to the groin. He went down; I was just about to stomp on him when Brother Beady's arms wrapped around me and dragged me away.

'Enough, Battler, stop! You've proved your point. Blind rage will get you in deep shit. He's not getting back up in a hurry.'

That mongrel was as feral as his younger brother, and they would both get their deserts over the next few weeks. There was a secret justice league around here. Not that I was aware of who they were, but I was glad that our humanity was not completely lost. Someone was balancing the books. For some reason, I was excluded from Friday night biffs-ups; it may have been that I was recently elected to our council of bothersome buggers for the year. On the other hand, Brother Beady's gym classes grew, and he'd also started wrestling training. Matches were scheduled to commence next week.

'Battler, I hear good reports from the dairyman regarding your work ethics; he tells me you are also competent at driving the tractor and our truck on the farm.'

'Yes, Thank you Brother.'

'If you keep this up, there could be a permanent position here for you.

'Thank you, Brother, certainly something to think about.'

Also, I've had a few phone calls recently from your brother Illy.

'My brother?'

'He will be coming up to see you this weekend.'

'Thank you, brother.'

Wow, I wondered what bought all this on. It has been so long since I have seen any family that I barely remember them. I wondered if someone had died; it seemed to be the only reason I ever heard about anyone these days. Still, it'll be good to see him.

He was the same brother, a quiet, easy-going bloke Deadly if provoked, besides boxing, he'd taken up two new hobbies. Drinking beer by the carton and attempting slack-arsed surfing. I loved his FJ Holden sedan, a base model that ran like a dream. Before visiting me, Illy would drop his mates, the *Clampetts,* down in the local town and pick them back up on the way out. This solved unwanted questions and gave his mates a chance for a beer or two, which was almost a religion with them.

I got to have a drive of his car when Illy organised a monthly day out. He had favourite places to show me in the surrounding hinterlands. Occasionally we visited our sister Betty and her family or brother Mal and his family. It was surreal to meet them and over time, we'd reconnect.

Not much changed during my final term of servitude at school. Life was what it was, although there seemed to be an increasing sense of unease. Some of the boys got caught smoking, but that was because of their stupidity. We all smoked at times; the best place was when clearing fields for cultivation. It helped that we were constantly burning off rubbish tree roots, which covered the smell of tobacco.

Our resident thief was finally nabbed and hung out to dry on a clothesline one night. A hessian bag was pulled over his head and he was swung around in circles. Several boys who had lost items of value gave him a wack with one thing or another, justice served. Another not so bright boy in our cottage thought it was hilarious to short-sheet beds. One night, someone sprinkled a pack of thumbtacks in his bed, which delighted him no end. He seemed to lose his enthusiasm for annoying others after that.

Mysteries Uncovered

I swapped my dormitory location with a young fellow who had developed anxiety to where he slept near the darkened amenities area. He reckoned it gave him the creeps. There were no objections from the houseparents, and neither of us had much to shift so with little fuss we exchanged places. He might have been concerned about payback for being considered the one who sprinkled the bed of the thumbtacked boy. Who knows innocence is no defence around here. For me his spot would serve another purpose, as one day I was lying down on Yao's bed chatting with Sami.

'You know if you lie here at an angle, you can see around the wall divider over there.'

'Shh, that's how we see who's coming.' Sam cautioned.

'We can improve on that. Give me a hand to move some of the other's furniture slightly.'

'Ok, that should have it; lie on Yao's bed; tell me what you see.?'

Sami responded, 'Tallboy mirror in the second section.'

'Give me a sec, how's that?' I made a further adjustment.

'Ceiling near the door, in the third section, move that wardrobe on a slight angle?' Sam suggested.

'Now, how is it?' I inquired.

'It's almost perfect; I can see out through the front door; how're we going to keep it like that? Some of the boys' stuff around with their mirrors?' Sam asked.

'Hmm, we'll have to work that one out, as we need better warning about who is sneaking up on us.' I replied. It improved the surveillance from my bed the most, as I could see from both directions.

'This cottage has a lot of doors; do you know there is another section locked off behind here? It leads out to that rear damaged verandah where all the junk furniture is stored; come on, Rickie, I'll show you.'

So, I went on Sam's mystery tour. I wonder why I hadn't noticed such a big section locked off. He had a hidden key to get into this area.

'Where'd you get that key from?'

'Found it. Some of us come here to smoke and have a hot cuppa. We just lay about the place for hours in our free time.' The brothers and some of the boys walk close by and don't even notice us.

'So, this's where you hide; I wander about all over the place looking for you buggers. 'Don't worry your secret is safe with me. Do you know what's behind those doors, Sam?'

'Don't know, can't get in there without breaking the glass. Sometimes I hear bangs and occasionally someone crying.'

Everyone's got secrets around here. Where do those other boys disappear to? I wondered.

***

The next day, I was at a loose end, wandering around the place, when I happened to run into him, who wanted answers to everything. 'Battler, where are you off to?' Brother FitBean had sprung me as I walked past the admin building.

'Going to give Skits a hand with the new bird enclosure, Brother.'

'He's not there; I spoke to him a while ago; he's gone down to do some welding. Come in here and have a talk with me.' Alarm bells rang in my head; the less time I spent in his company alone, the better it'd be for my health, both mentally and physically.

'So, you'll be leaving us in a couple of months. Have you had any thoughts on what you might like to do?'

'Maybe a horticulturist, electrician or an engineer.'

'You know those things cost money? and an education qualification higher than you've had. Perhaps you'll have to lower your ambitions.'

'Possibly, however, I've spoken to a federal politician, and he indicated there may be assisted education funds I can access.'

'Don't tell stories. When did you ever meet a politician?' Sometimes I wonder what world you're in.'

'It's not a fib, Brother. He's a friend of Bill's out at Chinchilla, and he was talking to us about life after high school. Night school, college, maybe even university.'

'Really, I didn't know that Mr Mann is so well connected; if you play your cards right, you may just get somewhere with our help.'

'How come this hasn't been mentioned before?'

'Don't push your luck, Battler; I've no time for young, smart arses.'

'No, Brother, I'm just asking a question.'

'Sometimes I think you grew up way too fast; you talk like someone much older. What are the boys up to in the old sheds and in the back area of Cottage One?'

Good try, you almost slid that one in.

'Don't know what you're talking about, brother.'

'Do you or these others have a connection with homophile activities? If you lie to me again, you'll find yourself on the way to Westbrook. See how long you last out there.'

'I still don't know what you're talking about, Brother. What's a homophile? Someone is certainly lying around here, but it's not me.' I was getting a little bit pissed off by his not-so-subtle bullying and innuendo. He was fishing for something; the problem was conversations with this bastard had more layers than an onion.

'Well, we'll fix that problem. I have witnesses. One of them happens to be here; come out, boy,' he called out. Shit, where did he come from? It was Red. He looked very dishevelled; they must have had him locked in a cupboard or something.

'Alright, here's some proof for you; Battler was with you other boys, wasn't he?'

'No Brother, he does live in cottage one, but he doesn't smoke, so he hasn't been with us out in the back section on weekends. He goes up to the gym training with Brother Beady's group in the gymnastics team, I think.' Red replied with embarrassment.

Brother FitBean almost spat the dummy, 'Get out of here, Battler.'

What the bloody hell is going on around here? Red was talking about smoking, and FitBean was talking about something completely different. I wondered what was happening in that locked unit at the back of Cottage One. Thank God Red spoke up. FitBean was up to something. I needed to avoid him; he could turn nasty when he didn't get his own way.

It was on the final few months until my Freedom Day. I had to be careful, or I would end up in the system of revolving doors of institutional abuse. I was beginning to understand the tension my old mate Bluebird felt in his final days here: don't rock the boat for any reason. *So, what'd I do, jump into the lion's den and rattle his cage? Gees, I get dumber by the moment.*

FitBean is soon being replaced by a brother, Pearly. It seems they all take turns at the helm. Over the years, my instinctive distrust of others was beginning to annoy people. A life of constant disappointments continued to muddy my world. Being forgotten, we lost souls most likely *developed idiosyncratic personalities to cope with our deep sense of loss.*

Recently, we have acquired a resident cabbie of sorts. A middle-aged guy who drove us boys to outside appointments. I wondered if they were all to do with medical issues. A month before my freedom, I and another boy were driven to a house in Brisbane. These events were beginning to fray my nerves as I thought it might be some sort of ruse. This trip was supposed to be for discussion on assistance funding for higher education. The other boy must've impressed them. I heard later that he eventually went to university and studied law. I, on the other hand, did not fare so well. While we were in Brisbane at the education funding discussion, we dropped into a halfway house at Albion. It was touted as an alternative option, somewhere to live at a set fee. To pay for this, we were found some dead-end factory jobs chosen by the brothers.

This didn't appeal to me. Instead, I decided to board with the parents of one of the other boys and find my own job. We were given no guidelines for our transition into mainstream society. No other support, financial or otherwise, was offered. It was a matter of you're on your own, boy, move along. For all intents and purposes, you were forgotten the minute you were shuffled out. Go lose yourself someplace else.

My final day had arrived. Without a backward glance, I jumped aboard the school bus with the rest of us 'graduates' on my last journey away from here. Back along the winding rural roads of yesteryear to the Greyhound bus terminus in Brisbane. Standing there, I felt the reality of my life finally sink in. Nine years locked away; my childhood had been stolen; my life forever fractured. Few of those miserable bastards gave a damn; after all, it was just a job. Here, I have learnt three things: work hard, don't complain, and don't bother anyone for any reason. Sort your own shit, out yourself.

I had become accustomed to people disappearing from my life, and it wasn't worth wasting time worrying about the why or the what. Worrying never solves a damn thing, it's just the way life was. The deep feelings of sadness and loss sank further, it would always follow me. The heady scent of freedom was calling me, place one foot in front of the other

The Greyhound bus departure to the western downs was announced, and it was time to move on with my life. At least in Chinchilla, people cared, and I was welcome. I could enjoy myself during my last holiday in the foreseeable future. I decided not to worry Bill and Gwyn about my prospects. I was one step away from being homeless, something I would experience more than once during my life. I felt a sense of abandonment, like that mangy dog over there wandering the streets.

I had seventy dollars and change in my pockets, a return bus ticket, and my worldly possessions in one brown suitcase. There's not a lot to show for all the years. I walked alone with the ghosts of a legion of lost souls, in hope that one day, God will deliver justice for us all.

I am three months short of my seventeenth birthday. What could possibly go wrong? Quite a lot, as things turned out. My resolve to succeed would be severely challenged. Life's choices come at a cost.

References

FICH. - Formerly in Children's Homes. Brisbane 1986
One of the self-help groups that pioneered the path to recognition of institutional childhood abuse.

Forde Inquiry-1999- Queensland- Commission of Inquiry order [No 1] 1988
Pg1- Pg 394.

Forgotten Australians – Senate Report 2004
Report on Australians who experienced institutional or out-of-home care abuse as children.

Australian Royal Commission inquiry into institutional responses to child sexual abuse.
December 2017- Volumes 2, 3, 4, and 11.